THE *ex* FILES SERIES

EXPLOSIVE

LISA RYAN CAMPBELL

Copyright © 2020 by Lisa Ryan Campbell

All rights reserved.

No part of this book may be reproduced in any form or by any electronic or mechanical means, including information storage and retrieval systems, without written permission from the author, except for the use of brief quotations in a book review.

This is a work of fiction. Names, characters, places, and incidents either are the product of the author's imagination or are used fictitiously. Any resemblance to actual persons, living or dead, events, or locales is entirely coincidental.

Cover design by Deranged Doctor Design
www.derangeddoctordesign.com

❦ Created with Vellum

GET YOUR FREE BOOK!

When you have a one-night stand with your next-door neighbor, and he turns out to be your boss.

Click here for your free copy of EXPLICIT!

For Lauren and for all sisters.

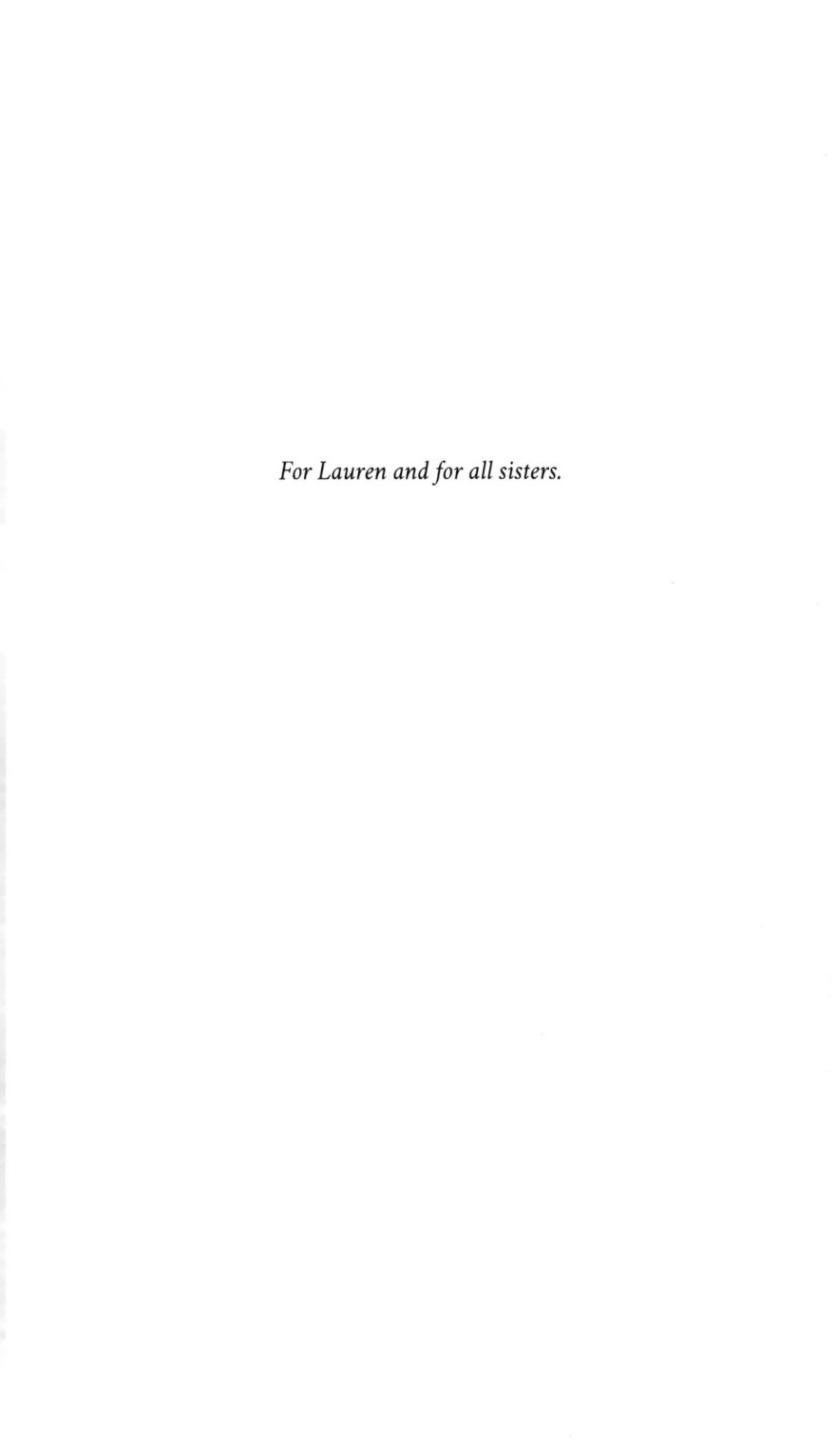

CHAPTER ONE

I grabbed another napkin from the middle console of my car. They were old napkins from various restaurants, collected over the many months I'd eaten in my car in between court appearances and depositions, and all were being put to use now to scrub the blood from my hands. With one eye on the winding road ahead, I pulled the visor down and bright light shined upon the blood spatter in my hair and across my face.

But it wasn't my blood.

I pulled another napkin from the collection, ran it across my face, and threw it to the side. I had to think about what I was going to say when I saw him again. How would I even begin to explain everything? But thinking about Brian only brought the nagging whispers back, and with each mile marker I passed, I had to convince myself not to turn around.

He doesn't want to see you.

That mantra replayed over and over in my head, attempting to talk me out of this foolish idea, but I continued on, becoming hypnotized by my car's headlights, which illuminated the road along the 101 freeway.

An hour and a half after leaving San Francisco, I arrived in Gypsy Bay, where Brian called home. It was quiet up there, maybe too quiet for me, but he'd found some freedom there after our divorce, and this was the first time I was going to see where he lived. No, it wasn't going to be the best of circumstances, considering I didn't have time to change out of my bloody clothes. I should have at least called him first and let him know I was on my way, so it wouldn't be a complete surprise when I showed up at his doorstep talking about a murder.

Out of habit, I reached across the console to the passenger seat to fish my cell phone from my purse. I dug inside all around, only to find it wasn't there.

"Dammit!" I shouted, knowing instantly that I must've dropped it in my rush to escape all of that death.

Suddenly, I became frightened. I didn't know what I was doing. I didn't even know why I was driving up there to see him. I just felt in my gut, he would know what to do. He always had a knack of making things all right. As a psychiatrist, he knew how to make problems seem not so surmounting, and I had to admit I was very curious to see how he planned to turn this mountain back into a molehill—that was if he agreed to help me.

I was so consumed with my thoughts I nearly missed the turnoff to the downtown district per the mechanical female voice of the GPS. When I turned onto the road, it felt as if I'd stepped into another world. It was nearly midnight, but I could still make out the sight of lit walkways, tree-lined paths and small business store fronts, and it all perfectly explained why Brian had decided to call this home. It had an old-town charm about it, kind of like Savannah, where we'd spent a long weekend once. He had always wanted some place to slow down and raise children. But I had my career to think of, and the last thing I needed was little people running around me and being away from the city and…

I shook away the torrent of excuses and realized with a pang of sadness and guilt, I no longer had to explain myself. My life with Brian was over, but I needed him just one last time. After all, he was the main reason I was driving around with blood and brain matter underneath my fingernails.

CHAPTER TWO

Two weeks later...
Brian Kessler exited the elevator on the fifth floor of San Francisco General, shook the rain from his jacket and looked around. He spied the nurses' station and headed there, but before he could ask the night duty nurses any questions, he was intercepted by a familiar face.

"Brian," Shawn said by way of greeting, and Brian didn't know whether to hug or shake hands with his ex-brother-in-law, whom he hadn't seen in more than three years.

"It's good to see you, Shawn."

Shawn took his hand firmly in his grasp. "Thank you for coming. I didn't want to call you at all, and I wasn't even sure you'd come down, considering how things had ended with you and Carrie."

"But you did call, and it only took you two weeks," Brian said, removing his wet jacket and tossing it over his arm. "Why didn't I hear about her car accident sooner? At least on the news?"

He knew his voice sounded brusque, and maybe Shawn didn't deserve it, but it was barely three in the morning, and he was still irritable. But what really pissed him off was that he was told to come to the hospital to see his ex-wife, whom he hadn't known had been in a car accident two weeks ago, much less in a coma that entire time. No other details had been given to him, but all of a sudden, Carrie's family needed his help.

"You can thank my parents and their lawyers for that," Shawn said. "Money and connections can go a long way when you want to keep things hushed up."

Brian knew all too well the extent of the Wallace's influence—especially in San Francisco. It had been powerful enough to bring his father down. He wanted to ask why they felt they needed to keep Carrie's accident quiet, but a more important question was on his mind.

"How is she?"

Shawn looked away for just the briefest moment and aside from his dark complexion, Brian was always struck by how much of a resemblance he shared with Andrew. From his coal black eyes and narrow nose to his hard jawline, Shawn could easily have passed for his father's twin.

"She's awake."

"Yeah, you told me that on the phone, but I'm more concerned about any neurological issues. She was in a coma for two weeks. Are there any lingering problems?"

"Well, that's why I called you."

Brian was growing impatient and wished he would just spit it out. Still, the counselor inside of him prevented him from bullying the man. He put one hand on his shoulder and spoke in the tone that made his patients comfortable enough to begin to open up to him.

"What is it, Shawn? Why does Carrie need me?"

"She doesn't need you for a damn thing."

Brian looked up past him to see an older and attractive,

statuesque woman with icy brown eyes coming toward him. Carrie had those same eyes.

"Natalie," Brian said, stepping away from Shawn and taking in the full view of his ex-mother-in-law. "It's good to see you again."

He knew the dull and dry tone in his voice wouldn't deter her. She stopped right in front of him and looked about ready to spit in his eye.

"Why are you here?"

One thing Brian loved about Natalie Wallace was that she didn't waste time mincing words, which oddly made him feel more freedom around her.

"As a matter of fact, I was just about to find that out," Brian said.

"I called him, Mom," Shawn said, stepping forward. "Carrie's going to need him."

Natalie immediately moved her piercing gaze to her son. "She's going to be fine. Your father said he would call Neil Jacobs in the morning. He's one of the finest in the city." Natalie looked once more to Brian and twisted her nose as if she'd smelled something rotten. "We don't need him."

Brian was sent on instant alert, despite Natalie's obvious distaste and rude manner. He knew of Neil Jacobs and yes, he was a top psychiatrist in San Francisco, but he specialized in patients who had suffered brain trauma.

"I thought you said Carrie was fine," Brian said, turning to Shawn.

"She is," Shawn countered.

"Then why are you calling in Neil? I know him and what he practices. What the hell happened to her?"

"That's none of your business," Natalie interjected. "I don't want you here, and Carrie definitely doesn't need to see you and whatever stress you plan on bringing into her life again."

"Mom, wait. He can help her a lot more than Dr. Jacobs."

"I want him gone!"

"Natalie!"

The three of them all turned to see Andrew Wallace, tall and distinguished with dark close-shaven hair and graying temples, come forward. He sent an apologetic look to the nursing staff, who had obviously grown uncomfortable from the raised voices, and then crossed to his wife and took her hand firmly into his own.

"I didn't call Neil. As much as it pains me, I have to agree with Shawn that Brian is the best hope for Carrie right now."

Natalie looked at the two men she loved as if they'd turned against her, then released her hand from Andrew's, gave Brian one final withering look, and then quietly turned and walked down the corridor to where Brian assumed was Carrie's room.

Andrew watched his wife go and then turned and eyed Brian with malice. "I share my wife's feelings on this one. I don't want you anywhere near my daughter."

Brian shook his head and spoke with derision. "She'll always be your little princess."

"You're damn right!"

That outburst seemed to surprise even himself. Andrew bowed his head and breathed in and out deeply for a few seconds before continuing.

"Did Shawn get a chance to tell you what's going on?"

"All I know is Carrie was in a car accident and has just awoken from a two-week coma. I assume now that you called me here because of some neurological issues."

Andrew was one of the top neurological surgeons in San Francisco. Brian had no doubt in his competency and would've bet money that his influence warranted the chief of neurology to examine Carrie. But when he paused, Brian knew immediately the news wasn't good. He could see through Andrew's dark eyes into the soul of a father who was afraid for his daughter.

"Carrie has completely lost her memory," Andrew said. "She can't remember anything. Not us, not where she lives or works, not even her own name."

CHAPTER THREE

She was kind, the woman who stood over my bed. She watched me as if she didn't know what to do with me, but I could see and feel the love she had for me. Her name was Natalie, and she was my mother. At least that was what she'd told me. It was bittersweet, really. She seemed like such a lovely person, that any girl would be blessed to call her mom, but on the other hand, I had to take her word for it. How did I know she wasn't lying to me?

How did I know any of these people who said they were my family weren't just lying to me? But to what end? Well, hell, if I knew who I was in the first place, then I could answer those questions and probably the thousand other questions before and surely to follow.

They said my name was Carrie Wallace. I was thirty-nine years old, single with no kids, and I was a senior defense attorney for a top firm there in San Francisco. There were other details my mother, Natalie, had tried to tell me—silly things like my favorite color was yellow, I love fried calamari and seemed to have recently developed a fixation for Sims games. I'd asked her why I never had kids, and she said there was still time for me. I then asked if there was a man in my life, and she simply said, "No."

She seemed to be doing most of the talking, my mother. There were two other men in the room—a tall and strikingly handsome older man who said he was my father, Andrew, and a younger version of him, a shy and attractive-looking man who said he was my brother, Shawn. The two of them looked stoic and uncomfortable, and I felt a little sorry for them. It must be hard to strike up a conversation with someone you know all about but doesn't know shit about you.

I had been relieved when they all left me on my own for once. They didn't know what to do with me, and the feeling was mutual. I just needed a moment on my own to think and softly beg my memory to come back to me. However, just before the door closed behind them, I noticed a uniformed police officer standing outside my door. He looked inside the room directly at me, and a slither of worry and foreboding trailed up the back of my spine, yet I had no idea why. Still, the possibility that I might be in some kind of trouble only made me redouble my efforts to get my mind to remember.

I grabbed for the mirror Natalie had left beside my bed, picked it up and began to speak to myself while getting to know my face.

"Who am I?" I kept asking myself. "Who are you? Tell me, please. Tell me before they all come back in this room. Tell me something so they can stop looking at me like a fucking zoo exhibit."

Ten minutes later, my mom came back into the room, and she looked pissed.

"What's wrong?" I asked.

She gave me a brief glance, turned away, and began to pace. Then she stopped and rounded on me.

"Sweetheart, I'm going to get you the best psychiatrist.

You don't have to worry about that. You don't have to do what they say."

I shook my head, confused. "What are you talking about?"

"Your father and brother have a specialist they want you to see to help recover your memory, but I think we can do better. We can find someone here in San Francisco. That way you can stay with me and your father."

"What's wrong with the doctor...um Dad and Shawn want me to see?"

She looked momentarily pleased I could remember my brother's name but quickly continued. "Well, he doesn't have as much experience as I'd like in these types of cases. Just do me a favor, honey, and consider all of your options."

"Sure," I replied, not sure what else to say. I could barely remember my own name, and she wanted me to research psychiatrists? I needed help now, and if they already had somebody lined up and willing to help me, then let's get on with it.

The door swung open and my father and brother walked in. Following them was a third man, whom I assumed was the specialist who would be in charge of rescuing my brain from this fog of confusion. Immediately, his eyes lasered in on me, and the way he was looking made me want to reconsider my mother's advice. This man looked at me not only as if he knew me, but as if he *really* knew me—and despised me.

I didn't know why, but I looked to my mother for comfort, and she wasted no time moving closer to my bedside. Maybe she really did birth me because I suddenly felt comforted by her presence.

"How are we doing in here?" My father asked, with the tone of a man who was trying to diffuse a room full of tension.

No one said anything for a long time, and then I realized everyone was looking at the mysterious man who walked into the room with my father and brother, as though waiting for him to say something. I looked toward him, too, and found he was still staring directly at me. His eyes had grown a bit softer then, and I could clearly see the stark blue beauty of them. Still, that small trace of animosity was there, and I began to wonder if I was the one who put it there.

My father ventured to speak again. "Carrie, this is Dr. Brian Kessler. He's a leading psychiatrist here in the bay area and specializes in brain trauma and memory loss, specifically amnesia."

He paused, and I wondered if I was supposed to say something at this point.

"Dr. Kessler practices less than two hours from here in a town called Gypsy Bay. He has agreed to treat you, and we think it's an excellent idea."

My brother, Shawn, spoke up. "He's a top specialist in the field. He's published and has also taught on memory loss and trauma."

I didn't really care to hear about his resume. If he was such an educated man, why had he yet to utter a word?

I sighed. "Is that where I live? Gypsy Bay?"

"No," Natalie rushed to say, moving closer to my bedside. "I told you, honey, you live here in San Francisco, where there are plenty of other qualified doctors to treat you."

"Natalie."

She ignored what sounded like a subtle warning from my father and continued on. "Like I told you before, you don't have to rush to make this decision. What's most important is that you rest."

"She'll get plenty of rest up north, Mom," Shawn said. "Gypsy Bay is a small quiet town off the coast. The ocean air will do her some good."

"It's already been decided," Andrew said. "Time is of the essence. We'll get some of her things moved up there, and she can begin her treatment immediately. I'm worried about any long-term damage."

"Don't say that," Natalie said, her voice rising in anger. "Her memories aren't going anywhere. At least not in the next few days it will take to decide other options."

"I don't want any other options," Andrew said. "I know your feelings on the matter, and while I agree with you, this isn't the time to bring all of this up."

"Well someone needs to," Natalie said, her eyes flashing.

"Mom, calm down," Shawn said, trying to appease her. "Dad's right. Brian is here and is willing to help her."

My family continued their debate around me, and I wondered to myself if this was usual. Did they often talk about my life and make my decisions for me while I stood in the room? I sat there observing and tried to follow along as each of them became passionate in their argument, but it only began to overwhelm me. I leaned my head back against the pillow and closed my eyes. But it was only for a few seconds because I still felt his stare. I slowly opened my eyes and met Dr. Brian Kessler's gaze from across the room as my family argued about whether to entrust him with my care. What was it about him? Amid all of this tension, he managed to stand calm and still. It intrigued me, but as the voices around us elevated, his silent demeanor became too intimidating. I couldn't take it anymore. I needed to hear his voice.

So, I asked him a question, and just like that—Pandora's box was opened.

It was a simple question, a logical question. Even better, the slightly raised voices of my family came to an abrupt silence. They all looked from me to Dr. Kessler, waiting for something to happen. But this mysterious and intriguing man said nothing; he left my room, taking the answer with him.

CHAPTER FOUR

Brian smelled the coffee long before the cup was placed under his nose. The strong aroma filled his nostrils, and he looked up gratefully to see Shawn standing there.

"Thanks," he said, taking the steaming cup and cradling it between his hands.

He remained sitting in the chair, leaning forward with his elbows resting on his knees. The coffee felt warm between his hands and served to ease the chill he'd felt standing in Carrie's room. Shawn sat down beside him, holding his own cup of coffee, and let out an exasperated sigh.

"I'm sorry about my mother."

Brian took a cautious sip and then shrugged. "You don't have to apologize for her, but thank you for your vote of confidence in there. I would thank your father, too, but he's not a big fan of me, either."

Shawn chuckled before taking a sip of coffee. "It would have helped if you had said a few words. It may have comforted Mom to hear your plans for treatment."

"I hadn't really decided I was going to treat her. I needed

to see her first. I needed to see if it was true, and not just some..."

Shawn looked over at him, his face twisted in disgust. "Jesus, Brian. You thought she was faking it?"

He shrugged. "I'm sorry. It's been three years since I've seen her, and things didn't end well at all. I didn't know what to believe."

Shawn didn't say anything for a long time. He was probably wondering what in the hell went on inside the home Brian shared with Carrie that would make him question her memory loss.

"Well, what do you think now?" Shawn asked.

"I'm sure you and your family have already been told she's suffering from Retrograde Amnesia, and from what I can tell, it's genuine. Even Carrie isn't a good enough actress to fake that vulnerable and lost look on her face. I've seen it before in brain trauma victims."

"Look, Brian, I'm sorry to spring this on you like this, and I'm sorry you had to see her like that. She only woke hours ago, and when I found out she'd lost her memory, you were the first person I thought of. She needs you."

"Who am I to you?"

Those soft words had sliced through him. What had made her ask him that? With her loss of memory, did she still sense some connection between them? He hadn't bothered answering her but turned and abruptly left the room like a fucking coward. But he could never tell her that at one time, she was everything to him—his lover, his confidante, and ultimately, his enemy.

He had to admit that the three years apart had been good to her. Wisps of her hair had gone askew and her face was devoid of makeup, which only highlighted the deep cuts, scrapes and bruises from the accident that were just beginning to heal. She'd lost a little weight, but there was still that natural beauty about her he could never deny and standing in that room, he couldn't keep his eyes off of her. He was in trouble.

"She can't know who I am."

Shawn frowned. "Don't you think that would help?"

"No. I don't want our history interfering with her treatment."

"But when her memory comes back, won't she know who you are?"

"I'll handle it then. For now, in the beginning stages, I want our relationship to remain professional. Doctor and patient, that's all."

Shawn nodded and stood to his feet. "I should get back in there and let Mom and Dad know before they say anything to Carrie."

Brian scoffed. "I doubt Andrew or Natalie will tell her about me. They'll be satisfied if that part of her memory never comes back."

Shawn gave him a sympathetic smile and outstretched his hand. "They may never say it, but on behalf of my family, thank you."

Brian rose from his chair, accepted the handshake, but kept his grasp on Shawn's hand to keep him from walking off. He looked to his right down the hallway toward Carrie's room, where a policeman stood vigil outside the door. Brian had noticed him when he first entered her room, but with all the excitement and the fact that he'd not seen or spoken to her in years, he forgot to ask about him.

"Why are the police here?"

Shawn looked uncomfortable. "I meant to tell you. They need to take her statement, but with her amnesia, it's been put on hold."

"Her statement about the accident?"

"Well, yes, about the accident and that night in general."

His discomfort became even more visible, and he slowly began to inch away. Brian put a hand on his shoulder to stop him again.

"Tell me what's going on, Shawn. Did something else happen that I need to know?"

He looked back toward his sister's hospital room and then shook his head.

"Before the accident, Carrie was seen leaving the apartment of one of her colleagues—a man named Harvey Adams."

Brian frowned in instant recognition at the name. "You're talking about the lawyer that was found dead?" He'd at least heard about that. One of San Francisco's ADA found murdered was a big story. "What does Carrie have to do with that?"

Shawn breathed in and let out an exhausted sigh. "A witness says when she left the apartment, her clothes were all bloody and she looked to be in shock. They thought she'd been hurt and called the police. But when the police arrived, Carrie was gone and Harvey was found dead with his face half missing from a gunshot."

* * *

Brian got home at nearly seven that morning and was both happy and disappointed to see the other car still in the driveway when he got there. Happy because the woman inside would give him the distraction he needed right now, and disappointed because he wanted to be alone with his thoughts. He pulled up next to it, shut off the engine, and leaned his head back against the headrest. He shut his eyes and breathed deeply in and out, trying to get the sight of Carrie's vulnerable and innocent look out of his head. In all the years he'd known her, she'd been neither vulnerable nor innocent, and he would have scoffed at anyone describing her that way. But that was how she'd looked, and it had been so foreign to him that he couldn't stop seeing it. Instantly, his eyes flew open in anger, and he punched a hand against the steering wheel, damning her for coming back into his life in this way.

He had to take several more deep breaths before he finally exited the car and walked into his house. The smell of fresh brewed coffee was enticing. He took off his coat and dropped his keys on a side table by the door. He went into the kitchen and saw Rachel standing by the counter, her back to him with one hand holding a mug of coffee and the other scrolling through her phone.

"Hi, babe," she said, without turning around but instead took another sip of her coffee.

Brian didn't return the greeting but walked up to her, put his hands on her waist and began kissing the back of her neck. Her body was warm and inviting, and he had the sudden need to drown himself inside of her.

Rachel didn't utter one protest but turned around and met his kisses with her own. Her aggressiveness momentarily surprised him. Normally, she would have said something about needing to beat traffic or having an early meeting, but he sensed she knew he needed this. He heard the loud clang of the coffee mug falling into the sink beside them followed by the thud of her phone onto the counter. Brian hiked up her black skirt, and Rachel wrapped her arms around his neck as he lifted her onto the countertop. She undid her blouse, revealing a lacy black bra as he tugged her panties down her thighs. She looked right into his eyes as she spread her legs wide, and Brian groaned as he undid his own belt buckle and tugged his pants down. He grasped her waist once again and pulled her forward to meet his erection. Rachel tilted her head back, giving him access to her slender neck and full breasts. Brian kissed his way down her now hot skin until he was pushing up her bra and sucking each nipple into his mouth.

"Do it Brian," she said, grabbing his ass and moving her body against him.

Brian licked and sucked each nipple just to tease her a bit more, then thrust himself inside her. They both moaned and cursed as they rocked back and forth on the countertop and in minutes, she was coming, followed by him. Brian nestled his face in the curve of her neck until his breathing slowed. When he could finally think, he felt like a creep.

"I'm sorry."

Rachel laughed. "For what?"

He couldn't tell her the entire truth of what spurred this session—that he needed to get his ex-wife out of his mind, so he settled for a partial truth.

"You don't deserve to be attacked like that."

She giggled again as she hopped down from the counter, pulled up her panties, pushed her skirt back down and buttoned up her blouse.

"Every woman deserves to be attacked like that by her man."

She tucked her blouse in, grabbed her phone, and kissed him on the lips. Then she stopped, and he guessed she must have finally noticed the tired look in his eyes.

"Rough night?"

He nodded. "I'm going to take a nap before my first appointment." He then slapped her on the butt playfully. "You're late."

"For once, I don't mind." She kissed him again, grabbed her purse and keys, and headed for the door. "I'll stay over tonight, makes us an early dinner and you can tell me all about it."

After the front door closed behind her, Brian felt relief,

and that made him feel worse. What the hell was going on with him? Rachel worked for the District Attorney's office in San Francisco. With both of their busy schedules, and the fact that she still lived in the city, they saw each other three times a week at best. Although she kept several of her things at his house for the nights she stayed over, she wasn't clingy, needy, or demanding of his time. It was perfect for him. At least, it used to be. Now, with one 2 a.m. phone call, he was being reunited with a woman he wasn't sure he'd ever see again, and it was knocking him sideways. He braced his hands on the counter where he and Rachel had just made love and surrendered to all thoughts of Carrie as they came rushing back.

CHAPTER FIVE

*E*ight years ago...
When Brian and his parents pulled up to the large home in Sea Cliff, they all sat in the car for a moment just to stare in wonder.

"You say he's a neurologist?" his mother, Marie, asked.

His father Gerald nodded. "One of the best in the city."

She pulled down the visor to check her makeup. "It shows. What about his wife?"

"She used to be a nurse and then moved up to an administrative position in the hospital where he works," Gerald said. "After they were married, she quit and came home to raise their kids."

Marie nodded, and Brian could see in the visor mirror that his mother slightly envied Natalie Wallace. She'd let it slip one time that she'd often wished she and his father had had more children together and that she'd been able to stay home with them. He leaned forward from the back seat and rested a hand on her shoulder in silent comfort.

She paused in retouching her makeup, turned around, and blew him an air kiss.

"Are we ready to go in?" Gerald asked, unlatching his seatbelt.

"Just one question," Marie said, returning her lipstick to her clutch. "Why the sudden interest in wanting to partner with you?"

"I already explained it to you. I have a celebrity client, and that has gotten me a lot of notice. He's not the first offer I've had of a partnership. His is just the most enticing."

Marie's brow creased with worry. "Just make sure to hear him out completely. You've made a great name for yourself without anyone's help. I don't want people to start using you."

Gerald scoffed and then leaned forward and kissed his wife. "No one's using me, honey. Now, let's go inside."

* * *

As soon as his family stepped into the foyer of the mansion, Andrew and Natalie Wallace greeted them as though they were old friends. They were a charming couple, and Brian immediately respected and envied them for the posh life they'd evidently made for themselves. But as much as he wanted to get to know the hosts who invited him into their home, he was even more so interested in the young woman who stood by their side.

They introduced their daughter, Carrie Wallace, who was stunning in a form-fitting black dress that reached just over her knees, high heels that showed off a pair of toned legs and curved into full hips, and an ass Brian wasn't ashamed to say he wanted to smack. Her breasts also had him hypnotized, but when he finally put his attention on her soft caramel-colored face with eyes to match, he saw she was giving him a smile that made him feel like the only man in the room. He wanted her, and because of that, he had to look away.

He tried to stay focused on the conversation between his father and Andrew Wallace. He was genuinely interested in their plans to expand the medical practice—the new building, the new offices, the staff and their projected profits. As a newly graduated medical student, he was itching to be on the ground floor and begin taking on new patients.

But after several minutes passed, he couldn't help himself anymore and finally dared to look Carrie's way. He was startled to find she was staring at him, too. When their eyes met, a slight smile formed on her lips as though she'd been waiting for him to give her his attention again and was feeling triumphant that he'd finally succumbed. But as arresting to his senses as she was, Brian didn't want her having a stronghold over him, so instead of returning her smile, he only nodded—a gesture that was kind enough to acknowledge her but not inflate her ego.

He then politely excused himself from the conversation and made his way to the bar. He ordered his drink, thanked the bartender, and looked around the mansion, admiring and taking it all in. Would he ever find himself living in a place like this? Would it be everything he hoped for?

"Having fun?"

He stopped admiring the home and saw that Carrie had followed him to the bar. She was still looking at him as if he fascinated her, as if he were a riddle she was desperate to solve.

"Um, sure," he said, and gave her a brief smile. He didn't want to be rude. "I thought you had a brother?"

"Shawn is at Stanford. He has midterms this week and couldn't make it to the party."

He nodded and then looked over at the curved staircase and eyed the ornate wood carving on the banister.

She ordered her own drink and then addressed him again. "You keep looking around."

He turned to find her watching him intently and looked away, embarrassed. "It's my first time being inside one of these homes." He thought for a moment and then looked at her again, this time annoyed. "I'm not going to steal anything."

Instead of looking embarrassed, she matched his annoyed look. "I wasn't thinking anything remotely like that."

She then also looked around the expansive great room, and he guessed she was trying to see it through his eyes, instead of the eyes of someone who'd grown accustomed to her opulent home.

"Did my dad ever tell you his story?"

Brian shook his head.

"He came from the south side of Chicago. A poverty and crime-ridden area. Like you, he was an only child, and his mother wouldn't let him go outside and play because she was scared of drive-by shootings and bad influences. So, his companion was the TV and board games they would play together."

Brian nodded.

"Well, one day he was watching one of his favorite shows, and there was a scene with the kids in school, and the teacher had them all pull out a blank sheet of paper and write their dreams down. As many dreams as they could think of and as illogical as they could make them. She said the more illogical the dream, the better."

"So, Andrew wrote his list that day?" Brian guessed.

`Carrie laughed. "No. That scene always stayed with him, but he didn't make his list until almost twenty years later when he finally left Chicago and moved to California for medical school. And even then, it was just one dream, but it was so illogical to a poor black man from South Side Chicago, that he may as well have not written anything down."

Brian waited and then finally nodded with understanding. "A home in Sea Cliff."

Carrie smiled, downed the rest of her drink, and handed the empty glass to the bartender.

She then gestured to his drink. "Finish that up and then let's go for a drive."

After assuring his parents he'd find a way home, he let Carrie take him to a nightclub, but it wasn't a place filled with twenty-somethings dancing to the latest songs. This club was filled with men and women closer to the age of their parents, partying to all the seventies hits. As soon as they cleared the entrance, she wasted no time pulling him to the dance floor and rocking her full and curvy hips back and forth to the beat of the music. It didn't take long for Brian to find himself dancing right along with her. He took her hand, twirled her around the dance floor, and then brought her back to him. With her back to his front, he put his hands to her hips and their bodies melded together as they moved in time to the funky rhythm.

* * *

"Why do you like that music?"

"My mom used to listen to it while my brother and I were growing up," Carrie said, taking a sip from the bottle and handing it to him. "She'd play it so loud, and we'd have dance parties."

They ended the night on Baker Beach, sitting on a blanket and huddled together under another blanket. His tie was long gone, and his shirtsleeves were rolled up past his forearms, while she'd let her hair down from its chignon and let the black tresses flow around her shoulders. They shared a bottle of cheap liquor from a convenience store while staring out at the dark waves, with the bright lights of the Golden Gate bridge to their right.

"The music is just the cherry on top. I mainly like the club because it's a place where no one knows me. I can be myself and not be concerned with keeping up appearances."

"Is that important to you?" He asked. "Keeping up appearances?"

She shrugged. "It's important to my parents. Even as a grown woman, I try to uphold a good name. They tell me as a black woman—especially a black woman of means, I'm even more prone to scrutiny. So, I try to be aware of my behavior at all times and not do anything to embarrass the family."

He couldn't argue with that. That was something about her culture and background he would never truly be able to understand, so he just had to take her word for it and respect it.

"So, Dr. Kessler," she said, turning her head to look at him. "What's your illogical dream?"

"I never really thought about it."

"Oh, come on! Everyone has one. What's yours? It's got to be something that you don't believe could ever possibly happen."

He took a sip from the bottle and handed it back to her. "I want to fly to the moon."

She choked with laughter on the liquor and bumped him with her shoulder.

"By 'fly,' you mean boarding a shuttle that will take you into outer space, right?"

"Hell no. I mean actually fly. I'm going to skip past centuries of evolution, sprout wings, defy gravity, break through the Earth's atmosphere, somehow learn to breathe in space, and be sipping margaritas on the moon in no time."

She was losing the battle at trying to keep a straight face. She nodded with tears of restrained laughter in her eyes.

"You're right. That's utterly ridiculous. Where would anyone get margaritas on the moon?"

When the laughter between them subsided, he turned to her and took the bottle out of her hands and asked with all seriousness:

"What's your illogical dream?"

She wrapped the blanket tighter around her shoulders and shyly looked at him.

"That you would kiss me tonight."

His eyes went immediately to her lips. They were full and slightly parted, looking all too delectable and inviting.

"Why would that be illogical?"

"Because it hasn't happened, yet. Because I want it to happen so badly, and the things we want so badly are the things that are always out of reach, right?"

He could hear her breath catch. Christ, she was nervous? She was nervous around him, when all night long, he'd forced himself to look at everything and everyone else besides her because he knew if he stole even a moment's glance at her, he would never be able to look away. Just like he was doing at this very moment.

He slowly traced his thumb over her lower lip and relished how moist and soft it felt. She matched his movements and traced her own slender finger across his lips, both of them making each other crazy with wanting.

"Brian," she said softly.

"You'll have to think of another dream," he said and kissed her, finally letting loose the feelings he'd been holding in the moment he set eyes on her.

She wrapped her arms around his neck, and the kiss became so satisfyingly deep. In that moment, Brian was so lost in her he would've bet money he *was* flying.

CHAPTER SIX

Fiona walked past Carrie's office but didn't really expect to see her there. She had been hoping, though, which was something she'd been doing for the past two weeks.

The partners weren't saying anything to her, even though she was Carrie's paralegal, but all she'd managed to get from the office grapevine was that Carrie had been in an accident and that all pending cases she had been trying were put on hold or reassigned. Fiona assumed she herself would also be temporarily reassigned, but as for now, her job was to get all Carrie's opened cases in order.

But just as equally huge was the news about Harvey Adams. His murder had been the top local story on all news stations for the past two weeks. The office gossip was spreading like a brushfire as most of the staff in the firm, including Fiona herself, tried to connect Carrie's accident to his grisly death. After all, everyone knew the two of them were dating, and now he's dead and she just woke from a coma. But the news wasn't reporting much about Carrie's car accident, and Fiona guessed her wealthy and influential parents had a lot to do with that.

"Fiona, you're wanted upstairs in conference room D." Roger, an assistant to one of the

partners, had come by to inform her.

"Why?" Fiona asked. She looked up from her work and was met with an appalled look as if she had no right to question anyone's orders.

"The partners are up there and so are the police."

"The police? Why do they want to see me?"

His look turned impatient. "I was only sent to get you, not answer questions."

She hesitated a moment longer and then stood from her desk and stalked past him toward the elevators.

In a few minutes, she arrived at her summoned spot but stood outside the conference room, looking at the men inside talking and wishing she could lip read. Soon, one of the partners looked up, noticed her and came to open the glass door of the conference room for her.

"Fiona, come in and join us, please."

He gestured to a man wearing a navy suit and badge, who was already sitting at the long conference table.

"This is Sergeant Harris with San Francisco homicide."

"Homicide?" she asked before sitting down in the chair provided. In the next instant, she shot up as though she'd been pricked by a needle. "Oh my God, my brother!"

Sergeant Harris also stood and quickly raised one hand as if to stop any further panic from her. "No, Ms. Richards. This has nothing to do with any member of your family. We're here on another matter that I believe you'll be able to help us with. It's concerning Carrie Wallace. You're her legal assistant, right?"

Fiona looked from the sergeant to the partners and then back to the sergeant. "I was assigned as her paralegal."

"Paralegal," he corrected, writing something down on a small notepad. He then lowered himself back into the chair and gestured for Fiona to do the same. She did so, but not before darting another glance at the partners seated around the table. She couldn't tell whether they were present for her protection or for the firm's.

"Tell me, Ms. Richards. When was the last time you spoke to Carrie Wallace?"

"You can call me Fiona, and I would say it was about a couple of weeks ago."

"And where was that?"

She paused. She wasn't sure if she should be forthright with him or not. Was she supposed to be protecting the firm, too? If so, it would've been nice if someone had coached her on what to say.

"Fiona?"

"She came to my apartment. I believe it was the night of her accident. March 17th."

"What time was this?"

"A little after eight in the evening."

He wrote down more notes. "And what was the purpose of that visit?"

Fiona recalled the seriousness in Carrie's eyes that night as she handed her the flash drive.

"Don't tell anyone about this or show this to anyone. Not even the partners. Just keep this until I come back for it."

"She wanted to give me some paperwork to file that had to do with the trial she was preparing for."

Sergeant Harris gave her a long look, and she knew that he knew she was already holding something back. But before his steady gaze could penetrate her defenses, one of the partners spoke up.

"Speaking of which, Sergeant, all of Attorney Wallace's cases have been reassigned to other senior associates for the time being. I'll be happy to have my assistant send you a list of the associates handling each case."

"I'd appreciate that." Sergeant Harris broke his stare for the moment, and Fiona took that time to control her breathing. She reminded herself to just continue to answer his questions but be as succinct as possible. She'd been present at enough trials to know how to do that.

Sergeant Harris gave her his attention again. "Now, Fiona, when you saw Ms. Wallace that night, did she seem upset, agitated, nervous in any way?"

"No, she just seemed hurried. We'd been working on this case for a while now, and the trial was set to begin next week."

"So, she only gave you paperwork to file and left?"

"That's right, Sergeant."

"Did she frequently visit your apartment?"

"Not socially, but she would occasionally come by after work if she needed to give me something regarding a case."

It was a lie, but she couldn't say anything more—not to him or the partners—until she spoke to Carrie.

Just keep this until I come back for it.

"Did she say anything about where she was going after she left you?"

"No, not at all."

"Did you ask?"

Fiona frowned. "Why would I? It's none of my business what she was doing or where she was going. I'm her paralegal. That's as far as our relationship goes."

Harris paused to study her for a moment. Fiona could see now he was trying to get a sense of Carrie's movements the night of Harvey's death. Had Carrie gone to see him after leaving her place?

"What do you think of Ms. Wallace? Is she pretty easy to work for or difficult?"

Fiona hesitated and looked around at the other partners. Was he serious? Did he really expect her to say anything about Carrie other than that she was the best boss in the world? The truth was Carrie was unapproachable. She made it known from the beginning there was an invisible wall between the two of them, and they would not cross it by any means. Fiona didn't take it personally, because she seemed to keep everyone at a distance. In fact, she'd been very surprised to hear that Carrie and Harvey Adams were dating. It meant she'd allowed someone to get close to her.

On occasions they stayed late, working on a case, Carrie kept to herself, shut in her office and only speaking to Fiona when she needed something. Fiona didn't mind the quiet or the distance Carrie put between them, but she often wondered if Carrie minded. There were times when Fiona would look up from her computer and through the closed glass door of Carrie's office only to find the woman staring forlornly out her window at the bright lights of San Francisco. Fiona wished she could read minds, because Carrie was nothing short of an enigma. She knew she came from a wealthy family, had a fine education, and was married briefly. The rumors were that her wedding had more than six hundred people—mostly friends and acquaintances of her parents. Now, she was divorced and married to her job. She seemed to be content with it all, but those long-lost looks Fiona saw said otherwise.

"Ms. Wallace is excellent to work for and a fine attorney."

Sergeant Harris let go a heavy sigh and closed his notepad. "I believe that's enough for now." He stood from his seat and handed Fiona his card. "If you think of anything more, please contact me. No matter how small."

Fiona nodded, took the card, and slipped it into her trouser pocket.

"Sergeant, we'd like to speak with you for a moment

before you go," one of the partners said, rising from his chair. "You may go, Fiona."

Fiona headed for the glass doors of the conference room, then stopped and turned. "Where is Carrie, I mean, Ms. Wallace, right now?"

They all turned to her, and Sergeant Harris cleared his throat.

"She's been released from San Francisco General, and at the moment, she's up north, recovering and doing therapy."

"Physical therapy?"

"No," he hesitated. "Psychiatric."

Psychiatric?

She stepped forward. "Where exactly up north?"

One of the partners spoke up. "I'm sorry, Fiona, but at this time, her location is not being revealed at the request of her family. We agree she should be given as much privacy and rest as possible."

"But I—"

"If you have anything pressing, you can give it to me or any of the other partners, and we'll make sure it's referred to one of the attorneys now handling her cases. For now, you'll be assigned to another senior attorney who will be taking over the embezzlement case Carrie was working on. Now again, you may go."

This time, she did adhere to the dismissal and quickly left, deciding she wasn't giving them a damn thing.

When she returned to her floor, she walked back to her desk and sat down, feeling defeated, unsure, and a little nervous.

She reached for her purse now at the bottom of her desk drawer and pulled out the flash drive tucked inside a small zipper pocket. It had given her a start when she heard Carrie's words, that night, but Fiona had shrugged it off.

Now Carrie was indisposed somewhere, and she was starting to wonder just what she held in her hands.

She looked around the small area of her cubicle and saw that the other paralegals were busy working and not paying her any attention. She looked down at the small flash drive again and bit her lip. It had to be important. Maybe something on it would at least give her a way to contact Carrie, and she never said she couldn't open it.

Without another thought, Fiona plugged the drive into her computer and pulled up the first document that was there. It was an Excel spreadsheet, and from what she could tell, it was a record of deposits and withdrawals to and from a bank account: $2700, $3000, $3500... The payouts seemed to have gone on for several months and then abruptly stopped. Fiona squinted and read that the last payment was made two weeks ago, the day before Carrie's accident.

Was this Carrie's financial data? If so, what was the reason for the money transfers, and why did she have to give it to Fiona for safekeeping? The depositor's name read, *Magnolia Trust.* Fiona searched her mind for cases she worked on in the past with Carrie, figuring the deposits were coming from a client. But no cases came to mind, and even so, all fees and billable hours were paid directly to the firm, unless Carrie was taking money separately.

Fiona shook her head, now regretting even opening the document. Maybe she should just go ahead and give this to the partners. They would be able to make sense of it because she suddenly felt like she was wandering beyond her pay grade.

She exited out of the financial document and saw an icon labeled *MP3* dated last month. She looked around again and saw she was still not being watched, then pulled out a pair of earbuds from her purse. She kept her music with her along with a spare change of clothes just in case she ever felt inspired to go to the gym and actually make use of the expensive monthly membership fee she was paying.

She plugged the earbuds into the computer, clicked on the icon and adjusted the volume. Immediately, she heard two voices. One was Carrie's voice and the other was a man's voice she didn't recognize, and they were arguing. Pressing her fingers tightly against her ears, she frowned as the conversation played out for her. Then the frown disappeared, and she immediately pressed *stop* and looked around again.

Fiona removed the headphones, pulled the flash drive from the computer, and stuck it back inside her purse. She slowly stood from her desk and announced to no one in particular that she was going to get coffee and made her way to the elevator. The entire ride down, she felt like a criminal carrying contraband. When she arrived at the lobby floor, she hurried out of the building, and it wasn't until she was several blocks away from the firm and among the crowd of the financial district that she felt safe enough to pull out her cell phone. She had three options: she could hand this over to the partners, making up some excuse that she'd forgotten about it, and let them take over from here; she could give this to Sergeant Harris because what she held in her shaking hands had to be evidence; or she could find Carrie, give it back to her, and pretend she hadn't heard a damn thing. But her researcher's brain was urging her to go with another option: find out what Carrie was up to. That idea seemed all the more intriguing because as Fiona replayed the recorded conversation in her mind now, she realized she did know the other voice. She recognized it from the many times he would come to the office and offer to take Carrie to lunch or dinner. ADA Harvey Adams. Carrie had been arguing with a man who was now dead.

CHAPTER SEVEN

A tense mood floated around the table and filled the room as Brian sat beside Shawn, opposite Natalie and Andrew Wallace. He'd made the trip up to San Francisco to have a discussion with Carrie's family to get prepared for his first counseling session with her in a matter of weeks. The meeting was being held in a conference room in Andrew Wallace's office. When he'd arrived, Brian deliberately avoided the spare office, now vacant, that used to belong to his father and Andrew's former partner—Gerald Kessler.

As he sat at the small conference table, he studied the faces of his ex-in-laws and saw they were still feeling reluctant about this entire arrangement. Natalie's eyes especially, told Brian she'd rather be anywhere else than sitting across the table from him. Andrew, stoic as ever, looked at his watch and then sent Brian an impatient look.

"Why are we here?" His deep voice boomed. "You know everything there is to know about Carrie's condition after speaking with her doctors."

"I'm not here to talk about her medical diagnosis," Brian

said evenly. "I called you all together to give me an idea of her emotional state before the accident."

"Her emotional state?" Natalie echoed.

"Yes. Carrie doesn't remember anything before the accident, so I need your help in filling in any gaps—anything I need to know that will give me an idea of what she was dealing with at the time."

They all remained silent. Three faces stared back at him, completely void of expression.

Brian tried a different tact. "During our marriage, I remember how close she was to all of you. She hated to miss Sunday dinners, as it was a time when you all would talk about what was going on in your lives."

He used to love those Sunday dinners at her parents' house as well. For one, they lived in Sea Cliff, a very wealthy and elite neighborhood in the city with multimillion-dollar homes perched along the water that gave its residents an enviable and unobstructed view of the Golden Gate Bridge. He'd grown up in San Francisco, and it had always been a dream for him to experience how the other half lived. However, he never told anyone that his dream had always been to be rich. He never shared it with anyone for fear it would make him appear shallow. But while other boys dreamed of being astronauts, firefighters, or President of the United States, Brian just wanted to be rich.

He'd grown up poor, his family living in a tiny, rundown apartment over a deli in Potrero Hill in the days before it was revitalized. While his father went to school, working on his doctorate and clinical studies, Brian's mother worked two jobs to make sure the rent was paid and the utilities stayed on. It was tough on her because there were many months she fell behind, and Brian often came home to find the lights shut off, no running water, or both. His father would be gone, abandoning the home for the library, with its lights and central air conditioning, to get his studies done.

Then came the day when his father graduated, got a position at a medical office, and things got better. They weren't wealthy, but they were miles ahead from where they'd been. Far enough ahead that Brian's parents were able to afford to move to a better neighborhood and send him to private school. But private school only increased his desire for wealth by seeing the opulence of his classmates. He knew before he even graduated high school that he was going to make a business for himself—no one ever got rich working for someone else.

Fast forward years later, his father began to develop a name for himself in the psychiatric field, specifically brain trauma. He got the attention of Andrew Wallace, a renowned neurosurgeon, and a partnership was formed. But that wasn't were it ended. Andrew not only saw a prosperous union with Gerald Kessler, but he had plans for Brian—plans that included his daughter, Carrie.

But after everything had happened with his father, Brian began to feel unwelcome at those dinners. And to his disappointment, Carrie, his wife at the time, silently chose a side, and it wasn't his.

Shawn spoke up. "It's strange, because the Sundays leading up to her accident, she seemed quiet and kept to herself a lot. Any time any of us asked her if something was wrong, she denied it, but I could tell something was bothering her."

"I figured she'd tell us when she was ready," Natalie said, dismissively. "Carrie always had a big case she was working on, and the closer she got to trial, the more reserved she became."

"You think her stress might have come from work?" Brian asked.

"It always had to do with work," she continued. "Ever since the divorce, she has dedicated herself to her career, and she's made a success of it."

Brian would have to be blind and deaf not to see the gleam of satisfaction in her eyes or hear the gloating in her words. He had been taking notes as they spoke and now put his pen down slowly and leveled his gaze at Natalie.

"Carrie has always been dedicated to her work. She's a brilliant attorney. I always knew that and never tried to stand in the way of her career."

Natalie narrowed her eyes. "That's not how I saw it. You nearly jeopardized her reputation when you practically threatened that she leave the firm."

Brian could feel his temper rising, but there was no stopping it. "You mean the firm that represented the family that was going after my father? You bet I told her to quit."

"Your father made a terrible misjudgment. Everyone knew that. After the tragedy with that actress—*Jesus!*" Natalie threw up her hands. "And you expected Carrie to risk her career to stand with you in that mess?"

"Yes, I did. But obviously, I was expecting too much. Your daughter may have been a good lawyer, but she wasn't a very good wife."

"How dare you!"

"Enough!"

They both looked toward Andrew Wallace, who'd slammed his fist down onto the oak table, demanding silence. He then put a steady but firm hand on his wife's shoulder.

"Bringing up the past isn't going to change anything. Let's just answer his questions and get through this meeting. This is for Carrie."

Brian could see she was having a tough time backing down, but she finally nodded and sat back in her chair, only to stare sightlessly at an invisible spot on the opposite wall.

Andrew then turned to Brian, pointing a finger at him. "As for you. I'll admit you're one of the best at what you do. I'm entrusting my daughter's care to you because I know you'll do whatever is necessary to heal her. But don't make the mistake of thinking I'm going to tolerate you bad-mouthing her in front of us. Whatever happened between the two of you is your business."

"That's the problem, Andrew," Brian said. "What happened between us was never just our business."

Andrew's glare lessened only slightly as if he heard the truth in Brian's words. He then also sat back and put an arm around his wife's chair. Shawn, who had stayed quiet during the entire exchange, finally spoke up now that his parents were subdued.

He leaned forward, clasping his hands together. "My mother is right that Carrie seemed to be nervous about a new case. She wouldn't even talk about it."

"Fine," Brian said and changed the subject. "What about this man—Harvey Adams. Who was he?"

"From what we could find out, he worked for the DA's office here in San Francisco. He may have been a colleague of hers. She developed a lot of relationships with ADAs since she often went against them in trial."

"I've been able to get from the police that he was found dead in his apartment and must have been killed sometime between nine and eleven p.m.," Brian said, glancing down at his legal pad full of handwritten notes. "What was she doing there so late?"

None of them ventured to give him an answer, and he was left to draw his own conclusions.

"All we know is that a neighbor saw Carrie running away from his apartment, and she had blood on her," Shawn said.

"The neighbor called out to her, but she didn't answer. She got in her car and drove away."

"Where did she go?"

"No one knows," Andrew said, cutting in. "We got a call about the accident on the 101. She flipped her car twice."

An involuntary shudder of fear for Carrie shot up Brian's spine. It wasn't the first time the thought came to him that she could've been killed, and it angered and scared him just as the many other times he thought about it ever since hearing she was in the hospital.

"Is there anything else I need to know?" he asked.

Natalie didn't bother responding but quietly stood from the table and grabbed her purse. Both Andrew and Shawn shook their heads no, and Brian was absolutely certain they were lying to him. But he said nothing and watched as the two of them also stood to leave. Shawn gave him a conciliatory nod and a wave, but Brian didn't respond. That entire conversation with the Wallace family only reminded him of the arguments he had with Carrie.

"What happened to Eliza was tragic, and the backlash Gerald got was terrible," Carrie said. "Still, he was my father's partner, and you have to understand the pressure my father was getting to cut ties with him."

"It's all just business," Brian concluded with cynicism.

She shook her head sadly. "I told you a long time ago that appearances and family honor—all that stuff matters to them."

"That doesn't mean they should matter to you. I'm your husband, Carrie. I'm your family! How about our fucking family honor?" He gestured his hand back and forth between the two of them. "You and me."

CHAPTER EIGHT

The town of Gypsy Bay was what I would describe as charming. It was a small town just sixty miles north of San Francisco and sat right along the coast of the Pacific. I got the feeling it was a place where people came to get away from it all, to hide from it all, or maybe like me, to remember it all. My family helped move me into the little furnished cottage home I would be spending my days in as I began my treatment with Dr. Brian Kessler. My father and brother left only a few moments ago, after helping us carry my things into the house. I got the feeling they felt uncomfortable with my condition, so I didn't balk when they made up some feeble excuse about wanting to beat the traffic back to the city. My mother, on the other hand, was in no hurry to leave me and even decided she would spend the night on the couch just to make sure I was situated.

"You don't have to do that," I said, not sure why I wanted to be alone. "I'm sure I'll be fine."

"Carrie, you don't know anyone out here," she said. "What if you need something?"

"I only planned to go through some of these pictures, watch a little TV, and then go to bed. Besides, if something happens, I'm sure Dr. Kessler will help—"

"No," she said sharply. "I'm your mother, and I'll stay here for the night."

I sighed, deciding it was easier to just let her have her way, and I was sure it wasn't the first time I conceded to her wishes. I then eyed the stack of photo albums she'd brought from home.

"Let's get started on those. Maybe something will jog my memory."

That seemed to please her, and for the next hour, she handed me photos of people who were unfamiliar to me. Grandparents, aunts, uncles and cousins, living and deceased, and with each picture she would say, "Do you remember her?" or "Surely, you remember that" or "Now I know you couldn't have possibly forgotten…"

After a while, I felt terrible. I knew she meant well, but as far as I could tell, the people in these photos were strangers, except for her, Dad, and Shawn, and the only reason I knew them was because they were the first faces I saw when I woke from the coma.

As my mother talked, I nodded, taking in as many details as I could hold and studied each picture she placed in front of me. I started recognizing the same group of relatives from previous pictures, but now it seemed as if these same people were all in one place and dressed up.

"Were these taken at some party?" I asked, picking up one picture of my two cousins. The women were both dressed in short cocktail dresses, holding glasses of champagne and smiling for the camera.

I found one of my brother. It was the same party-like setting, maybe a fancy restaurant, and he was in a tuxedo.

Mom leaned over and frowned at the pictures. "I believe so, yes, but for the life of me, I can't remember what we were celebrating."

I looked at her, but she had already bowed her head and resumed flipping through another album. I frowned with suspicion. For more than an hour, she'd spoken nonstop and in great detail about every photograph. She even had anecdotes for nearly everyone. Now suddenly, she wasn't sure about this one event. She was hiding something from me. But why? Wasn't the idea to tell me everything and let my mind connect the dots? Why keep secrets from me now?

I let it go, finally putting the pictures aside, and closed the album. "I think I'm done for tonight. I don't want to overdo it."

"Of course, honey," she said, closing her own album and gathering up scattered photos.

I looked around the small living area and into the equally small connecting kitchen and wondered how long I would have to be there. How long would it take my mind to start remembering?

"Mom," I said, trying out the word. "You said I was a lawyer?"

"Oh, how stupid of me," she said. "I didn't bring your diplomas. Yes, you're a lawyer, a senior litigator to be precise." She leaned forward and winked conspiratorially. "And I'm not ashamed to say a very good one."

I smiled at the compliment. "Was I working on any cases before the accident? Maybe getting back to work would help."

She was already shaking her head before I finished. "The partners have already begun reassigning your cases. At the moment, you're on paid leave, and they want you to just focus on getting better."

I tried again. "I overheard Dr. Kessler talking to Shawn and Dad. He suggested I get back to my daily routines as soon as possible."

If I hadn't been looking at her, I would have missed the glare that came over her lovely face. She masked it with a smile.

"I know Dr. Kessler is a leading psychiatrist in this area, but there are other options, Carrie, and I wish you hadn't been in such a rush to use him for your treatment."

"Okay, that's enough," I said, my voice rising. "My memory might be gone, but it didn't make me oblivious. You don't like him. Why not?"

She was momentarily surprised by my tone but recovered quickly. "I—I don't even know him. I just want you to know there are other options."

She was lying again, but I was too tired to try to pull the truth from her. Sighing to myself, I started to help gather up the scattered photos and came across the picture of a car lying on its hood. I gripped the picture in my hand as visions came racing at me that didn't make any sense. I was in a car, driving fast with tears streaming down my face. I had seen something, and now I was running away. Suddenly, I was screaming, the car was toppling over and over and then darkness.

"Carrie! Honey, I'm so sorry," my mother said, snatching the photograph from me and gripping my hands. "Are you all right?"

I nodded, putting a hand to my forehead to stave off an oncoming headache. "I think I was seeing a memory of the accident."

"That picture was taken for your insurance claim. I should have taken it out." She paused and looked at me, alarmed. "My God, you're shaking. Are you cold?"

"I was shaking that night," I said, softly.

"What?"

I looked at her. "I was shaking that night, Mom, just before I flipped my car. But I wasn't cold. I was shaking because I was scared."

CHAPTER NINE

"Help me understand," Rachel said, pouring coffee into a to-go canister. "There are other psychiatrists residing in San Francisco that specialize in memory loss and brain trauma. Why does she have to move sixty miles north to have you treat her?"

Brian leaned against the counter, holding a mug of steaming coffee, and replied with a smirk, "Because I'm the best, sweetheart."

Instead of laughing, Rachel leveled a look at him that told him she wasn't in the mood for jokes. He sighed, put the mug down on the counter, and folded his arms.

"You sound just like her mother."

"Her mother? What does she have to do with this?"

"She's not a fan of this idea either. In fact, she's never been a fan of me, period. She's always believed Carrie could have done better than me and was only too glad when we split up."

Rachel didn't respond, so he took that as an opportunity to further plead his case.

"Despite her mother's misgivings, the family knows me,

and I know Carrie. I guess it makes them comfortable knowing we already have a built-in relationship."

"So, you're there for the personal touch," she said. "Did you give them the ex-husband discount?"

"Come on, Rachel."

She grabbed her canister and stalked past him to her briefcase, where she began shoving papers inside of it. "It was a joke, but you can at least understand my misgivings about this. You were married to the woman once. It was bad and you divorced each other. The end. Why is there now a sequel?"

"She completely lost her memory," he said. "She doesn't remember me or what happened between us."

She snapped the briefcase closed and glared at him. "But you do."

He paused to frown at her. "What's really going on here? I've counseled women before and you were never this…"

"Never this what? Go ahead, say it."

"Jealous."

Her eyes flashed, and then she inhaled deeply, held it and let it out slowly. "I don't know what's wrong with me. Maybe it's her. You told me so many horror stories about the things you two said and did to each other. Then there was that business with your father…" She paused, eyed him warily, and something in his eyes must have stopped her from continuing down that track.

She turned her back to him. "Never mind. I guess having her back in your life, our lives, is rubbing me the wrong way."

Brian nodded, rounded the counter and moved up behind her. He wrapped his arm around her waist and kissed the side of her neck. She leaned her head back against his shoulder, giving him easy access to nuzzle her neck. His hands moved up her blouse and undid the top few buttons. He then pulled the blouse down over her shoulders until her tattoo was visible. He smiled at the sight of an inked hummingbird hovering over a flower and kissed it lightly.

Rachel chuckled. "You always go for my tattoo first."

"I like it," he said, kissing it again. "I especially like the story, little Ray bird."

He felt her still beneath his hands and knew it was due to the memories he'd conjured up. He stopped and slowly turned her around to face him.

"I'm sorry. I don't mean to make light of it. I know that name is special to you."

She'd told him her sister, Lily, had given her the nickname when she was little. Lily drowned when they were just girls, and Rachel paid tribute to her with the tattoo.

"It's okay," she said, shrugging. "It was a long time ago. Talking about her doesn't hurt as much as it used to."

"That nickname sounds familiar to me, and it suits you. Maybe that's why I like it."

She shrugged. "Lily got it from an old movie she saw and just started calling me that one day."

He bent his head forward and kissed her until the vulnerable look in her eyes was gone. As soon as their lips separated, the doorbell to his office sounded, signaling his patient had arrived. Brian dropped his hands from her waist and moved away from her. He started toward the door that led to his office and then turned to look at her, silently asking if she was okay.

"Go on," Rachel said, chuckling. "The sooner she remembers that she hates you, the sooner she'll be gone."

CHAPTER TEN

"I've been here before. I remember this house."

The last time I saw Brian Kessler was in the hospital. I'd asked him if we knew each other, he stormed out of my room, and that was it. Now, it appeared he agreed to be my psychiatrist and help me regain my memory. But judging from his demeanor and the look on his face, he didn't seem too happy about it. Maybe he was forced into it by my family. They seemed like the type of people who threw their weight around—especially with money. Was I the same way? Did I believe everything could be solved by tossing a few bills at someone?

When he gestured silently for me to take a seat, I decided to lighten things up a little between us by stroking his ego.

"Thank you for agreeing to help me," I said. "I hear you're one of the best..." I trailed off and looked around his office. I noticed the books with his name on the jacket spine, his framed degrees from prestigious universities, and photos of him with people who were most likely well-known in the psychiatric community.

"Very impressive," I finished softly.

"Thank you," he said, grabbing a blank notepad and pen from his desk, and sat down in an armchair across from me. "Let me start by explaining the way I work. I want you to start with anything you remember about yourself and about the night of your accident. This first session is just going to be a nice, easy chat. Think of it as getting to know each other, only we'll both be getting to know you."

I nodded, a little taken aback by his brusque manner, and the fact there was still a trace of hardness behind his tone and his eyes when he looked at me. I still didn't know what to make of it, and he never really did answer my question in the hospital room. But something told me this wasn't the time to push him into admitting something when I wasn't even sure there was anything to admit.

"In the coming weeks, I'll start to probe you a little, but not too much, to see if we can loosen up some more memories. We'll meet twice a week and when you're not here with me, I expect you to do exercises at home to aid your mind in remembering. A lot of your healing will depend on you and how committed you are to working with me."

"I understand."

"Good," he said, sitting back in his chair. "Now, tell me anything. Anything you remember about yourself."

I started by closing my eyes. It was a trick I picked up in the hospital, and I found it helpful when I was trying to recall something. But everything right now in my brain was still a fog.

After a moment, I shook my head, irritated with myself. "No, there's nothing."

"It doesn't matter how small or mundane, Carrie," he said, trying to prod me. "Maybe your favorite color, favorite food, or a song you like to sing?"

"Why doesn't my mother like you?"

He frowned at the sudden change in subject and cleared his throat. "Isn't that more of a question for your mother?"

"I already asked her."

"And what did she say?"

"She said she doesn't agree with some of your methods."

"Well, then, I guess you have your answer."

I stared, waiting for him to say more, but he didn't. Neither one of them was going to tell me what I wanted to know, so I decided to let it go for now.

"Now what?" I asked.

"Do you want to talk about the night of the accident?"

I closed my eyes again and gave way to the scrambled visions that came to me.

"I remember driving, with blood on my hands." I paused. "They tell me the blood wasn't mine."

"That's what the police are saying."

"I want to tell myself, tell everyone that I would never hurt anybody, but I can't because I don't know that about myself. Maybe I am a dangerous person."

"You're not."

For the first time in our session, his blue eyes softened toward me.

"How do you know that?"

"There would be signs. I don't see anything like that in you."

"The police want to question me. My mother is getting me a lawyer to be there with me, but I thought it would also be good if my therapist was there. In case I have any breakthroughs.

Do you mind?"

"Not at all. I'll be there."

"Thank you."

"I want you to try journaling any and every thing that comes to you, especially in your

dreams. When you're ready, I'd also like to take you back to the scene of the accident to see if anything more is triggered."

I nodded, feeling reassured by his plans. "How long do you think it will be before I remember everything about myself?"

"That's impossible to answer. You're going to hear me say this over and over again, but every mind is different. We file things away until we're ready to face them. Time will pass, the mind slowly heals, and then one day, a memory returns."

Brian spent the rest of the session walking me through more exercises he wanted me to try, and by the end of it, I was feeling overwhelmed. He walked me to the side door that served as the entrance to his office and held my coat open for me. As I slipped my arms into the sleeves of my coat, I could feel his warmth surrounding me from behind, and I immediately felt calm again.

"Thank you," I said and opened the door. Then I turned back to face him. "I have one more question. It's the same one I asked you in the hospital, but you never answered me."

"Carrie—"

"I'm sorry for being persistent, but I have this feeling you and I know each other. It's the same feeling I had with my family. I don't remember them, but it's hard to deny the feeling of familiarity. So, Dr. Kessler, who am I to you?"

I watched his blue eyes, looking for any hint that I wasn't just imagining this feeling.

"Nothing," he said, his tone cold and unfeeling. "We have no relationship whatsoever."

CHAPTER ELEVEN

Brian couldn't help it. As soon as the door closed behind her, he moved to the window and pulled the curtains back slightly to watch as she got into her car and drove away. It wasn't until she was further down the road that he began to feel himself breathe easier. It was still hard to believe that Carrie was back in his life again. Having her occupy the same space as him, having her sitting only a few feet away from him, conversing with her as though she was just a stranger... It all felt surreal. He hadn't seen or contacted her in three years, and with a simple twist of fate, she was back in his life. Only this time, she knew nothing about him, while he knew everything about her. It had been so tempting to help her fill in the details when she was telling him about herself, such as her favorite color being yellow, she loved key lime pie, and she used to sing softly in the shower because she thought she was tone deaf. Brian, however, had loved her singing voice.

Before she lost her memory, Carrie knew just as well as he that their marriage had been part of an arrangement, however, they both chose to ignore it, even though it was always there like an invisible wall between them. He wondered if she ever knew he blamed himself for entering into that deal with Andrew, all because he'd been tempted by money and prestige. He blamed himself every day, thinking that if he'd only married Carrie because he loved her and wanted to be with her, instead of for financial gain, their marriage would never have been tainted from the beginning.

* * *

As Brian exited the elevator onto the seventh floor of the medical office building, he admired the sleek look of the place. Plush carpeting and dark wood furniture decorated the waiting room. Framed prints of post-modern art lined the walls. Even the patients had an elite and exclusive look about them. Brian coveted the lavish surroundings and secretly filed every detail away in his memory for later inspiration when he finally had his own practice.

He walked up to the receptionist desk where a young woman with brilliant red, wavy hair smiled up at him.

"May I help you?"

"I'm Dr. Kessler, here to see Dr. Wallace."

"Oh yes, Dr. Kessler!" Her smile turned radiant. "He's expecting you. His office is in the back. Can I get you anything to drink? Coffee or tea?"

"No, thank you."

She stood and hit a button that silently unlocked the door leading to the back, where more sleek-looking offices waited. Brian thanked her and with her directions found his way to Andrew's office.

When Andrew saw him, he stood and gestured him inside with a welcoming smile. "Brian, come in."

"Thank you for inviting me over," Brian said, looking around as he took a seat. "You have a very nice place here."

Andrew waved it off, as though his obvious wealth was no concern to him.

"Did Regina offer you something to drink?"

"Yes, but I'm good. Thank you."

Andrew Wallace's deep, baritone voice made him the kind of man who commanded attention. Although he was in the process of partnering with Brian's father, they hadn't taken the time to get to know each other. Brian figured that was what this meeting was about. He admitted to himself that being near the man both intimidated and impressed him. He was an African-American man who could've used his humble upbringing as an excuse to take the wrong path in life. Instead, he used it as motivation to become a leader in his field. Brian felt a connection to him because he, too, wanted to rise above his station in life. He wanted to achieve success in his career. The kind of success that made him so prosperous, he never had to look back and be reminded of his poor beginnings.

"I don't want to take up too much of your time," Andrew said, leaning back in his chair. "But I wanted to tell you that since your father and I are joining practices, I've begun to take an interest in your work, and I have to say I'm very impressed with you."

Brian sat up straighter. "Thank you, sir."

Andrew continued. "I hope you don't mind, but I took the liberty of requesting your academic records from Berkeley, and I see that not only have you started publishing extensively in psychiatry, you were called upon many times to lecture."

Brian nodded. "As a doctoral student, sometimes my professors would give us the opportunity to lecture to the underclassmen."

"You're being modest," Andrew said. "After your thesis was published, you were even asked to lecture to faculty members."

Brian didn't say anything to that. Yes, he was considered top in his class, but he didn't like to talk about it. Andrew called it modesty, but Brian just didn't see the point when his record spoke for itself. He never liked the idea of interviewing for a job, and he had a sneaking suspicion that's what Andrew was trying to get him to do.

"Your father tells me you have another month to go with your residency. I'm sure you've received offers from many practices."

"Yes."

"Have you thought about being your own boss, instead?"

"Sir?"

Andrew grinned. "I already talked to Gerald about this, and he wholeheartedly agreed. Because of your stellar academics and what you've managed to accomplish in such a short time in your career, I'd like to offer you your own practice."

Brian kept his face void of emotion, but inside he was battling between standing still in complete shock and doing back flips in excitement.

"Dr. Wallace, I appreciate your confidence in me, and owning my own practice is of course a goal of mine, but what my record doesn't say is that I have massive school debt. Like my father, I worked and took out loans to pay for school. I appreciate your faith in me, but my own practice is years off."

Andrew nodded indulgently. "I believe that someday, you'll be as brilliant as your father, and given time, you may even surpass him. I want to help you get a head start. I want to invest in your practice, and of course, that includes taking care of your student loan debt."

Brian could no longer keep his emotions at bay. He was stunned.

"Why?"

"I think I've kissed your ass enough to explain why," Andrew said on a chuckle.

Brian slowly stood and reached out his hand to shake Andrew's. "Thank you, sir. You're very generous, and I accept."

Andrew returned the handshake and smiled. "You're welcome, but sit back down. It's only fair that you hear my entire offer before making a decision."

There it was. No one would be this generous without wanting something in return, and Brian wasn't ashamed to admit to himself that he was willing to give almost anything the man asked of him. He took his seat and watched as Andrew threaded his fingers between his hands. He paused to look down at them, then slowly looked up to return his focus to Brian.

"This may sound strange, but tell me something. What do you think of my daughter, Carrie?"

CHAPTER TWELVE

Widow Lake 11:01 p.m.
The two of them sat together on a park bench in solitude. The trails along the lake had been closed hours ago, but they always found a way to get in. He stared out at the vast lake and dark silhouette of forest beyond it. It was a beautiful place to be, but there was no warmth in his heart.

She looked over at him and wondered if he was thinking about her, who sat beside him like this every week, patiently waiting for the day when all of this plotting and scheming would be over. Or was he thinking of Eliza—his first love, who was the reason she, herself, could never have his heart.

She promised herself she would hold her tongue and just enjoy the feeling of his arms draped around her shoulders, pulling her close to him and staring out at the moonlit waters. But a lot had been on her mind recently, and if she couldn't talk to him, who could she talk to?

"I'm worried. With Harvey's death, don't you think we should pull out?"

"Hell, no," he said, quickly. "His death was an accident, and yeah, it may have set us back, but we're not going to stop. We can find another greedy ADA to do the job."

Even in the darkness, she could see he was holding a steady, sly smile.

"You already have someone in mind."

He turned to her, clearly proud of his own cleverness, and his smile turned wide and brilliant. "Always have a backup, baby. It's a woman this time."

"Will she agree to pursue the indictment? We got a lot of flak from Harvey about the flimsy evidence."

"Yes, but like Harvey, this one has a few skeletons she would rather not see come to light. She'll take the case."

She looked away. Now came the part she hated. "How much is it going to cost?"

At least he had the grace to hesitate. "Well, with Harvey's death, she was a little apprehensive in taking over, so I had to sweeten the deal a little. I agreed to two grand more than we were paying Harvey."

She wanted to scream. This money they were paying out, the money from her inheritance from Eliza, it should be going toward a future together. They could take this money, leave and start a new life anywhere they chose. Instead, they were here, and she was being bled dry to finance a revenge plan—*his* revenge plan.

He must have sensed her darkening mood because he turned to her, tightened his arm around her, and tilted her chin up to look at him.

"I'm sorry. I know what you want for us, and I want it too. You have to believe that. But I don't think I'd ever be happy with you, knowing that the man who defamed Eliza's name is walking around free. The man who couldn't accept the fact that his father was a fuck-up and took Eliza away from me—from us. I want him to pay, and then I want a life with you."

God, she wanted to believe that.

CHAPTER THIRTEEN

I climbed out of my car in front of a coffee shop in downtown Gypsy Bay. It was not quite a small town but also not a bustling metropolis. Still, having been there a week, I needed to find my way around. I wasn't sure how long I planned to stay, but I assumed it would be until I got the bulk of my memories back. But, however long I planned to call this a temporary home, I should at least get to know it a little better. The day had dawned sunny for Northern California, though the fog was expected to roll into the town later in the day, so I planned to enjoy the light and warmth while I could.

As soon as I entered the coffee shop, the perky young girl smiled from behind the counter and greeted me.

"Welcome to Beans and Brews. What can I get you?"

"Just a medium black coffee."

"Right away," she said.

Moments later with my to-go cup in hand, I left the shop and bypassed my parked car, deciding instead to take a walk around the downtown area. I strolled past boutiques, hardware stores, antique shops, and a bar and grill on the corner of Seventh Avenue and Evangeline called *Charlie's*. I slowed as I passed the large picture windows because inside the restaurant, I saw a familiar face.

It was Brian.

I stopped and stared, watching my therapist have lunch with a young woman who had her back to me. I moved to the side out of Brian's line of sight, but not so far away that I couldn't still see them. I didn't want to disturb them, but my curiosity got the better of me. Before I could tell myself to stop staring, the two of them rose and shared a long embrace. Then they walked arm in arm out of *Charlie's*. I turned around so my back was toward them and allowed them to pass by me unseen. However, that move made me miss my chance at seeing her face. I turned and began to follow them as they crossed the street, holding hands and looking like a loving couple. I didn't know why, but I wanted a look at her.

The two got a block ahead and then stopped to look at something in a store window. I took advantage of their pause to catch up to them. This would be my chance to get to see the woman in full view. I had the idea to pretend to bump into the two of them under the guise that I'd been wandering around town. Brian would then have to introduce us. Soon, they continued on their walk, and I followed suit, waiting for the opportunity to accidentally on purpose bump into them.

I was so entirely focused on my two targets I didn't see the woman coming out of an office with her head down, not seeing me either. As a result, we collided into each other, our purses fell, and small black and white photos scattered to the ground.

"I'm sorry," I said, grateful I'd managed to hold onto my coffee. I kneeled down to help her pick up the pictures. As I got a closer look at them, I could now see they were sonograms, and the grainy images were of a tiny fetus. I looked up at the building she just came out of and saw it was an obstetrics office. I then glanced at the woman who shared my same complexion, only her eyes seemed to hold more warmth. I studied the photos for just a moment more and then handed them back to her.

"Thank you," she said, rising to her feet. "And I should be the one apologizing. I wasn't looking where I was going."

I gestured to the pictures she now clutched in her hands. "You obviously have a lot on your mind right now. Congratulations, by the way."

The brightest smile came over her face, and it was contagious. I found myself smiling and sharing in her excitement.

She held out a hand. "Shannon Spencer."

"Carrie Wallace," I said, returning her handshake. "It's nice to meet you."

I didn't want to be rude, but I glanced around Shannon to see if I could spot Brian and tried not to look too disappointed when I saw that I'd lost him and his female companion.

Shannon cocked her head to one side. "I haven't seen you around town before. Did you move to Gypsy Bay or are you just visiting?"

"A little of both."

She frowned with confusion, and I continued to explain. I couldn't follow Brian anymore, and this was the first person besides my mother and therapist that I'd had a conversation with since going out there.

"I was involved in an accident and unfortunately lost my memory. So, I moved here temporarily as a patient to Dr. Kessler."

Recognition flashed in her brown eyes. "Oh, yes, Brian. I know him well. You're in good hands."

"That's what I keep hearing."

"It's true. He's a terrific psychiatrist. My husband suffered from memory loss a few years ago, and Dr. Kessler was very helpful. I'm not sure where Gray and I would be had it not been for..." It was now Shannon's turn to look over my shoulder, and when she did, her face went from calm to panic-stricken. "Oh shit," she hissed and began stuffing the sonogram pictures into her purse. "Don't say anything about these. He doesn't know yet."

"Who?"

I turned around to see a tall, broad-shouldered man in a tan law enforcement uniform with handsome features climbing out of a sheriff's vehicle. He made his way over to us, and I couldn't help but smile at his imposing figure and striking honey-brown eyes.

"Good afternoon, ladies," he said, giving me a smile and giving Shannon a kiss on the lips that was brief but rife with deep love. I suddenly felt envious of the two of them. Not because I wanted Gray for myself, but because I wanted someone to feel that way about me.

"I was looking for a lunch date," he said, looking down at her with a smile. "Are you free?"

"It so happens that I am," she said, returning his warmth. Shannon then turned to me. "Gray, this is Carrie Wallace. She's in town to see Dr. Kessler."

Gray returned his attention to me and held out a hand. "Gray Spencer. I'm the sheriff of Gypsy Bay. Welcome."

"Thank you," I said. "Shannon tells me you've worked with Brian before for memory loss."

"I have," he said, shoving his hands into his pockets. "Just remember to do the exercises and anything else he suggests. You're going to be frustrated with him and especially yourself, but it all helps. Trust him. He knows what he's doing."

He wrapped an arm around Shannon and shared a long look with her I couldn't decipher. Then they both looked back at me.

"You should come by the office some time if you need to talk about your experiences. It might help since I know what you're going through."

"That's a great idea," Shannon said.

I could see his offer was sincere, and I immediately felt grateful. "Thank you. I may just take you up on that since I'm feeling a little isolated." I looked around as people passed by on the sidewalk. "I guess we take for granted that we always know who we are."

"It's not something that happens every day. You have a right to feel out of sorts," Shannon said. "I can't even imagine what it would be like."

Another look passed between the couple as though they were sharing the same thought. I wondered briefly what their history was and then realized I had my own story to sort out before I could delve into anyone else's.

CHAPTER FOURTEEN

After saying goodbye to the Spencers, I explored a little more of Gypsy Bay. Truthfully, I was hoping to get another chance to see Brian and that woman he was with. Was he married? Dating? Was it any of my business? But I hadn't seen them again and decided it was time to return to my car and go back home.

When I pulled into my driveway, I turned off the ignition and just sat there with the windows rolled down. I could smell the salt in the air carried by the breeze from the sea. I felt at peace there. For some reason, this place spoke to me, but I didn't know what it was saying.

I had so many questions that no one was willing to answer for me. Parts of my life that I wanted to know, but either no one knew the answers or they just didn't want to tell me. The latter possibility roused more questions.

It was an odd feeling in some ways, not knowing whom I was and where I came from, and yet perfectly normal in other ways. This was my new normal—at least for the time being. I was getting to know myself all over again.

I finally climbed out of the car, and looking up at the sky, I noticed that the predicted fog was finally coming in.

When I opened the door, I saw that my mom was pacing the floor and looking very dignified in a pair of navy slacks, a white cashmere tank, which only seemed to make her chocolate skin glow, and dark brown loafers with her hair pulled back and styled in a French twist.

"Finally, you're back," she said.

"What's wrong?"

"Your lawyer called."

I put my keys in a basket by the door. "What did she say?"

"She wants to meet us at the police station in San Francisco. I already called your father, and he's going to be there, too."

"Why do the police want to speak to me?"

"Eve said something about the sergeant getting impatient. Your statement was very vague, and he wants to know if you've remembered anything else."

"A simple phone call will answer those questions," I said. "Number one, I had just awoken from a coma and number two, I still have amnesia and don't remember anything."

"Honey, he thinks you're holding out on them. But don't worry, Eve will take care of it. Let's just go down there, answer whatever questions he has, and then we can come back home."

I thought for just a moment. "I'm calling Dr. Kessler."

She actually looked insulted. "What? Why?"

"Because it will help to have my therapist confirm that I'm not playing some kind of game. He can tell this Sergeant Harris that I really can't remember anything," I said.

"Eve can tell them that. She's there to protect you."

My eyes fell closed. Why did we keep having this argument? "Dr. Kessler is an expert in the field."

"I don't think he should be there," she said, definitively.

"I'm sorry, Mom, but I'm calling his office."

I dug inside my purse for my cell phone. My mother stood in front of me with her arms crossed and a disappointed look on her face, but I ignored her and dialed Brian's number. His voicemail answered, and I figured he was still out enjoying his free time with his date. An unexpected feeling of jealousy rose up inside of me, and I quickly left a message, explaining the situation, and then hung up and looked at my mother.

"What time do they want me there?"

"In two hours. We should leave now."

I moved to the kitchen. "Let me make a sandwich first for the road. Do you want one?"

"How can you be so calm?" she asked, following behind me to the kitchen and standing in the doorway.

"Looks can be deceiving. I'm anything but calm. But the truth is, I can't tell them anything. No matter how impatient they get, I don't know anything." I spun around to look at her. "Why are you so nervous? Is there something you know that I don't?"

My mother stepped back as if I'd slapped her. "No. Nothing."

I looked at her a moment longer and then turned back to the refrigerator to pull out items for sandwiches.

"I'm going to stick with the belief that I'm innocent and that I haven't done anything wrong until someone can prove differently."

"I don't think you did anything wrong, Carrie. You're a truly good person."

"But I see how you look at me. It's as if you're not so sure anymore."

"I'm sorry, honey. I'm just stressed about this entire situation."

I paused in spreading mayonnaise on the bread and looked at her, exasperated. "You think I'm not?"

She sighed. "Yes, of course you are. I just don't know what to do here."

We stared at each other in silence, and I saw she was now looking exactly how I felt. Scared and defeated.

CHAPTER FIFTEEN

"We'll be recording this. Anyone have a problem with that?" Sergeant Harris asked as he walked in with a file and a blank yellow legal pad.

With my lawyer, Eve Hamilton, sitting beside me in the sergeant's office and my parents waiting just outside, I had all the support I needed, but it wasn't putting me at ease. A cup of tepid coffee sat in front of me, but I hadn't taken a sip. I simply wanted this over with. Nothing else had come to me, and I didn't know how many times I could say the same thing. My story hadn't changed, because there were no new memories to change it.

Eve nodded her consent to the recording. She wore a dark gray pencil skirt with a baby-blue blouse, and her tall stature and narrowed gaze only added to her air of confidence. I wondered if I had that same demeanor when I'd been practicing. Did my clients feel assured by my presence?

Harris sat down at the table across from us and cleared his throat. "Interview with Carrie Wallace on…" He proceeded to tell the date and time, all those present, and the fact that I'd been informed of my Miranda rights, and then before the questions could begin, a brisk knock sounded at the door.

He paused the interview and announced for whomever it was to come in. A female uniformed officer stepped in with Dr. Kessler on her heels. I started to smile but quickly caught myself. He'd obviously gotten my message, and I was glad he was there, but he was my therapist and this was an official police interview—not a date. Sergeant Harris, on the other hand, didn't seem too excited to have him present, but he accepted the circumstances, gestured for Brian to take a seat, and resumed the interview. Brian looked at me, smiled briefly, and sat on the other side of me. Our elbows barely touched, and God, he smelled good. After announcing for the recording that Dr. Brian Kessler was now present, Sergeant Harris began his questioning by sliding a photograph across his desk to me.

"Do you know that man?"

I picked up the photo and recognized it instantly as the man the police were questioning me about the morning I woke up from my coma.

I nodded. "It's Harvey Adams. I only recognize him from his photograph in the papers and what the police have showed me. I haven't had any concrete memories of him, yet."

His gaze tried to bore into me. "According to the statement you gave to the officers, you don't remember visiting him."

"That's right, Sergeant. I still don't remember visiting him that night."

"We have eyewitnesses who say you did. In fact, they say you were a frequent guest at his home. Many times, you stayed overnight."

I stiffened at Brian's presence beside me and suddenly regretted asking him to come down there and hold my hand.

For some unknown reason, I was embarrassed he knew I'd been involved with another man.

"I have no recollection of any of that at this time."

"He was killed the night of your accident, Ms. Wallace. He was shot through the head."

"Yes, I've been told that."

"After your car accident, you were admitted to the hospital with blood on your clothes, face and hair. We tested it, and it's his blood type. Now, I know this isn't easy to hear, but we also found other traces of his DNA that confirmed his identity on your clothing…brain matter."

I choked back nausea and resisted the urge to quake with fear. I wanted to run out of there. What the hell happened that night?

Harris let the silence go on for a moment and then continued.

"I'm going to conclude from the witness statements that you and Harvey Adams had an intimate relationship."

"Sergeant," Eve said. "You can conclude that all you want, but unless these witnesses saw the two of them sharing a kiss or more, I'm going on record to say you have no physical proof of an intimate relationship."

"Oh, for Christ's sake, Eve. The doorman says he often saw her with an overnight bag, and they left the lobby on multiple occasions holding hands. What more do you want?"

"I want my client to say for herself that she was involved with the late Mr. Adams. Not you."

"She doesn't remember."

"Then we'll just have to wait until she does."

Now Brian stiffened beside me. This was making him just as uncomfortable, and I wanted to crawl into a hole.

Harris finally let it go and changed tactics. "Ms. Wallace, I read the statement you gave to the officers, but I'd like to hear in your own words what you do remember from the night of March 17th and if there's anything new you recall."

"The first thing I remember is traveling south on the 101. It was dark and the road was winding. I remember being so scared, but I can't remember why."

"Just a moment. You're absolutely certain you were driving south on the 101?"

"Yes."

"Were you leaving San Francisco?"

"No, I believe I was headed back to the city."

"You were headed back to San Francisco," Harris reiterated. "Back from where?"

"Gypsy Bay."

Brian had been facing forward during most of the question and answer, nodding his head to support Eve's claim that my memory was still gone and monitoring me for any sign of a breakthrough or unnecessary duress. But for the most part, he'd kept a silent vigil. It was at that moment I sensed him slowly turning his head in my direction and could feel his eyes laser onto me. Was this important to him?

He lived in Gypsy Bay. I could've been visiting him. But that was nonsense because I didn't know him before the accident. I thought back to those feelings of familiarity when I saw his house at our first session. Something told me I'd been there before, but I didn't have any way of proving it.

Harris, however showed no reaction. In fact, his face remained carved in stone. "Gypsy Bay? Why do you say you were coming back from Gypsy Bay?"

"There's a memory that keeps coming back to me. I see a sign that says *You Are Now Leaving Gypsy Bay*."

Did you go there that night?"

"I suppose I did, but I still can't make out why."

Brian quickly stood but said nothing. Sergeant Harris, Eve, and I all looked up at him.

"Dr. Kessler, are you all right?" Harris asked.

"Excuse me, I have an important call to make."

He didn't offer any further explanation but left the room just as quickly. Harris noted his exit for the recording and continued to question me about my foggy memory that night. But my mind was now distracted from thinking of Brian.

Did he know why I was in his town that night?

CHAPTER SIXTEEN

*B*rian paused outside the door of Harris's office. He didn't want to leave Carrie, but the news that she was on her way out of Gypsy Bay when she had her accident took away his breath. What was she doing there, and why had her family kept that detail from him?

He pushed off from the wall and stalked out to the lobby in search of answers.

Both Andrew and Natalie looked up at the sound of his approach and stood to their feet.

"What's going on in there?" Andrew demanded.

Instead of answering his question, Brian asked one of his own. "Why didn't you tell me that Carrie's accident happened some time after she left Gypsy Bay?"

Natalie stared at him for a moment.

"What makes you think she was leaving Gypsy Bay?"

Brian pointed behind him. "Because that's what she just told the cops."

Natalie frowned. "Maybe she's confused."

He narrowed his eyes in anger. "Are you going to keep

lying to me? I'm treating your daughter. All of the information, all of the details are important."

"I wouldn't know if she was going to or coming from Gypsy Bay," she said. "None of us was with her that night."

Exasperation tightened his fists. He let out a few breaths to try to relax. "Natalie. Please. If you want me to help your daughter give me all of it. All that you know about that night. The more details I know, the more I can help Carrie piece her memory back together. I will know if something is significant. I can't do my job properly with only part of the story."

Natalie sighed, shared a knowing look with Andrew, and then looked back to Brian. "We didn't want you to know about it."

"Why? Why would you withhold something like that?"

"When the cops told us where her car was found, Andrew and I thought that maybe she was coming to see you for a reconciliation."

He took a step back. That was quite a leap. "I haven't talked to Carrie in years. Why would you think that?"

None of this made sense. Not in any twisted way he could think of. But if it wasn't the insane possibility of a reconciliation, why else had she made the drive up there? As far as he knew, she didn't know anyone else who lived there, and it wasn't exactly the type of place she would normally frequent. She preferred the hustle of the city and wasn't one to take vacations since her career had been her priority before, during, and after their marriage.

Andrew interrupted his thoughts. "Brian, we honestly don't know why she was on that road at that time. Just like you, we can only guess."

If Carrie was in Gypsy Bay, why hadn't she contacted him? Why didn't she knock on his door? He didn't like to deal in what-ifs, but if she'd knocked, she might not have been in the accident. He wasn't a monster. He would have opened the door for her. He was sorry how things turned out for them, and if she'd been in need or in some kind of trouble, he would have let her in his house and done all he could to help her through whatever it was. Carrie had to know that. But if she had come up there for what her parents suspected, then what? Would he have tried to reconcile with his ex-wife? It wasn't as if he'd never thought about it. Especially in the early months after their divorce when he was painfully missing her.

Footsteps alerted him that the interview was done, which meant he was no longer needed there. It was best he get home. He needed to get his head together before he dealt with Carrie.

However, before he could escape, he heard her calling out to him from down the hallway.

"Dr. Kessler."

He turned and waited until she was upon him. The flats she wore made her a foot shorter than him, and she was looking up at him with those piercing dark brown eyes that always made him feel as if she could see right through to his nightmares and his pleasant dreams.

"Could we go and talk somewhere?" she asked.

He hesitated and then shook his head, looking at his wristwatch. "Now's not a good time. I have to get back home. I have another commitment."

She tried again. "We could drive back together—"

"No," he said, instantly. He regretted his tone, but this latest news had him wondering what was going on. He needed it all sorted in his head, and he knew she wouldn't be able to give him any clarity. Besides, he couldn't take seeing the vulnerability in her eyes anymore or the way her thighs and ass were perfectly molded into the black leggings she wore. It made him want to do something crazy, like take her in his arms, comfort her and ultimately do things to her body that used to make her cry out his name.

She was frowning and looking a bit hurt. "Well, I guess another time then."

"We can talk at your next appointment."

"Okay. Sure."

With that, he left her and her parents standing there.

Now more than ever he wanted to help Carrie regain her memory. He doubted that she was the perpetrator of a crime, but what worried him was that she was possibly the victim of one.

CHAPTER SEVENTEEN

I woke up remembering my mother.

It was the first memory of a member of my family, and I sat straight up in bed, exhilarated. But as soon as the memory came to me, I was afraid it would disappear just as quickly, so I took a moment, steadied my breathing, and let the details roll through my mind.

I stood before the full-length mirror and admired how the soft white fabric complemented my brown skin tone. The mermaid-style gown clung to my breasts and full hips, and the ruffles that flared out at the bottom made it look as if I were standing on top of a blooming rose.

"You look beautiful, Carrie," she said, looking at me in the mirror over my shoulder.

"Thank you, Mom," I said. Then I thought, I hope he thinks so, too.

"Have I forgotten anything?" I asked.

"You've got your something old, something new. What's your something blue?"

"My garter is light blue. I didn't want it too dark so it wouldn't show through the dress," I said.

"Makes sense. You borrowed my pearl drop earrings. Are you nervous?"

I shook my head no but couldn't hide the subtle frown creasing above my brow.

"You're still bothered about it, aren't you?" she asked.

"Wouldn't you be?"

"I'll admit it could've been handled differently, but it got you here, didn't it? And you told me you love him. Why should that change because of some silly deal?"

"Would he have still agreed to marry me?"

"Of course, he would have. Honey, let it go. You love him. That's all that matters."

"But does he love me or does he love my money?"

She stopped looking at me through the mirror and came around to stand directly in front of me.

"Carrie. Why are you asking me that question and not him?"

I shrugged. Suddenly, in this gorgeous dress, I felt so insecure. "Because I'm afraid of the answer."

That was where the memory ended. I shook myself again. I'd been married. Or had something happened? No, I'd bet I was married. It felt right. I felt as if I'd been married.

I didn't know if I should feel relief that I remembered something so huge or pissed off that no one had told me. I shifted out of bed to start my day. When my feet hit the floor, I said it out loud. "I was married."

I started my shower. As I waited for the hot water to come out in the stream, I said it again.

"I was married."

No one had told me. My family hadn't told me. My mother who was in the memory hadn't told me.

I showered, then wrapped my wet body in a towel and sat on the edge of the tub for a moment, trying to wrap my head around this memory. Was I still married? No, I couldn't be. My husband would have been at the hospital.

I quickly dressed for the day, not knowing what it would bring and then finally got up the courage to call my mother.

"Carrie? Is everything okay?"

I ignored the concern in her voice. "I had a memory about you."

"Oh, honey, that's great! What was it about? What were we doing?"

She sounded so excited and relieved that her daughter now remembered her, and I hated to take away that happiness, but she'd lied to me.

"You were standing behind me, and we were admiring my wedding dress together. I was about to get married, Mom."

There was a moment of silence on the line. Then a quiet, "Oh."

"Yes. Oh. Why didn't you tell me I had a husband? Why didn't any of you?" I asked, referring to my dad and Shawn.

"Carrie—"

"I have a lot of questions now, and I want you to tell me the truth. Is he still alive? Am I still with him? Where is he?"

There was silence on the other end of the line.

"Hello? Mom, are you there?"

"I'm sorry, but I don't want to talk about this."

"What?" I asked, incredulous. "Are you serious? Why not? This is important. I want to know who this man was."

"I said I don't want to talk about it, Carrie, and I don't have to give you a reason why."

The next sound I heard was the signal of the call ending. I took the phone from my ear and was shocked and even more angered to find that she'd hung up on me. This didn't make any sense to me. Why would she avoid this conversation? Was the situation that horrible?

I dropped the phone on the table while I debated calling her back. She probably wouldn't answer. I could give her space, but she wasn't the victim here. I was. Too many people weren't telling me things, and I was getting tired of it.

Someone knocked on my door, and I turned to it, irritated by the interruption. I wasn't expecting anyone, so I went and peered through the peephole. It was Brian. I sighed. Maybe it was good he was here because I needed to talk to someone.

I opened the door with a fake smile pasted onto my face. "Hi."

"Hi." He frowned. "Are you all right?"

Apparently, I wasn't good at disguising my anger. "No." I stepped out of the doorway. "Come in. I have coffee."

"Just a small cup, thanks."

He followed me into the kitchen. Like me, he was dressed casual in jeans and a lightweight, crew neck, gray sweater. No matter how he looked, he always struck me as handsome, but there was something else. It was a sense of comfort and familiarity I felt whenever he was near me.

"What brings you here?" I asked, grabbing two mugs out of the cabinet.

"You want to tell me what's going on, first?" he asked.

"You first," I said, pouring him and myself some coffee from the pot.

"Now that I know the exact location, I wanted to take you to the scene of the accident."

"Oh?" I slid the mug of coffee across the table to him.

"Yeah, just as an experiment. We'll see if it helps. Ideally, it should be night since that's when your accident was, but I don't want to overwhelm you."

I leaned against the counter with my coffee mug in hand, staring at a blank spot on the table. "Sounds good."

"We can take it slow and if it bothers you, you can leave."

"Okay," I said.

"Carrie."

I broke away from my daydream and looked up at him.

He put the mug of coffee down and looked at me earnestly. "What is it?" he asked.

"I was married."

CHAPTER EIGHTEEN

The entire ride to the 101, he feared she'd come right out and accuse him of keeping this monumental secret from her. He was her ex-husband, he'd been the man in her memories, the man she was speaking of, and he hadn't told her. But as the time passed and he listened to her recall the memory of the wedding dress, he realized she'd only seen her mother. She hadn't yet recalled the memory of walking down the aisle toward him.

"I called my mother," Carrie said, looking out the window at the passing scenery. "She was absolutely no help. She flat-out refused to tell me anything more about him. Maybe he was a complete asshole."

Brian's back went up, and he had to resist the urge to defend himself. "In time, your own memories about him will resurface and you can make your own judgment then."

She turned to face him. "Speaking of my mother, I want to apologize for her and my father for keeping the accident location a secret from you. I only just remembered a few days ago, otherwise I would've brought it up at our first session."

"It's all right. Actually, I'm kind of used to it."

"Do a lot of families keep secrets from you?"

Not as much as your family.

He nodded. "Sometimes, people are ashamed of something they did and would rather not mention it. It's just the reality of the beast. The amnesia is often a catalyst for a lot of family secrets to come out, but like a lawyer, it helps if I know everything. It will aid me in helping the patient put the puzzle pieces together."

"Then you have to wade through all sorts of family issues," she said.

He turned and smiled at her. "I'm a psychiatrist. I'm used to dealing with issues."

"Still. You end up with more than one patient."

Brian chuckled. "Yes, that's true."

Suddenly, he felt guilt overtake him. Wasn't he doing the exact thing her family was doing? He wasn't being honest with her or upfront by keeping their marriage a secret. Most of the problems they'd faced stemmed from neither of them being forthright with the other, and now it was continuing on. It had become such a natural way of behaving around her, that he didn't even realize he was still doing it. Carrie was used to it, too, only she didn't know it. But he couldn't let her find out about him or what they had been to each other. At least, not now. The therapist in him didn't think she was ready to confront that, but the man in him didn't think *he* was ready.

"Let's stop here, first," he said, pulling to the side of the road. "There's the sign you talked about in your statement. Remember to take your time and don't strain."

They both got out of the car and Carrie walked slowly toward the sign that read, *You are Now Leaving Gypsy Bay* and stood in front of it for a long while. She had been leaving. She had wanted to see someone there.

Had that someone been him? He couldn't get past that idea. But why? Why hadn't she just called? Even if his phone number had changed, she had many ways to get his number. But even more importantly, what had made her change her mind about seeing him? Why had she made it all the way up there, only to turn around and head back to San Francisco?

Or maybe she hadn't been *coming to see him at all.*

After several minutes passed, she turned back toward him and shook her head. "Nothing very clear. Just flashes of me driving. I can feel my mind wants to remember, but it's still all confusing."

"It's okay. Let's go. The next stop will be the actual scene of the accident."

As he pulled out onto the 101 and headed south, he realized this must have been the exact route she took to leave Gypsy Bay, and the question assaulted him once again: What was she doing there?

The ride was mostly silent this time. She stared out the window, and he guessed she was trying to reacquaint herself with the surroundings. In the light of day, things were bound to look different, but he was hoping her mind would recall something. He pulled over onto the side of the highway and consulted the notes he took down from Sergeant Harris. They were in between mile markers 173 and 174. He looked up to see the metal rail fencing had been bent and small shards of glass still littered the road. She was lucky the fencing had stopped her car from going over the edge. His heart stopped at the thought of losing her and not even knowing she may have been coming to him for help.

"Is this where it happened?" she asked.

He nodded. "Take a minute and look around."

Carrie opened the door and climbed out, and Brian followed, watching her as she studied the area. She went to stand by the metal railing and carefully looked over the edge, pulling her hair back from her face. The breeze carried in from the ocean was much stronger up there where they were out in the open than in the city.

Suddenly, she stepped back, her eyes wide with excitement. "I'm remembering something."

"About the accident?"

"No." She shook her head. Her eyes were closed, and she was doing the breathing exercises he'd taught her. "I don't think this is related at all. It's just an older man. I'm laughing with him."

"Is it your father?"

No, but he's a white man, about the same age as my father. Maybe older. Sixties I'd say."

"Does he have any defining characteristics?"

"He has a close-cropped beard. A head of full white hair, and there's a small mole or maybe it's a birthmark under his right eye."

Brian nearly choked. She was describing his father.

"What else?" he asked, holding his breath.

"That's about it. We're not talking about anything. Just laughing. When I get home, I'll go through the photo albums again. Maybe I missed him the first time around."

She frowned and a crease appeared on her forehead. She was trying too hard.

"Don't force it," he said. "The fact that some memories have returned is a good sign. It will come again."

She rubbed her forehead and he recognized the look of aggravation on her face. "You've said that, but I just want to remember. I want my life back."

"I understand, Carrie."

"But you don't," she said, her eyes flashing with annoyance, "because it hasn't happened to you."

"You're right, but I've studied, observed, and treated it long enough to come close. You're in limbo until you remember, but your brain has chosen to keep memories from you. It's very possible for us to heal ourselves, but we have to take our time."

She let out a breath and walked back to the car, but Brian stayed back now plagued by his own thoughts.

Whatever the reason for her being on this road that night, it had to have been very important. It had been a dark, cloudy night, with strong winds, and he knew that kind of weather had never been her favorite time to drive.

Could it have something to do with his father? Was that why that particular memory returned to her at this moment?

CHAPTER NINETEEN

Brian dropped Carrie off at home, feeling her frustration rolling over her in waves. She'd had two memories come back to her today, but he could tell that wasn't good enough. He recognized this a lot in patients, especially the ones who suffered retrograde amnesia like her. They grew tired of being fed the memories of their lives in bits and pieces and tried everything they could to get their mind to open up well before it was ready.

He watched as she opened the front door, turned to give him a half-hearted wave, and then closed it behind her. He waited there a few more minutes, wanting to go in after her and say something, anything that would bring her a little bit of comfort. But that wasn't a good idea. Today on the highway, while she recalled details of his father, she'd had her eyes closed and was breathing deeply in and out, while the wind blew her hair into her face. She'd look so beautiful standing there, and he'd found himself reaching forward to move the strands from her face before he caught himself and stepped away from her. No, it wasn't a good idea for him to be alone with her right now.

Instead of going home, he detoured to the coast and pulled off at a scenic overlook. He needed a quiet place to think.

He climbed out of his car and walked to the fence that kept tourists from falling off the rocky edge. He rested his arms on it and looked out, not really seeing the ocean but seeing the past unfold in front of him.

* * *

She was sitting on the couch when he came home. He was fuming, ready to throw something but seeing her sitting there, still in her overcoat, brought him up short. She was looking up at him with so much pain and regret in her eyes, that he wasn't sure how to react. It had been over a week since they'd been in the house at the same time. Most days she was asleep, and he got home so late he'd pass out in the den. Other times he'd feel her crawl into bed at night, but when he woke in the morning, she was gone. They had become strangers living in the same house—both committed to careers they'd work so hard for, but somewhere along the way, they'd forgotten they were life partners.

"You heard?" she asked, solemnly.

He shrugged off his own coat and tossed it over an armchair. He then stalked past her to the mini bar in the living area to make himself a drink.

"Yeah, I heard. My mom called me at work crying. She's afraid she and Dad will go bankrupt."

"I'm really sorry, Brian."

He poured scotch into a glass and downed it in one swallow. "Forget the apologies. This isn't your fault. I was going to call you, but I'm glad you're home. I need you to use your connections and find someone in the firm to represent them."

They hadn't been the most loving couple to each other in the past few years; he'd been so busy chasing the prosperity and wealth he'd promised himself as a child, and Carrie was on the fast track to be the first black female to make partner at her firm. Their passion for each other had become non-existent, but he still cared for her, and he knew she felt the same about him and his parents.

So, it came as a complete surprise when he turned from the bar to find her standing and giving him an odd look.

"What's wrong?"

"I can't do that."

That response floored him. "You can't find a lawyer who specializes in civil suits to represent my parents? Why the hell not?"

She rounded the couch and came to stand directly in front of him. "How much has your mom told you?"

"Only that the Watleys are suing Dad for civil liability. They couldn't make the malpractice suit stick, because Eliza was diagnosed with depression."

"What else?" Carrie asked.

"Isn't that enough?" He was losing patience, and as a result, he was raising his voice. But why the fuck was she asking these questions? Time was of the essence. The sooner he could find some stellar representation for his dad, the sooner he could put his mom at ease. She was scared right now, and a slither of hope could make all the difference.

"Listen, if you don't want to get involved, I'll call that damn firm myself and find somebody."

"Brian, wait." She grabbed his arm to halt him

"What?"

Whatever she was hesitant to tell him was making her nervous, and when she did spit it out, he understood why.

"My firm is representing the Watleys."

He finally had to sit down. The hits that were coming at him were becoming too much to bear. His strained marriage, Eliza Watley's suicide and the subsequent attacks against his father, now this civil suit, and out of all the law firms in San Francisco, it had to be his wife's employer.

She came to stand in front of him, and once again, he noticed she still had on her coat. Maybe she'd come straight home, shocked by the news as he was and just never thought to take it off.

"So, what are you going to do?" he asked.

"What do you mean?"

"That firm is taking part in going after my parents' life savings. Your father has already bought him out of the practice, and he's under review from the medical board whether to have his license revoked." *He bent forward, resting his arms on his knees and looked directly at her.* "What are you going to do?"

She nodded slowly, and a knowing look passed through her dark brown eyes. "You want me to quit."

He didn't say another word, allowing his silence to speak for itself.

"I've worked hard for this career, Brian. I'm going to make partner here. You're asking me to leave and start all over again somewhere else?"

He stood. "This is about my father. Do you honestly think it would be okay with me for you to stay there while they're screwing with his life?"

She turned and began to walk away.

"I'm your family, Carrie. Not that law firm. They've dangled a partnership in front of you and no one else matters."

She stopped, turned and stormed right back to him. His five feet ten inches dwarfed her five-two frame, but she didn't let that stop her as she marched right up to him with anger flowing over her and unshed tears in her eyes.

"This isn't as easy as you think."

"It's not so difficult to me. I would leave a practice if you asked that of me."

"You would never have to! It's a lot easier when the business belongs to you—thanks to my father."

His jaw hardened. "Be careful, Carrie."

But it was as if she couldn't hear him through her fury. "You *remember my father. The man you now despise. Are you going to give him back the money he funded into your practice? That is why you agreed to marry me, right?"*

He knew she had to know about it, but in the four and a half years they'd been married, she'd never once brought it up, and neither had he. Just like everything else, they pretended it didn't exist. Andrew Wallace had offered him Carrie's hand in marriage, and although he'd fallen hard for her, Brian couldn't deny that he'd also fallen for the Wallace's wealth and connections. Not to mention, the investment he'd gotten from Andrew Wallace had instantly propelled him into entrepreneurship years before he'd expected. But he didn't expect it to ever come back to bite him like this. The truth was kicking his ass, telling him he'd married a woman who was the same person as himself. The sad part was, he understood everything she was feeling when he put it into the context of her ambition, because he was the same way. She wanted to be partner more than anything else, and he'd wanted wealth and success more than anything else. Somewhere along the way, they both forgot what was really important. They'd not only lost each other, but lost themselves in the process.

He took her hands in his, and when she jerked them away, he grabbed for them again and clutched them.

"This is something we should talk about. And we will talk about it, but not now. Right now, I need your answer. Where do you stand?"

The tears he knew she'd tried with all her strength to hold back, finally fell as she slowly backed away from him.

"I'm staying at my parents tonight."

"Why?"

"Because I don't want to spend the night arguing with you."

His hold on her hands tightened with the desperation of not wanting her to walk out on him. "Don't go. Argue with me, ignore me or make love to me, I don't care. Just don't walk out that door."

She unclasped her hands from his as the tears streamed furiously down her cheeks. "I'm so sorry. We can talk in the morning."

She left the house without looking back, and he realized then why she was still wearing her coat. She never planned to stay.

CHAPTER TWENTY

"*How do you justify this? You're taking a bribe in order to bring an indictment against a man.*"

"*Bribe or no bribe, there's enough evidence, and I'm going forward with it.*"

"*Are you insane? If anyone finds out that you, an ADA, took a bribe to bring murder charges against someone, your case will be dead before it even starts.*"

"*There's no reason for anyone to find out.*"

"*I found out.*"

A long pause.

"*Listen, Carrie just come by so we can talk about this. I'll explain everything. Just don't go to the board or the DA or anyone. Let me see you first.*"

Fiona paused the recording, looked at the time and groaned aloud. It was just past ten thirty at night. She'd listened to the audio clip of Carrie and Harvey arguing so many times that she'd practically memorized it.

After she left work, she'd gone straight home to sit with her laptop and the flash drive Carrie gave to her. She'd set herself up at her kitchen table wearing an old t-shirt, sweats, and fluffy socks. It was her favorite way to research if she wasn't at the law library.

What she'd been able to work out was that Carrie had recorded a phone call between her and Harvey, where she accused him of taking bribes for a case. He was guaranteeing someone that he'd bring a murder indictment and conviction against someone if they paid him enough, but neither he nor Carrie ever mentioned who the case involved or what exactly the details were. She pulled up the bank documents again. At first, she believed they were Carrie's but now her gut was telling her these were Harvey's financial records and the mysterious benefactor was whoever owned Magnolia Trust. But she'd never be able to find out who owned that trust, and there was where her research had ended.

She saw from in the notes that Carrie used Sam Collins, the private investigator for the firm, to do her digging for her. But he hadn't seemed to be able to find out who owned the Trust either, or he would've included that information in there. Fiona had tried calling Sam and sweet-talking him into giving up more information about this job he was doing for Carrie, but he wouldn't budge. Even after she proved she had the documents he'd given to Carrie by reading his notes verbatim, he still didn't tell her anything.

"It's against my policy, Fiona," he said. "Until I get permission from Carrie, I can't disclose any details about the job."

She wanted to yell at him that if she could get ahold of Carrie, she wouldn't need him at all. For now, however, she was alone in figuring this out herself. But she was no investigator. She could research case law, but this was not as easy as finding references for cases to use as precedents. This was a different kind of research, and it was incomplete. And the only woman who could connect the dots was Carrie.

Fiona grabbed for her cell phone and scrolled through her contacts until she got to Carrie's number. For what had to be the hundredth time since the day she found out about Carrie's accident, she hovered her thumb over Carrie's number and hesitated before pressing the dial button.

Even if she came out and told her everything about Carrie's visit to her, the flash drive, and what Fiona had managed to uncover, would Carrie even be receptive to any of it? Fiona didn't know the extent of her amnesia. Maybe it was short-term memory loss, and she only forgot about the accident. But if it was long-term memory loss, she could be calling a woman who didn't even know her anymore.

But that nagging feeling kept creeping up on her that something was going on, and making contact with Carrie was something that needed to be done. At least if she did remember her, the flash drive, and everything else, Fiona could get her address and hand everything over to her. Maybe she was planning to bring her investigation to light. Harvey Adams might be dead, but whoever paid him off was still out there and obviously had money to buy convictions.

She pressed the dial button and held her breath as it rang over and over again until finally, Carrie's voice sounded loud and clear. Only it was her voicemail greeting.

"Dammit," Fiona said, as she listened to the greeting. She was prepared to hang up and muster up her courage another day, but she'd already come this far. She'd never left a message before, but maybe if Carrie heard her voice this time, she'd instantly remember her and call back.

When the recording beeped, she hesitated for several seconds, and then finally found her voice.

"It's me, Fiona. I don't know if you remember me, but I'm your paralegal. It's very important that I talk to you. Please call me back at this number."

She started to hang up, and then continued on. "You trusted me when you came to see me that night. You can still trust me."

CHAPTER TWENTY-ONE

I lightly kissed the birthmark on the inner left thigh of his creamy pale skin while grasping the hard length of him between my fingers. I then moved my palm up and down, creating a friction I knew would get him going. My mouth traveled from his inner thigh to the very top of his length, where I licked slowly and torturously in a circular motion. I heard him groan with both irritation and desire but concentrated on my task.

He wasn't going to run this show just yet, I thought devilishly as I enveloped the rest of my mouth over him. He gripped my hair in his hands and undulated his hips, trying to give me more of himself, trying to get more of him to go deeper into my mouth. I relaxed my throat muscles and obliged him, taking in as much as I could handle. The animalistic sounds that came from him were worth it, and I felt myself getting wet and excited for him. More than anything, I loved to pleasure him because there was no end to the pleasure he gave me in return.

"Get up here," he said, and I squealed with delight, knowing what was coming next.

* * *

It had been two days since I'd seen him, and showing up like this was completely unprofessional. I nearly turned around and headed back to my car when the porch light came on, and I was standing under its spotlight, looking like an intruder who'd been caught.

The door opened a crack, and when he saw who it was, it widened even farther until I could see all of him.

Brian frowned. "Is everything all right?"

"Yes, I just needed to speak with you. It's about a dream I had. But, I don't think it was a dream."

He sighed heavily. "It's late, Carrie."

"I know, and I'm so sorry. This dream just rattled me, and I couldn't go back to sleep for thinking of it."

"You could've called."

"Yes, I know, but this was important, and I didn't want to wait until morning or our next session on the chance I'd forget about it."

That was a lie. I just wanted to see him. I wanted to see his face when I told him. I wanted validation that what I suspected was right.

He sighed again, rubbed a hand through his hair and down his face, then gestured me into the foyer. I had clearly woken him up, and how was it possible he looked even more handsome when he was sleepy?

"Come in."

"Thank you," I said, swallowing nervously. Seeing him in a T-shirt and pajama pants made me feel foolish all of a sudden. I glanced up the stairs, certain I'd find the same woman I spotted him with at *Charlie's*, only this time, I'd see her face, and she'd look very annoyed with me for choosing to bother the household at this time of night.

Brian led me through the short hallway and into an attached room that connected to his office. I had always entered through the side door that opened directly into his office. This short walk through the rest of his home had me once again believing that I'd been here before.

He turned on the lights and gestured for me to sit down in my normal seat on the couch. No doubt, he wanted to keep this visit clinical.

"So, tell me about this dream," he said, moving to the back of his desk in search of a fresh notepad and pen.

"Well, it was about the two of us."

"What were we doing?"

I watched him very closely. "Making love."

There was only the slightest hesitation—a half second pause before his hand touched on a pen and closed his desk drawer.

"This could get interesting," he muttered.

He passed by me to sit in the chair opposite mine, and I took in his sweet masculine scent, masked by the fragrance of the shower gel he must have used before going to bed. I wanted more of that natural scent of his. I wanted it all over me.

Jesus, I must be still hopped up after that dream. It was the only way I could explain this sudden urge to pounce him. I refocused my attention on the subject at hand. I had gone there to get at the truth.

"Don't misunderstand me," I said, raising my hands to forestall any preconceived ideas in his head. "I didn't mean that as a come on, and I'm not at all trying to be inappropriate."

"It's all right."

"It just confused me."

"Why?"

"Because it felt so real."

"Dreams often do."

"No, I don't mean like I thought it was happening, but real like...real like I've already lived it."

Now he was regarding me closely. "Like a memory?"

I nodded.

He put his legal pad and pen to the side and leaned forward in his chair, bracing his elbows on his knees.

"Where were we?"

"What?"

His piercing gaze slanted up toward me. "Where were we making love?"

I shrugged. "It was a bed."

"Anything about that bed or the room strike you as familiar?"

"No. Just you." I paused a moment and then continued. "To be fair, I didn't actually see your face."

"You didn't?"

"No, but I knew it was you," I rushed to say.

"If you didn't see my face, how do you know it was me?"

"I don't know. I just felt in my heart it was you."

I held my breath as he looked to be lost in thought. Moments later, however, he sat up and leaned back in his chair and an indulgent smile spread across his face. My heart plummeted. He was about to explain it all away.

"The difference between dreams and memories is that only one gives us the full picture. We experience all five senses and everything in the picture is familiar. Dreams just give us a glimpse, a taste of what's going on in our subconscious. I'm the first man you've had any sort of intimate relationship with since waking from your coma."

I frowned. "Are you…are you saying I'm horny?"

"No. I'm saying that our relationship could be seen as very intimate. You've been through a traumatic event, and I'm helping you recall memories. Sex is also very intimate, so it's perfectly normal for your subconscious to portray me as a lover—even though I'm not."

His gaze didn't falter from mine, and suddenly the air in

the room felt suffocating. This had been a really bad idea. Did I actually show up here at nearly midnight, expecting him to tell me it was a memory I was experiencing? Or had I been *hoping* he would tell me that?

I stood abruptly and grabbed for my purse. "I should go."

He stood, too. "There's no need to feel embarrassed, Carrie. Like I said, it's completely normal. You were in a coma for two weeks. Your mind is just doing what it's supposed to do. Also, you've had two memories return to you this week. You may be forcing yourself to remember more and mistaking the dreams for the real thing."

I kept my eyes focused on the collar of his T-shirt, suddenly unable to look at him.

"I guess so. Sorry for disturbing you. Please apologize to your wife for me," I said, then

stepped past him toward the office door.

"My wife?"

At the door, I paused and then turned and forced myself to look at him. "I saw you with a woman at a restaurant downtown sometime last week. I just assumed..."

"Oh, right. That was Rachel. She's my girlfriend, but she's not here tonight."

I nodded and suddenly felt something shift between us. It was the first time he ever mentioned anything personal about himself to me, and I could tell he didn't like it one bit.

"Maybe you should call first the next time you want to make a late-night visit."

My back went up at the bite in his tone, even though he had every right to be annoyed. But I was annoyed, too. No screw that, I was pissed. I didn't like being lied to or having my feelings dismissed. He was keeping something from me, and I couldn't understand why, but it hurt.

I opened the door, then paused and turned around again,

the night's chilly breeze wafting at my back. "Do you have a birthmark on your inner left thigh?"

He didn't answer.

"I only ask because the man in my dream did. I kissed it just before I—"

"That's enough, Carrie."

I turned and walked out.

* * *

I didn't go home. I couldn't just drive myself home, get back into bed, and stare up at the ceiling for the rest of the night, wondering to myself why Brian and everyone else around me seemed to be withholding information from me. Instead, I drove around the downtown area of Gypsy Bay, desolate and quiet at this time of night. The only establishment that still had its lights on was the bar and grill where I saw Brian and his girlfriend, Rachel. I pulled slowly into the lot, hoping I could get a late-night snack, but one look at the bar stools resting atop the bar and one lone man mopping the floors, I knew the diner had also closed its doors for the night. I looked past the restaurant to a wall of trees. But, with the moonlight casting its glow, I was able to see a clearing through the forest and what had to be Widow Lake beyond it. I remember overhearing some of the townspeople talking about it, and since I was killing time, I figured now might be a good time to see it. I left my car in *Charlie's* lot, and walked the rest of the way to the trails behind the restaurant that would eventually lead me to the lake. Thankfully, the trails were strategically lit in different places or I may not have had the courage to venture that far into the trees. I buttoned my jacket, slipped my hands deep into my pockets, and began a quiet, lonely walk that would hopefully clear my head.

But as my trek took me deeper into the forest and toward

the lake, I realized I'd only managed to make a fool of myself in front of Brian. Yes, I'd had a dream about him, but maybe what he said was true, and it was only a dream. Maybe, I just wanted it so much to be a memory that I took it upon myself to basically ambush him in the middle of the night in hopes he would confess. Yes, I remembered my mother. I was even beginning to remember some things from my childhood and teenage years. My memory was slowly coming back, but it didn't mean that *everything* was a memory, no matter how much I wanted it to be. Still, there was something nagging inside of me that just wouldn't go away. Sergeant Harris said I was romantically involved with Harvey Adams, but why can't I remember being with him, yet in the same moment, I can remember being with Brian?

But Brian was just a dream.

"Please, just listen to what I'm saying!"

The raised female voice stopped me dead in my tracks. Farther down the trail, at the edge of the water, were a set of park benches where people could stop and take in Widow Lake. There, I saw two shadowed figures who apparently also had trouble sleeping. But instead of enjoying the silent night and peaceful waters, they seemed to be arguing. I didn't want it to appear as though I were eavesdropping, so I slowly turned around to head back to my car. Then came the man's reply, his voice also raised and carried by the water.

"Fuck Kessler!"

Kessler? As in Dr. Kessler? Brian? I stepped closer, careful that my booted heels didn't make any sound.

CHAPTER TWENTY-TWO

Widow Lake 12:36 a.m.

"She just dropped the case, without any warning?"

"That's what I said! The bitch called me, said she was done, and hung up on me," he said. "No explanation. Nothing!"

Secretly, she was relieved the new ADA decided not to take on the case against Brian. She was hoping it would make him see what they were doing was no more than a fool's errand. They still had a chance to leave everything behind and go make a new life somewhere. But he was so angry, and now even more determined to see this through.

She tried her best to make him see reason. "Maybe this is a sign. We have the money, we have our freedom, let's just pack up—"

"I told you before I'm not going anywhere until that fucker is behind bars. I'm getting my payback."

"All he did was write a book and try to exonerate his father. Wouldn't you have done the same thing for your father?"

Fury entered his eyes, and he grabbed her by the shoulders and hissed in her face. "Whose side are you on?"

"I'm on your side, honey," she said, quickly trying to console him.

"Fuck, Kessler! Do you hear me? Fuck him! We find someone else. We continue with the plan, see it through to the end and then get out of here. Do you understand?"

She nodded her agreement purely out of trepidation, but she realized he wasn't looking at her anymore but at a spot over her shoulder, and his eyes were narrowed. She turned around to see what had caught his attention just in time to see the figure of someone in the distance.

"Who's there?" he shouted.

Whoever it was didn't reply but instead ran away.

"Who the hell was that?" she asked, panic rising up inside of her.

"Who knows?"

"Do you think we should go after them?"

"No," he said. "It's probably just some kids who snuck out to come down here and start trouble. We just scared them away."

She exhaled a long, heavy sigh. "So, what now? If we go looking for another ADA, it will begin to look suspicious. Eventually, someone is going to wonder about the sudden interest in this four-year-old case and bring the cops in. It's a wonder they're not knocking on our door already."

"Relax, I got the cops handled. The DA's office, on the other hand, is your territory. You know those people. You know who can be turned and who can be trusted to keep their mouth shut."

She backed away. "You want me to find another ADA? I told you, it's going to bring us unwanted attention. Not everyone is as corruptible as Harvey was. Is this revenge plan really so important to you that you're willing to risk your freedom? You won't be happy until we're behind bars!"

"That's not true, I want—"

They both went quiet at the sound of an unrecognizable ring tone. It took him just a few seconds to realize that it was coming from his back pocket. He pulled out the cell phone he'd grabbed from Harvey's apartment that night and watched the screen light up with an incoming call.

"Whose phone is that?"

"It belongs to that bitch Harvey was screwing. It fell out of her purse that night, and I grabbed it before I ran out of there, hoping she'd come back looking for it or that it would give me an idea of where she's hiding."

They watched the phone ring and ring until it instantly went silent. Seconds later, the voicemail icon showed, indicating a message had been left. He pressed the appropriate buttons and the sound of a female's voice came through.

"It's me, Fiona. I don't know if you remember me, but I'm your paralegal. It's very important that I talk to you. Please call me back at this number. You trusted me when you came to see me that night. You can still trust me."

They listened to it once more, and then he ended the call and frowned.

"Who the hell is Fiona?" he asked.

CHAPTER TWENTY-THREE

Sergeant Derek Harris sat at his desk updating his report on the Harvey Adams case, even though there wasn't much to update. He still had jack shit, mainly because his only witness and possible suspect had a convenient case of amnesia, and her lawyer was enjoying every minute of it. Any time Derek even hinted at charging Carrie Wallace for Adams's murder, her lawyer would slap him in the face with her diagnosis. It was aggravating to say the least, because Derek was damn sure Carrie was the key to all of this. Even if she didn't pull the trigger herself, she saw something, but for now, the memory of it was trapped somewhere her mind couldn't get to.

His desk phone rang, disturbing him from his brooding thoughts. He gave it a dismissive look, but then picked up the receiver, deciding he could use the distraction from a case that was currently going nowhere.

"Harris," he answered brusquely.

"Sergeant, this is Sophie James."

"Sophie, you have the wrong desk number. But I guess I have time to flirt while your man is out working a case."

"You're too funny, Derek."

He chuckled at her sarcasm. Sophie James was an ADA for San Francisco County and a good source of information to the SFPD, specifically the homicide division. That may have had something to do with the fact that her love, Ethan Markham, was a sergeant there as well. Derek respected the man and had petitioned to be his new partner on more than one occasion, but for now, Ethan was content to work alone. After the debacle with his last partner, Derek couldn't blame him.

"So, what do I owe the pleasure?" he asked.

"My boss has been going through all of Harvey Adams's open and pending cases, and reassigning them to other ADAs. The office keeps logs of all pending cases the ADAs are working," Sophie said.

"Okay," he said, not yet sure where she was going with this.

"Well, his assistant was going over the logs, and there seems to be a case missing, but we still have the name of the defendant. That's why I'm calling you."

"Who's the defendant?"

"Brian Kessler. His name sounded familiar, and then I remembered he's indirectly connected to Harvey's murder investigation."

Derek had been leaning back in his chair in a relaxed pose, but with Sophie's words, he sat straight up. "You're telling me Brian Kessler is listed as a defendant in a case Harvey was trying?"

"It doesn't look like it went to trial yet, or we'd all have heard about it. These seem to be preliminary records that went missing."

Derek stayed quiet, not sure what to make of this information. He'd found out early on that Brian Kessler was once married to Carrie Wallace, but for reasons only Brian and the

Wallace family know, they refuse to let Carrie know. However, Brian is counseling her to regain her memory. Now, Carrie is either a suspect or a witness in the murder of Harvey Adams—the man who was about to indict Brian for whatever reason.

"Listen, there's nothing concrete. We have no idea what Harvey was doing. Without the file, I couldn't tell you if he had a solid case or not," Sophie said. "I only called, because I know you're investigating Harvey's murder."

"Yeah, thanks, Sophie. I appreciate it. And if that file turns up—"

"I'll let you know, and I'll be waiting for your warrant."

He scoffed. "I thought being with Ethan was supposed to make you nicer."

She hung up.

He chuckled, hung up the receiver, and sat there at his desk and tried to get his mind to sort out the jumble of thoughts. What did Brian allegedly do, and did he know that Harvey had him in his crosshairs? Did he find out from Carrie? Were the two of them working together to get Harvey out of the way? But what about Carrie's car accident? Surely, she wouldn't flip her car over twice on purpose. Unless of course, she'd become a liability to him and he caused her accident. However, Carrie didn't die, and with her amnesia, Brian could keep an eye on her and monitor exactly what she begins to remember.

Maybe all this time, he was looking at the wrong suspect. Derek grabbed his car keys and jacket. It was time he started finding out more about the good psychiatrist.

CHAPTER TWENTY-FOUR

I walked up to the front steps of the small cottage home that I'd come to know well and had been my source of comfort here in Gypsy Bay and knocked briskly on the side door. A few days had passed since the night I showed up here and told Brian I'd had an erotic dream about him, so I wasn't sure what to expect. However, when I woke up this morning, I felt restless and inactive. We were working on recovering my memory, but all around me was a murder investigation involving a man whom I was apparently the last to see alive—which meant I was the number one suspect.

Brian opened the door, his eyes widened slightly in surprise, and then he looked down at his wristwatch.

"You're early," he said. "Our session isn't for another thirty minutes."

He looked so good in his jeans and black sweater, and his arctic blue eyes now held warmth in the mid-morning sun.

Why did this man affect me like this?

"Do you have another patient right now?" I asked.

"No, I was just reviewing some notes," he said, and then his eyes turned curious. "Something the matter?"

You know me, but you won't admit it.

"I'm sorry I couldn't give you more information about what I heard the other night. Whoever it was sounded very angry with you, and I wish I'd seen their face."

After I ran away from Widow Lake that night, I went home and spent the rest of the night in a restless state. I tossed and turned in bed only barely getting snatches of sleep and waiting for a decent hour the next morning before I called him to tell him I'd heard voices at Widow Lake and someone shouting his name.

But Brian didn't sound too concerned about it on the phone and looked even less concerned now when he shrugged. "I wouldn't worry too much about it. It was probably just some kids letting off steam. I've had to report a few incidents of vandalism around the neighborhood to the Sheriff's office during the past year. Maybe some of them got in trouble for it and now think I'm a prick."

He paused and must have seen my apprehension. "It's okay, Carrie. I'm sure it's nothing. Do you want to come inside?"

"No, I'll wait out here while you get your jacket. I want to do another reconstruction for our session today."

A slight smile tugged at the corner of his mouth. "Is that right? You want to go back to the scene of your accident?"

"No," I said, making sure my voice held firm. "I want to go to Harvey Adams's apartment."

He studied me for a long moment, and then came out onto the porch and closed the door softly behind him.

"I'm not sure you're ready for that, Carrie."

"I think I am."

"What brought this on?"

"I don't want to sit around and wait anymore for Sergeant Harris and the rest of the SFPD to come and arrest me. I want to take responsibility. Visiting the apartment might help me remember something…" I paused before continuing. "Even if it means remembering something awful."

He sighed. "I understand how you feel, but it's a crime scene."

"Then get me as close as possible."

He still looked as though he wanted to refuse, and I began to lose patience. "If you won't take me, I'll plug the address into my phone and find it on my own."

He nodded. "Yeah, I'm sure you would. I'll call Sergeant Harris. Maybe he can meet us there."

* * *

By early afternoon, we arrived in downtown San Francisco where Harvey Adams once rented a condo in a high-rise building overlooking the financial district. It looked to be a newly renovated building, and I found myself wondering how a public servant could afford the rent this place no doubt carried.

When Brian and I entered the lobby, Sergeant Harris was there to greet us and looking very eager. I noticed he cast a narrowed gaze in Brian's direction, but I filed it away to ponder over later. The three of us rode the elevator in silence up to the sixth floor, and it wasn't until we came to the door of apartment 632 that Sergeant Harris finally turned to me to speak.

"I appreciate you doing this to help with the investigation, Ms. Wallace, but are you sure you don't want to call your attorney?"

"I'm sure," I said.

He nodded, turned, and unlocked the door and went inside. Before I followed him, I felt Brian's tug on the sleeve of my coat. I turned and met his silent yet concerned gaze.

"It's all right," I said.

"You start showing any signs of distress, and I stop this," he said firmly.

I didn't answer but turned to follow Sergeant Harris into the apartment. Sunlight strewn in from the open blinds that showcased a spacious area with floor-to-ceiling windows. Even from here on the sixth floor, there was an excellent view of the financial district. I looked around, noting the open floor plan with living area, kitchen, and dining room all sharing the same space. I ran my hands along the couch and stepped into the kitchen. It was definitely a man's place, with all hard lines and dark wood furniture. Only the basic necessities were present, but none of the soft touches that indicated a woman had lived there. I sent a quick glance at Brian whose gaze was directly on me. It gave me a start to see he looked angry, and I wondered what he was thinking.

"Does any of this look familiar to you," he asked, the anger gone that quickly.

I kept looking around, waiting for something to spark, and shook my head. "I don't recognize any of this."

"Keep looking around," Sergeant Harris said. "Take your time. From what the neighbors say, you came here multiple times. You knew him, Carrie."

"That's enough, Sergeant," Brian admonished. "I don't want her influenced by the power of suggestion. Let her mind come to the truth on its own."

I whipped around to Sergeant Harris, who had raised his hands in mock surrender. "What did you say, Sergeant?"

"What?" he asked, frowning.

"Say the last thing you said."

"Okay, this is what I'm talking about," Brian said, "Carrie, figure it out on your own. You can do this."

"Dr. Kessler, please, there was something he said." I turned to Sergeant Harris again. "Say it again."

Harris shrugged. "I said you knew him."

"I knew him," I said to myself, quietly. "I knew him." I walked around the open space some more.

"I know him," I said. "I know him. I know—"

A rush of nausea came over me. I bent down at the waist and tried breathing deeply as Brian had coached me that day on the highway. I focused on getting the nauseous feeling to pass, but somewhere in the distant background, I heard voices—a mixture of Brian's and Sergeant Harris's. They were asking me if I was all right, but I didn't want to answer because something else, something more important was happening. A memory was resurfacing, and I didn't want to lose it.

"I don't even know you anymore," I said, standing in the middle of Harvey's living area and staring at him with disbelief.

"The evidence is clear and damning. I'm prepared to take this to trial."

"Yes, and I'll bet that money you're getting is to ensure a conviction."

I stopped in my search for my jacket and got a good, long look at him. "What's the matter with you? How could you even consider something like this? You're about to dig up the past and destroy his life all to suit your mysterious sponsor."

"Whether I take the bribes or not, this is still a strong case. If I win, it will do great for my career."

"You're really going through with this?"

He exploded, slamming a fist down onto the high-top counter that separated us. "You weren't even supposed to find out!"

"Well I did find out, so now what?"

"Carrie, can you hear me? If you can hear me, I need you to keep breathing."

The memory faded away, and I could now hear Brian's voice coaching me in a deep and soothing tone.

"That's it," he said, rubbing my back. "In and out. Slow, cleansing breaths."

"Is she all right?" Sergeant Harris asked.

"I'm fine," I said, rising to my full height. I side-stepped away from Brian's touch, only because it felt comforting… and familiar.

"What just happened?" Sergeant Harris asked. "One minute, you were fine, and the next, you're staring, not at me, but through me. Did you remember something?"

I didn't want to tell him the truth, because in doing so, I would also need to tell him exactly what I'd remembered, and I wasn't even sure what I'd been recalling. Harvey and I were having an argument about him taking bribes for a case. Then, suddenly, I was afraid to be around him. Now, he's dead. Did he come after me, and did I somehow get a gun and shoot him in self-defense?

"Did you find the gun," I asked the sergeant.

He didn't seem to like it that I was answering his question with a question of my own, but he shook his head. "No. It was .45 caliber round, but the gun was never recovered."

I turned to Brian. "I need to go."

"You don't want to see the rest of the apartment?" Sergeant Harris followed us to the door. "It might help."

I shook my head and started to walk through the door Brian held open for me.

"Ms. Wallace?"

I stopped and turned to look at Sergeant Harris.

"I know you remembered something. For whatever reason, you don't want to tell me what that was, and that's okay. But know that I will eventually find out what happened to Mr. Adams, and if I find you held back anything pertinent to my investigation, I'll be throwing you in jail." He paused and looked to Brian. "Along with his murderer."

***

Brian was unusually quiet as we left the downtown area. He remained silent as he wove his way through the lunch-hour traffic until he found a public park. There, he pulled his car into an available space, shut off the engine, then finally turned to me.

"For someone who was so desperate to get answers, we didn't stay very long."

I lowered my head to pick at the cuticles of my fingertips.

"I know you remembered something back there, Carrie. Are you going to tell me what it was?"

"We were arguing—Harvey and me."

"What about?"

"A case he was working on. I don't know the specifics, but it sounded as though he was taking a bribe to bring a case to trial. I was angry with him. I threatened to report him."

"Then what?" Brian asked.

"Harvey…he looked so angry, and I suddenly felt like I was in danger."

I watched the children playing in the park, with their parents standing nearby in case they were needed.

"I don't know what happened after that, but what if he came after me, I defended myself, and accidentally killed him? What if Sergeant Harris is right, and this is all a lover's quarrel gone wrong?"

"Don't get ahead of yourself. Until you can remember what happened, don't let the opinions of the police, your family, or even me influence you. These are your memories, and only you know what happened."

I shook my head, feeling tears welling up in my eyes. "I know you're right, but I'm so scared. I don't think I could ever kill anyone, but everyone is looking at me as if I did, and I can't stand it!"

"Hey, listen to me," he said, turning in the seat toward me. "You didn't kill anyone. So, get that out of your head."

"How do you know?"

"Because I do. I know it's not much of an answer, but you'll just have to trust me. You're not a killer. Do you understand me?"

I slowly nodded and took solace in his determined tone. "That look you're giving me, right now...please don't ever stop looking at me that way. You believe me. I need you to keep believing me."

He raised a hand to the side of my face and used his thumb to brush away a lone tear that had fallen down my cheek. "You can count on it."

His touch against my skin and his words were such a comfort to me I didn't want the moment to end. Any second now, he was going to take his hand away from my face and then drive us home. But I wasn't ready to go back to a doctor and patient relationship. I just needed to bask in this feeling with him for just a little longer.

I took my hand and touched the side of his face, feeling the rough surface of a close shave. I then slowly moved in close to him and hesitated before lightly touching his lips to mine. The kiss was warm and inviting, but I only indulged for a few seconds and then pulled back. Brian looked at me strangely and then immediately took my face in both of his hands and brought my lips back to his. This time, it was deep and sensuous. I wrapped my arms around his neck and moaned at the instant pleasure it brought me. We explored each other as much as we could in the tight space of the car. But as he tasted me and moved his hands all along my back and waist, something told me this wasn't an exploration. It felt like he was reacquainting himself with me. I became so wrapped up in the way he tasted, his warmth and the overwhelming desire I felt for him at this moment that I couldn't help but moan. But at the same time I moaned, he said something that I barely heard, but the words I thought I heard surprised me so much that I pulled away to look at him.

"What did you say?" I asked, breathless. He didn't answer me, and I instantly regretted breaking contact because the look he gave me was now accusatory.

The moment was lost, and I knew what he was thinking: This was not supposed to happen.

However, he didn't say or do anything, except to face forward in his seat and turn the ignition.

"I'll take you home."

"Thank you," was all I could say as I savored the memory of his lips and the words I knew I'd heard. But I also knew he'd forever deny saying them.

I missed you.

CHAPTER TWENTY-FIVE

*E*ver since she contacted Carrie a week ago, Fiona had been checking her phone for missed calls every half hour. She had so much she needed to tell Carrie that she was nearly bursting with it. Fiona was certain she wouldn't have changed her phone number, not without notifying the partners or even herself, because she would have to update her clients. Yet, and still, Carrie hadn't responded.

It was Thursday evening and Fiona was working in her home office, which doubled as her kitchen table. In between typing up briefs and motions for a new attorney she'd been assigned to temporarily, she was searching for any and all information about Harvey Adams. She still didn't know what his death had to do with all of this, but the rumor was that Carrie and Harvey had been dating. Sam still wouldn't give her any information and insisted he had to hear from Carrie first before he told her why he'd been following Harvey Adams. From what Fiona could decipher, he'd been tailing Adams for a few months, and he'd also obtained copies of bank statements that showed large amounts of cash deposited every two weeks into an account owned by

Harvey. All deposits continued to come from that same blind trust, and it had proved next to impossible for Fiona to find the name of the owner.

So, on one hand, she had notes from a five-year-old scandal, and on the other hand, she had a murdered ADA who was receiving payouts from a mystery trust all recorded on a flash drive Carrie had given to her for safekeeping. What connected them? She needed to talk to Carrie, but what were the chances Carrie would even remember *her*, much less explain what the hell she'd been up to?

She removed the flash drive from her computer and thumbed it between her fingers. A smaller part of her was urging her to call Sam and offer him some money to find out where Carrie was staying temporarily. Then she could put the flash drive and all of its unanswered questions into an envelope and mail it to Carrie with a note explaining everything as best she could. At least then, Fiona would be rid of the headache and could get back to her own life.

But, it was only a small part. The larger part of her told her to make sure she put the drive in Carrie's hands. Not only that, but Fiona just wanted to make sure the woman was okay. No, they hadn't been close, and before that night Carrie came to her apartment, Fiona had no idea Carrie even knew or cared where she lived.

She picked up her cell and started to dial Sam's number to work on finding Carrie's whereabouts, but before she could scroll to his number, her display flashed that a call was coming through. She frowned at the number, not recognizing it at all, and then a surge of excitement shot through her at the thought that this might be Carrie calling from a new number. Fiona quickly answered the call before voicemail took over.

"Hello?" she said with eagerness. "Carrie?"

Silence came from the other end.

"Hello? Who is this?"

A man's voice finally spoke, and it was deep and menacing.

"That's not important, Fiona. What's important is that you listen to what I'm going to tell you."

"Who is this, and how do you know my name?"

"This will be my one and only warning. Drop this. Stop looking for that bitch. Stop calling this number. Stop searching for answers."

"I want to know who I'm speaking to," she said.

"You're speaking to someone who will make Mark and Veronica's lives very bad unless you back the fuck off!"

Fiona paused, her eyes widened in fear as she took the phone from her ear and stared at it as if she couldn't believe what she was holding in her hands.

"And let's not forget their baby girl, Janelle. You just became a new aunt, Fiona. Don't make it a short-lived experience."

Tears of pure fury came to her eyes. "Whoever you are, you leave my family alone. Do you hear me? I swear to God, I'll kill you if you come near my brother, his wife, or that little girl."

Mocking laughter came from the other end as though her threats were utterly ridiculous to him.

"Back off, Fiona."

The call ended, and Fiona resisted throwing the phone against the wall. Instead, she scrolled through her contacts with shaky fingers until she came to Sam Collin's number.

When he picked up, she wasted no time and came straight to the point. Screw Carrie's amnesia. Screw her rehabilitation. Fiona was going to find her and make her remember.

"Sam, if you don't want to tell me what she was doing, at least tell me where I can find her."

CHAPTER TWENTY-SIX

The secretary pointed me to the sheriff's office, and because the door was open, I walked in on Gray Spencer staring at the same small black and white photos Shannon had dropped to the ground the day I met her. I couldn't decipher the look on his face, so I wasn't sure if what he was looking at was good news or bad news to him.

I rapped on his open door, and he looked up with a start.

"Sorry to bother you, but I had some free time today, and I remembered you offered to help me if I ever needed it."

Recognition washed over his eyes, and he quickly put the sonogram pictures to the side and stood up with a smile.

"Carrie Wallace," he said, coming from around his desk.

His tall, broad frame was just as imposing as the day I met him when he surprised his wife for lunch, but the smile that crossed his lips was enough to put me at ease.

"Please, sit down," he said, pulling out one of his guest chairs for me. He then turned to close his office door, correctly assuming that this would be a private conversation.

"How have you been adjusting to our town?" he asked, returning to his seat.

"It's definitely a place I would choose for a weekend getaway, but something tells me I'm a city girl at heart."

He laughed. "I can understand that. Speaking of which, I wanted to tell you the day we met to always listen to those gut feelings you have about yourself. Even though your mind is still healing, there are thoughts and beliefs you have about yourself that will never go away."

I nodded. "Thanks for the tip. That insight is the reason I came to see you."

"I figured as much." He paused. "How are your treatments and sessions coming along?"

"Slowly."

He let out another laugh. "I remember those days. Trust me, no one understands your frustration like I do. Dr. Kessler and every other specialist will tell you not to force it, and it will become the most annoying shit you've ever heard."

I laughed and nodded at the truth of his words.

"But they're all correct," he continued. "Sooner or later, you will remember. Just be patient with yourself for a while longer."

I set my purse on his desk and leaned forward in my chair. "I'm going to go out on a limb and tell you something, because like you said, you're the only one who really understands what I'm going through. But I would like this to remain between us."

"Of course."

"I know you're right when you say I need patience, but there's one night in particular I desperately need to remember. The details of what happened that night could mean the difference between me being charged for murder or being a witness to a murder."

I looked down at my lap and then back up at Gray. "After I met you and your wife, Shannon, I went to the local library to do some research. Apparently, there was one night in question you needed to remember, also."

His eyes turned somber as he nodded. "The night my brother died on the cliff. Knowing what happened that night would mean knowing whether Shannon was a murderer or not."

"I know the events were painful," I said. "I just want to know what finally shook that memory loose. I was hoping that maybe it could help…"

I trailed off, realizing now what I was saying. I closed my eyes and shook my head slowly, suddenly feeling very foolish.

"Listen to me. I'm asking you to tell me the exact steps you took to recall a memory as if it were a 'one-size-fits-all' kind of thing." I grabbed my purse and stood. "Sorry again to bother you, Sheriff."

"Carrie, wait," he said, also rising and rounding his desk. "Sit back down. I want to do what I can to help."

I paused to look at him, saw the sincerity in his eyes, and slowly retrieved my seat. This time, Gray sat in the chair next to mine and turned toward me, resting his elbows on his knees in an earnest gesture.

"To answer your question, a simple sentence was all that was needed to help me finally remember, but I honestly believe that all the sessions, the journaling, revisiting the location, and anything else that Dr. Kessler told me to do helped to loosen that memory and led up to that final moment."

His eyes looked away to stare at some distant spot beyond me, and I knew he was recalling events that would forever be a mystery to me.

"There's something else I've come to believe," he said. "Sometimes, the mind will do what it can to protect you, and that might be what's causing the delay in your memory of that night."

"What do you mean?"

He focused on me once again. "You said that night could mean the difference between you being a murderer and a witness to a murder. Whatever you saw or did that night, it might be so horrible to you, that you don't want to remember."

Tears burned the backs of my eyes, but I refused to let them fall. "I do want to remember. I need to know."

He nodded, and I could feel the empathy he had for me. "Then give it time. You'll never know what the final trigger will be."

"Thank you, Sheriff."

"Gray," he corrected.

I smiled and then angled my head toward the sonogram pictures. "I see she told you."

He followed my gaze, stared at the pictures, and it warmed me to see the joy pass through his eyes.

"Shannon was raised by her aunt, who died a few years back. My parents also died a while ago. Then after everything with my brother..." He paused and shook his head in wonderment. "She gave us a family again."

CHAPTER TWENTY-SEVEN

Derek Harris took a swig of his soda and popped up instantly out of the booth when he saw Natalie Wallace breeze into the diner with a confidence and stature that a woman of wealth wore naturally. She was dressed in a beige knit sweater and chocolate brown slacks with flats, and Derek surmised that even with her efforts to appear casual, her style and grace could not be contained. She had a no nonsense look on her face, but he couldn't see what her eyes were telling because of the large shades she wore.

"Mrs. Wallace, thank you for coming," he said, gesturing for her to sit opposite him in the booth.

Natalie Wallace remained standing. "You told me on the phone this would not be about Carrie. It's the only reason I didn't tell her lawyer I was meeting with you. But if I get one whiff of you trying to get information out of me about the night Harvey Adams was killed, I'm walking out of here."

"It isn't about Carrie—at least not directly."

"Sergeant—"

"It's about Brian Kessler."

She stilled and then slowly removed her shades. When

Derek gestured to the booth again, she sat down this time. The server was immediately at her side, asking if she wanted to order breakfast, and Natalie said she only wanted coffee.

Derek waited with her in awkward silence as the server returned with a cup and pot of coffee. She filled Natalie's cup, refilled his, and then finally went away.

"What about Dr. Kessler?" she asked.

"I had a talk with some of the hospital staff at San Francisco General. They remember hearing arguments between you, your husband, and your son about Carrie's treatment—namely her psychiatrist. From what I gather, you weren't in favor of Dr. Kessler, even though he's one of the top in his field."

"I believed we could do better. There are other top psychiatrists in that field."

"Okay, now tell me the real reason you didn't want him to treat Carrie, and I'm guessing it has a lot to do with the fact that they were once married."

She gave him a smile that hinted at her waning patience. "If you've already surmised everything, Sergeant, then you don't need me."

Derek didn't say anything to that but decided to wait her out. She looked away to focus on the people passing by the window of the diner, and then turned back to him.

"Yes, of course it had to do with the fact that they'd been married. I saw the whole thing as a disaster in the making."

"Why?"

"For obvious reasons. How could it ever be considered a good idea for Carrie to be treated by her ex-husband?"

"You're telling me it was a bad divorce?"

"Sergeant, it was a bad marriage. I doubt the two of them would've even been together if Andrew hadn't dangled bait in front of Brian."

She paused to look down to examine her manicured

hands. "My husband wanted to merge practices with Brian's father, Dr. Gerald Kessler. I'm sure you've heard of him."

Derek leaned back against the booth and nodded. "As in Gerald Kessler and Eliza Watley? Yeah, I did my research."

"Andrew offered Brian a very sweet deal in exchange for marrying Carrie. He believed if Brian and Carrie wed, then that would cement the partnership he had with Gerald."

"Andrew Wallace the neurologist and Gerald Kessler the psychiatrist," Derek said. "Sounds profitable."

"It was for a while. Then after that debacle with Eliza Watley, Andrew was forced to cut ties with Gerald—and anything and anyone associated with him."

"Are you trying to tell me the two of you convinced Carrie to divorce Brian because of his father's legal troubles?"

"No! Listen, Sergeant, I may not have approved of Brian and Carrie's marriage, but I do respect the bond of matrimony. She was married to him, and I expected her to support her husband, even though we had to distance ourselves from his father. We only asked him to keep a low profile until everything calmed down. But Brian…"

When she trailed off, Derek arrived at the conclusion on his own. "Brian wouldn't keep quiet. He defended his father's practices and upheld that there were absolutely no mistakes in his treatment of Eliza Watley."

Natalie nodded. "Things got worse. Gerald was sued, he lost his practice and went into isolation. Then when he was found dead, Brian blamed us for turning our backs on him in the first place. Carrie, naturally got in the middle of the crossfire, and their marriage was even more strained than it had been."

Derek thought for a minute. "Forgive me for saying, Mrs. Wallace, but everything you've told me has only proven that

Brian was a loyal son. What does all of this have to do with why you don't want him treating Carrie?"

Her eyes flashed with renewed anger. "Because while Brian was being the loyal son and defending his father's actions, he was being a terrible husband by forcing Carrie to choose sides. Carrie, however, only saw reason and agreed with us that Brian should keep a low profile. She was there for him when he was mourning his father's death, but I saw that Brian hated her for not leaving her firm or even us. You have to understand, Sergeant, that my daughter is a very proud woman. Throughout her teen years and into adulthood, I'd never seen her fall head over heels in love with any man—not until Brian. He may have entered the marriage based on a bribe, but Carrie genuinely loved him. I was so happy for her, but I despised him for not seeing the love she had for him. Or maybe he did, and he just used it in hopes he'd get her to do what he wanted."

Derek ran his finger over the rim of his mug of coffee. He then leaned forward across the booth and spoke softly. "Is that your only objection to him, Mrs. Wallace, or is there something in your gut that believes he would cause harm to Carrie?"

She returned his stare and then expelled a heavy sigh. "I really don't know. All I can say is that Carrie may have temporarily forgotten him, but Brian has definitely not forgotten her or everything that happened between them. And I wouldn't put it past him to use it against her."

CHAPTER TWENTY-EIGHT

I woke up remembering my father.

It wasn't some cutesy or sentimental memory where he was tying my shoelaces for me or teaching me how to ride a bike or embracing me at my high school graduation. No, the first vision I had of my father, I was shouting at him.

"Why don't you just stay out of my life!"

"Lower your voice. I was trying to help."

"How? How exactly was bribing him going to help me? Are you so sure that I can't get a man to marry me without offering him something worthwhile?"

"I know you like him. I saw the way you were drawn to him from the moment we invited them to the house. I just thought it would be beneficial to move things along."

"Beneficial for you, that is."

He took a hesitant step toward me and raised one hand as if trying to calm a wounded animal. "What's the problem? Do you love him or not?"

"Yes, Dad, I love him, but I have no idea how he feels about me, and since you made him an offer he couldn't refuse, I guess we'll never know, will we? The last thing I want is for him to think he's *stuck with me because of some stupid deal he made with you. I want him to see me as his wife, not the rich bitch with the influential father."*

"Don't you ever talk to me that way again, Carrie."

I stormed away from him.

It was further proof that I was married. Or at the very least, I'd been close to being married. Where was he? We couldn't have still been married because he would've now shown his face to me. But were we divorced? Did he die? I always had the feeling when I woke up that my family was hiding something from me, but I'd assumed it had something to do with the night of my accident. Was it really about my husband? Was he the secret they didn't want to tell me about? There had been no pictures with me and another man in the photo albums or digital files my mother brought me. I thought back to that day I called her and asked her about my husband. She'd hung up on me as if it was too painful for her to say anything more about him. Calling her again was out of the question, but maybe if I called my dad and told him that my memory of him came back, he'd be more receptive to telling me about this faceless man. But something told me he and my mom made a pact to not discuss it with me. Maybe they were waiting until my memory of him returned when they'd have no other choice but to tell me what they knew. But I wasn't going to sit around and wait for that to happen.

After getting out of bed, showering, and eating a simple breakfast of yogurt, toast, and juice, I spent the morning sitting at my desk, going through the old photo albums my mother had left behind. I was making my way to extended family—aunts, uncles, and cousins. With each picture, I stopped and studied it, giving my mind a chance to catch up and hopefully latch onto a memory that would eventually become crystal clear to me.

In between flipping through album photos and swiping

through digital images on the computer, I occasionally glanced up at the clock and watch as the time approached and then slowly ticked past 9:30 a.m. When it reached 9:51 a.m., I was officially twenty-one minutes late for my appointment with Brian. Considering I was never late, he was bound to realize by now I wasn't coming. Yet, he didn't call and that hurt more than anything because it solidified my belief that I'd crossed a line with him, and it had affected him more than he'd let on.

After that searing kiss, he refused to even look at me, much less say a word to me as he drove us home. If I hadn't said, "Thanks for the ride," I wonder if he would have even acknowledged me with a simple nod.

That kiss happened three days ago, and we'd been avoiding each other ever since, and just like me, I was sure he'd been dreading this upcoming therapy session. So, I decided to make things easier on the both of us and forego this one and instead spend the day looking at photos and doing some journaling. Next week however, we would both just have to grow up, because my treatment was still important.

As I thought about stolen kisses with Brian, an idea occurred to me. I went to the internet on my computer and pulled up the courthouse website for San Francisco County. Marriage licenses were public record. I was betting I'd been married here in California, so this was the place to start.

As I began to navigate my way through the court's website, a sudden and firm knock sounded at the door. I turned from my seat at a corner desk in the living room to stare at it warily. Maybe Brian wasn't going to allow my sudden lapse in professionalism to get in the way of him doing his job. But that would mean having to face him much sooner than I was ready.

A second knock came, this time sounding more insistent,

and I rose from the chair and walked to the door. When I opened it, I saw a woman of my same height and build sporting a blond pixie cut and standing on the other side of the threshold.

"Hi, can I help you?"

The stare she gave me lasted a bit longer than what was comfortable, but eventually, a hesitant smile began to form at the corners of her lips.

"Hi, Carrie. I'm glad to see you're okay."

As soon as she spoke, the sound of her voice unleashed a torrent of memories—memories of seeing her in an office, memories of her speaking to me in a courtroom. This woman obviously knew me, and I just realized I must know her, too.

"I'm sorry," I began. "I don't know if you've heard, but I suffered amnesia from an accident—"

"I heard," she said. "I've tried to be patient and give you time and space to recover, but I need your help." She stepped forward. "My name is Fiona Richards. I'm your paralegal at Smith, Downing and Whitaker."

I tossed the name around for a moment, but nothing struck me as familiar about it. Only her face was recognizable. Then, for the first time, I noticed the look of distress and worry in her eyes.

I stepped to the side. "Do you want to come in and tell me what's going on?"

Fiona looked around as though she expected someone to be following her and then nodded and stepped inside the house.

"Have a seat," I offered and closed the door behind her.

I didn't know why she came and had no idea how I, as an amnesia victim, would be able to help her, but I wasn't about to let her go. I was brimming over with questions, and aside from my family, she was my only link to the outside world.

She could give me answers about myself, my job, and my colleagues.

"You said you needed my help. What can I do?"

Fiona was sitting in a soft armchair across from me but looked anything but relaxed as she sat forward, clutching something between her hands.

"How much do you remember about the night of your accident and Harvey Adams's death?"

"Only small snatches but nothing concrete. I haven't been able to piece together much about that night. Why do you ask?"

"The police questioned me—a Sergeant Harris. I told him you came to see me that night."

I was taken aback. "I came to see *you*?"

No one, including Sergeant Harris, had ever mentioned that I visited this woman that night. Everyone was more focused on me being at the scene of Harvey's murder than my whereabouts beforehand. Fiona nodded and finally unclasped her hands to reveal what she'd been clutching.

"Yes. You came by my apartment, and you gave me this."

It was a thumb drive. I leaned forward with one outstretched hand, and she immediately handed it over.

I frowned, turning it over in between my fingers. "What's on it?"

"Surveillance records and financial documents about Harvey Adams. It looks like you tracked his movements for two weeks."

I looked at her, feeling confused. "You're saying I was having him followed?"

"Not just followed. I think you were having him investigated. We have a guy named Sam Collins who does investigations for the firm. He says you hired him to follow Harvey, but he wouldn't give me any more than that without your permission."

I shook my head, not ready to explore that bit of information just yet. "You said I gave it to you the night he died. What did I say to you?"

"You said you wanted me to keep it for you, and that if anything happened to you, to give it to one of the partners."

I frowned again. "Is that all?"

Fiona nodded. "You looked worried. I tried to get you to tell me what was going on, but you refused. It was the last time I saw you."

I sighed and stood to pace around the sofa, suddenly feeling frustration overwhelm me. "I can't remember any of that. Did I say where I was going?"

"No."

"My accident happened several miles away from here on the 101. Did I say anything about coming up here to Gypsy Bay?"

"You didn't say anything, Carrie. You just handed me the thumb drive with the instructions to keep it safe until you came back for it. Then you left."

"What time? What time did I leave?"

"It was past nine thirty."

So, just like Sergeant Harris said, I had plenty of opportunity to kill Harvey. But what he didn't know was that Fiona's account had now given me motive to kill him. If he knew about this thumb drive and its contents, I would find myself arrested before the end of the day.

This was getting beyond my control. I needed to see what was in those files, what I was up against, and then get the flash drive to my lawyer as soon as possible. I stopped pacing, grabbed for my jacket draped over an armchair and turned in search of my car keys.

"Can you get in touch with this Sam Collins?"

She nodded slowly. "Yes, but—"

I shrugged on my jacket. "Good. Call him and tell him to meet us, and you can take me to him."

Fiona stood. "I can't do that."

I paused in my search for my car keys and looked at her. "Why not?"

"I only came to return those documents to you. I can't do anymore. I hope you get well, soon."

I watched in puzzlement as she picked up her purse and began to head for the door. As she opened it and stepped onto the porch, I was right behind her.

"Wait a minute," I said. "You give me this thumb drive, answer a couple of questions, and then leave? What's going on?"

She stopped and turned around, and for the first time, I noticed something in her eyes that had been there all along, only I chose to ignore it. She was afraid.

"Someone called me. They warned me to leave this—all of this about you and Harvey—alone."

"Who? Who called you?"

She turned back around and continued in her stride to her car, and I had to race up behind her and grab for her arm.

"Fiona, wait! Tell me who called you."

"I don't know! All I know is that the son of a bitch threatened my life and the lives of my brother and his family. After I leave here, I'm going to the police."

"No, wait, please! I need your help."

I couldn't lose her just yet. I still had more questions, and I wanted them answered before she told Sergeant Harris everything. At her car, as she fumbled in her purse for her keys, I continued to plead my case.

"If you can just take me to this investigator, he can tell me what I was doing. Then I'll be able to talk to Sergeant Harris. Just give me some time to work this out. Don't you see I'm blind to everything that's going on?"

She snatched the car keys out of her purse and turned toward me with eyes that were furious.

"You may have lost your memory, but you're still the same person—you only care about getting what you want."

"What are you talking about? You came to see me, and I'm asking for your help."

"I came to see you to give you back that damn thumb drive, which has been nothing but trouble to me since you gave it to me that night. Now, it's your problem. I'm going to the police to get some protection."

"Fiona I—"

"They want to hurt me and my family, and this is all your fault," Fiona said, her voice rising in panic. "This was between you and Harvey, but you put me in danger. Don't you fucking care?"

"Of course, I care, but I can't help you when I don't even remember you or anything else about that night!"

She shook her head, turned away from me in disgust, and then got inside her car. She turned the ignition and in the next instant, I had to jump back as she tore out of the driveway and sped down the street with tires squealing. I continued to stand there, hoping she'd turn around and come back. But after a few minutes passed, an empty street was all I saw. She was going to the police, and I had no idea what she was going to tell them.

Without another thought, I ran to my car, got inside and peeled away to follow after her.

CHAPTER TWENTY-NINE

Fiona sped away down the quiet, tree-lined street, out of the neighborhood, through the downtown district and out of Gypsy Bay. It wasn't until she was on the coastal highway leading back to San Francisco that she felt tears burning the backs of her eyes. One had managed to trail down her cheek, and she wiped it away—angry at herself for letting her emotions get to her.

Screw this, she thought to herself. This trip had been a mistake. It had been a mistake to take that USB key from Carrie in the first place. But Fiona had always admired the woman, apart from the fact that she'd been too demanding. She'd always treated Fiona with respect, as if she'd seen more in her than a paralegal whose job it was to do her bidding. For that, Fiona wanted to help in any way she could, and after Carrie's accident, she wanted to continue helping her. She had a vision of the lost and confused look in Carrie's eyes, the complete opposite of the woman she was used to seeing around the firm, preparing for trial. Feelings of guilt at leaving her without answers were slowly creeping in, but she tucked them away and kept driving because circumstances had changed. Now Fiona was the one who needed help. Someone was stalking her movements, and she couldn't go on protecting Carrie from whatever she'd done or forgotten she'd done that night. She had to look after herself and make sure her brother and his family stayed out of harm's way.

Keeping her eyes on the road, Fiona pressed the button on her steering wheel that dialed the contact number she'd saved in her phone. As the sound of the ringing filled her car, she realized if she was going to him for help, she'd have to tell him everything she omitted the first day he came to see her.

"Sergeant Harris." The commanding boom of his voice broke the silence in the car.

"Sergeant Harris, this is Fiona Richards."

A brief pause as she figured he was trying to place her name in his memory.

"Ms. Richards," he said, finally. "Yes, you work with Carrie Wallace. What can I do for you?"

"I need to speak to you. I'm being stalked, and it has to do with the night of Harvey's murder and Carrie's accident. She gave me something that night to keep for her, and it's because of that I'm being threatened."

"Slow down, Ms. Richards. Where are you?"

She could hear papers rustling, and she guessed she'd caught him at his desk, and he was rifling through it, trying to find a piece of paper and pen.

"I'm on the coast highway heading back to the city. I just came from seeing Carrie."

"You saw Carrie Wallace?"

"Yes." Fiona took a deep breath before continuing. "I told her I was coming to see you after we talked."

Another pause. "Are you in danger now?"

"No."

On instinct, she checked her rearview mirror to see if she was being followed, but only a tractor trailer and a minivan with a family trailed behind.

"It's nearly eleven thirty," he said. "I can meet you halfway. Say about forty-five minutes at Rudy's Café. Do you know the place?"

"Yes. I can tell you everything I know, but I'll need your help in protecting my family."

"I'll tell you what: I'll radio one of the officers in that area to wait with you until I arrive. I can help you, Fiona," he assured her.

"Thank you."

"Forty-five minutes. I'll see you then."

Fiona disconnected the call and felt a modicum of stress and fear leaving her body. This had been the first right move she'd made since opening her door to Carrie that night.

* * *

She made it to the café in just over a half an hour. Sergeant Harris wasn't there, but true to his word, she did see a police cruiser parked in front. As Fiona drove up slowly next to the cruiser, she slowed down in order to get the officer's attention and signal to him or her that she was the person waiting for the sergeant. But no one was inside the car. She parallel parked in front of the police car, shut off her engine, and waited. She pulled out her cell phone and scrolled through her texts and emails just to give herself something to do. In all honesty, she was nervous to meet with the sergeant. After all, she had withheld information from him. What if he gave her a hard time and didn't trust her? Fiona would just have to make him believe her. It was too bad she hadn't thought to make a copy of the flash drive and bring it with her. She'd returned to Carrie the one given to her that night, but she hadn't thought she'd have this sudden change of heart, nor the urgent need to finally seek help from the police.

A sudden and quick succession of raps on her window startled her out of her thoughts. The fear that had gripped her slowly dissipated as she took one look at the man in uniform. Fiona hit the button for the automatic window, and as it rolled down, she had a feeling of recognition from the man, despite the aviators covering his eyes.

"I'm Officer Lowell. Are you Fiona Richards?"

"Yes," she said.

"Sergeant Harris radioed. He asked me to wait with you until he arrived. It shouldn't be much longer. In the meantime, he wanted me to get a preliminary statement from you. If you'd be more comfortable, we can do it inside the café."

"That's fine," she said. "I need to use the restroom anyway."

She grabbed her purse and keys, stepped out, and locked the door. They walked into the small diner together, and a server gave Fiona directions and a key to the bathroom.

"I'll order us two coffees," Officer Lowell said.

Fiona smiled her thanks and headed toward the rear of the café where there was a private bathroom. She walked in and locked the door behind her. She relieved herself, washed and dried her hands, and stared out of the one dingy and dusty window. She was beginning to feel a bit more at ease. When Sergeant Harris arrived, she'd insist that he put a detail on her brother's house. Speaking of which, she should at least give him and Veronica a call to let them know what may be happening. The last thing she wanted was to alarm them when a policeman showed up at their door for something she was involved in.

She pulled her cell from her purse and started to scroll to her brother's number when something outside the window caught her attention.

Fiona squinted and leaned closer to the small glass pane for a better look. Was that...was that Carrie's car?

Someone knocked on the door, and for the second time that day, she was startled.

"Just a minute," she called back. She looked out the window again. She didn't see anyone inside the car, and it could just be a car that looked like Carrie's.

Silence followed, then another knock, and this one was louder.

"I said just a minute," she said.

Someone tried the knob, twisting it, but the lock was on.

Fiona turned toward the door in both surprise and anger. She stared at the knob as it twisted and turned, but whoever was trying to get in was stopped by the locked door. Something curious went up her spine, something that resembled fear, and that only angered her even more. This business with Carrie and the threatening phone calls had her jumping at shadows, and she was completely over it. With her phone call forgotten, she tossed her cell into her purse, twisted the lock with a snap, and snatched open the door, ready to give whoever was on the other side a piece of her mind. But as soon as the door swung open, a strong hand grasped her neck and forced her back inside the small space. She looked at her attacker with wide-eyed terror as she clawed at the hands squeezing the life from her neck. The fear she ignored earlier rose to full-blown panic as she saw the bathroom door slam and lock, trapping her inside.

CHAPTER THIRTY

A cold feeling of dread fell upon Derek Harris's shoulders when he pulled up to the roadside café and saw the police cars swarming the place. He knew immediately something terrible must have happened, and goddammit, his gut was telling him it was Fiona. His first clue had been the fact that she hadn't answered when he called to see if she'd made it to the café safely. But he did radio Officer Lowell, who confirmed Fiona was with him. At the time, however, the officer reported she was in the bathroom, and he was getting ready to take down her preliminary statement. Still, Sergeant Harris broke a lot of traffic laws in his rush to get there and see for himself that she was okay.

But obviously, he hadn't gotten there quickly enough. He had to lay on his horn for several pedestrians and media who were in his way until he finally found a convenient enough parking space near the entrance of the café.

He got out, approached the officer in charge of keeping people behind the yellow caution tape border, and produced his badge. The officer nodded and quickly lifted the tape for Harris.

"Where am I going?" Harris asked, tucking his badge away and pulling out latex gloves.

"The restroom. Towards the back and to your left," the officer stated, barely above a whisper in case the media or anyone other than law enforcement was listening. "Officer Lowell is back there waiting for you. He held up the ME from taking the body until you got here."

"Thanks."

He entered the café, and the only people inside the dining area were an older couple, a server, a cook, and a middle-aged man who looked to be the manager of the place. They all sat in booths, no doubt waiting to be questioned or released as witnesses. Harris kept moving toward the back until he found Officer Lowell and the crime scene investigation team all crammed together in the solitary unisex bathroom.

The moment Officer Lowell spotted him, his broad shoulders seemed to slump from exhaustion, and his hardened eyes dulled with relief.

"Sergeant," he said, shaking his head. "I'm so sorry. It was my duty to look after her and—"

"Stop." Derek held up one hand to forestall any more apologies. "This is on me. She told me she'd been threatened, but I underestimated the level of danger she was in."

"I feel responsible, sir—"

"Well, don't. Just tell me what you know."

The firm command in his tone seemed to be just what was needed to shake the officer out of his self-pity. He paused to take a breath and then relayed to Derek what had happened after Fiona arrived at the café."

It all sounded pretty straightforward, but when Lowell

got to the part about her leaving to use the restroom, Derek's ears perked up.

"Did you notice anyone following her in there?"

"No, no one."

"What about the people up front?"

"The server said she noticed Ms. Richards, but she was in the middle of taking the couple's orders. The cook and manager both say they were in the freezer at the time, checking the meat inventory. If anyone did follow her in, no one noticed."

"Cameras?"

As soon as he asked, Derek felt a wave of disappointment at the look on the officer's face as he shook his head.

"No cameras. It's a small, out-of-the-way, kind of place. They never saw a need for them."

"All right," Derek said. "I assume you got everyone's statement, but I want to talk to them myself, again. Get everyone's contact information and let them go. Also, get in touch with the victim's brother. She was worried about them, and I want a uniform to get over to their house right away. I assume he's her next of kin."

"Yes, sir."

As soon as Officer Lowell left, Derek turned his attention to the medical examiner, who was looking impatient to have the body.

"What can you tell me so far?"

Doctor Sonya Ruiz, who worked in the ME's office, stepped forward and used her pointer to gesture to Ms. Richard's body lying on the ground.

"There's bruising around the neck and the left cheek, and a heavy blow to the back of the head. She was choked, but that's not what killed her. It seems the victim was stunned first by being hit across the face. She tried to turn and run, possibly out that small window and was hit on the back of the head with a heavy object. No sign of the murder weapon anywhere, and there doesn't look to be too much struggle. The murderer must've easily overpowered Ms. Richards and didn't take too long. He or she likely couldn't risk someone walking in or hearing the sounds of a fight."

Derek turned and eyed the lock on the bathroom door. "I agree with you that she must've been ambushed. Maybe just as she was coming out, she was pushed back inside and locked in."

He paused to look at the window. "That's pretty small for a normal-sized adult. I'm not so sure Ms. Richards would've fit through there."

She was desperate," Lowell supplied. "You'll try anything when you're under attack."

"Maybe," Derek mumbled, now lost in thought.

Another scenario went through his mind, and that was the fact that maybe Fiona knew her killer. He could be wrong about her ambush because she simply let the killer inside, and even felt comfortable enough to turn her back on them. His gaze went from the body to the door and then again to the window, trying to get the pieces to fit in his mind. If Fiona knew her attacker, a bathroom was a strange place to have a meetup. Then the sight of something, or rather, someone outside the bathroom window jolted him completely out of his thoughts.

"What the fuck?" he muttered, and then moved like lightning.

He bolted out of the bathroom, ran through the dining area past the frowning witnesses, and then outside to fight through the growing crowd.

"Out of the way," he ordered, trying his best not to shove people to the side, but he didn't want to lose sight of her.

But with all the commotion he was causing, she spotted him, and—big mistake—she turned to run.

"Carrie!" he shouted, as he gained speed to chase after her.

She ran across the road, ignoring blaring car horns of drivers that missed her by inches and was almost to her car. Harris kept moving but was stopped for just a few seconds when a car nearly hit him, which was followed by a loud and long angry horn. He spared only a second's glance for the driver, and then continued after Carrie. By this time, she had her car door open and was climbing inside. Derek barely managed to grab hold of one arm, pull her back out, and slam the car door shut. He then turned her around so that the front of her body was facing the hood of her car and pulled her wrists behind her to slap on the handcuffs.

"Why did you run?" he asked. "Why did you run?"

"Because I didn't do it."

He turned her around to face him. "Do what?"

"Kill her!"

"Innocent people don't run, Carrie. What are you doing out here?"

She looked up at him with defiance. "You've already made up your mind about me. I know you think I'm a murderer."

"You're not doing a good job of convincing me otherwise. Now, I'll ask you again: What are you doing out here?"

She cut her brown eyes away from him, and her lips stayed closed.

"That's how you want to play it? Fine. Let's go."

He walked her back to the café and put her in the back of his car. "You can call your lawyer and the rest of the cavalry when we get back to the city."

CHAPTER THIRTY-ONE

*B*rian's cell phone was ringing, but he ignored it as he looked at Rachel in bewilderment.

"You're really going to continue to deny it?" She asked.

"Deny what? I told you, there's nothing going on with me."

She stared at him as if she didn't believe him. "You've always given me the respect of being up front with me," she said, keeping her voice calm and even. "Don't start keeping things from me, now."

He stared back at her, knowing her words to be true. And the longer she stared, the more he felt the guilt washing over and consuming him.

"I'm sorry," he finally said.

They'd been standing at opposite ends of the family room for the past five minutes, arguing about his recent change in behavior—more to the point—the woman who was causing his recent change in behavior. Rachel must have seen the agony in his eyes because she slowly made her way to the couch and sat down. She then patted the empty space beside her.

Brian's phone began to chime again, but he quickly put it on silent without looking at the display and joined her on the sofa. As soon as he sat down, he leaned forward, resting his elbows on his knees and cradling his head in his hands. He had made a terrible mess of things, and now was the time to face the woman he'd disrespected and confess.

"Just tell me what happened," Rachel said. "I know it has something to do with her."

"We were in San Francisco. I was taking her back to this place as a memory exercise. That's all it was supposed to be. I never went there to do anything except counsel and treat her..." He paused in what he felt sounded like rambling and just said it. "I kissed her."

Rachel nodded somberly and then turned to look at the blank screen of the TV in front of them surrounded by shelves of books. For a moment, she was silent and Brian wished to God she would yell and curse at him for being a jerk, a prick and a bastard.

"You kissed *her*?"

In actuality, she'd kissed him, but all he remembered was her full lips and soft cheeks brushing against the stubble of his shaven beard. All he remembered was that he didn't want it to stop. All he remembered was wanting more, and not being able to stop thinking about it. So, what was the difference?

"Yeah, I kissed her."

There was that look again of not believing him, but she must have decided it wasn't worth the trouble disputing it, especially since she hadn't been there.

"I know you're expecting me to be angry, but the truth is, I'm not. I've been expecting this for a while now. Maybe all that time of waiting for it to happen, I grew used to the idea. But the fact that I'm not angry that my boyfriend kissed his ex-wife also makes me sad. It tells me a lot about our relationship."

"Don't," Brian said. He knew what she was leading up to, and he wasn't about to let a kiss in the heat of the moment be the cause. "Don't do this."

"Why not?" she asked, turning to face him. "Something is different about you. I've sensed it all along. You're pulling away from me."

"That's not true."

"Because of her."

"No."

"Give me some credit, Brian. You're still in love with her."

"I'm not. At least, not the woman I married. I fell out of love with her a long time ago."

"What about the woman she is now?" Rachel asked.

He remained silent, which was all the answer she needed.

She sighed. "Let's spare ourselves the unnecessary drama. There's no need to pretend with me. Something is going on with you. I've noticed it for a long while now, no matter how much you've tried to ignore it."

Brian had no more words. She was right. To continue to stand there and deny his feelings would have been insulting to her, and if nothing else, she at least deserved his honesty. In fact, he owed her much more than his honesty. She'd been there, helping him investigate his father's murder when everyone else had told him the case had gone cold. He suspected the people blamed Gerald for the death of one of their own and didn't bother to look too hard for his killer. But Rachel took his notes, pulled some strings at the DA's office and got renewed interest in the case. Unfortunately, nothing much had come of it, yet, but he was still thankful for what she did. Part of him wondered if he was using that as an excuse to stay with her long after he knew in his heart nothing would come of it.

With that possibility on his mind, Brian did the only thing he could do.

"I'm sorry. I know that doesn't excuse any of this, but I'm so sorry. Just know that nothing other than that kiss happened between us."

"I know," she said, holding up a hand to stop him. "I know you'd never intentionally disrespect me. I know you care about me. I know all of that."

"Then why are we breaking up? I'll refer Carrie to another counselor. Hell, it's what her family wants anyway. She'll move back to San Francisco, and you and I can get back to our lives."

Rachel was smiling and shaking her head before he finished. "You and I both know that's not what you want."

No, it wasn't what he wanted, but dammit, it was what he needed.

His phone began to vibrate against his hip. Brian cursed, fished the phone from his pocket, and looked at the display this time. He saw that it was Shawn Wallace's number, and instantly thought of Carrie. If Shawn was calling, something must have been wrong. It continued to ring, and he looked up at Rachel with regret.

She smiled sadly. "Answer it. Otherwise, you'll hate yourself for not being there when she needed you."

"We're not done talking."

"Yes, Brian, we are. I'll try to have my things moved out by the end of the

week." She turned and headed up the stairs, giving him no excuse but to answer the call.

"What is it, Shawn?"

"I'm sorry to bother you, but it's about Carrie."

"What about her?"

"I just got a call from my mom that she's been taken down

to the precinct again. Apparently, she tried to flee the scene of a murder."

Brian stilled and his prolonged silence forced Shawn to continue. "Listen, I'm in San Diego right now for business. Mom or Dad won't call you, but you and I both know that having you there will lend some weight. I know things are tense right now, but—"

"I'm on my way," Brian said, heading for the door with his jacket and car keys. Before he shut the door behind him, he looked up in time to see Rachel on the landing of the second floor. Their looks mirrored each other's as they both silently apologized for not being what the other one needed.

CHAPTER THIRTY-TWO

For the second time, I was the last person to see someone alive. For the second time, I was a prime murder suspect. And not for the first time, I had no clue what the hell was going on. However, what was new was that my interview had been upgraded to an interrogation, and I was placed in a room with a one-way glass mirror and no coffee. Sergeant Harris was obviously not playing patty-cake with me anymore. He had two unsolved murders on his hands, and the common denominator between the two was me.

At the start of the interrogation, Sergeant Harris tossed several colored photos of Fiona's crime scene across the table at me. Eve threw a fit, gathered them up, and accused the sergeant of being unprofessional. While they argued briefly back and forth, I still couldn't get the sight of Fiona out of my head. Her twisted body and dead, sightless eyes would haunt me for a long time. I wanted so much to just escape somewhere and scream until all of my anger, frustration, and fear were gone. But there was no escaping this nightmare.

"Ms. Wallace, do you need me to repeat the question?"

I sat up straight and looked at Sergeant Harris, who was now composed and sitting across from me. I turned to my lawyer, who was giving me a quizzical look, and then looked to the sergeant once again.

"I'm sorry. Yes, please repeat what you said."

"How did Fiona Richards know where to find you? From my understanding, your parents only shared your address with the partners of your firm, and they assured me they did not release that information."

I shrugged. "I don't know, but from what I hear, she was a very good paralegal with great research skills. It isn't that difficult to get my new address."

"Why did she come by?"

Instead of answering, I flashed on a memory that had returned to me. I was in an apartment. Fiona's apartment and I was handing her the flash drive.

"What do you want me to do with it?" she asked.

"Just keep it for me. I'm working on a case the partners don't know about, and I'm going to need your help with it. We'll have to work after hours. Don't worry about the billing. I'll make sure you get paid."

"Carrie—"

"Just do it, please. I'm still your boss."

The memory was quick and clear, but I kept my face still and void of all emotion as I answered the question. "She said she'd been worried about me and wanted to see how I was doing. She also had some personal things from my office that she'd figured I'd want."

"Like what?"

"My gym bag with a change of clothes and my iPod."

He waited, and when it was apparent I wasn't going to volunteer any more information, he spread his hands wide. "Is that all?"

"She stayed for a little while, we had coffee, and she brought me up to date about what was going on around the office. It was a friendly visit."

Sergeant Harris gave a low, rumbling sigh. "This will all go a lot easier if you're upfront with me, Ms. Wallace."

Oh no, Sergeant. I'm going to lie, I told myself. *I'm going to lie until I know for sure what the hell I've done.*

He continued to look at me, and I matched his stare without blinking. He then pulled his cell phone from his belt holster, put it the middle of the table, and pressed a few buttons. In just a few short moments, I heard Fiona's voice and knew that I'd royally fucked up.

"I need to speak to you. I'm being stalked, and it has to do with the night of Harvey's murder and Carrie's accident. She gave me something that night to keep for her, and it's because of that I'm being threatened."

"Slow down, Ms. Richards. Where are you?"

"I'm on the coast highway heading back to the city. I just came from seeing Carrie."

"You saw Carrie Wallace?"

"Yes. I told her I was coming to see you after we talked."

He paused the recording. "So, here's where I'm confused. You say it was a friendly visit, but not moments after leaving your place, she calls me, sounding frantic and afraid. She tells me she's being threatened because of something you gave her the night Harvey Adams was killed. Clear it up for me, Ms. Wallace, and before you say anything, I'm letting you know now that the amnesia defense won't work anymore."

I scrambled, trying to find an excuse, anything to explain that damning phone call, but my mind was coming up blank.

"What did you give her, Carrie?"

"I don't know, Sergeant. I have no idea what she's talking about. If I gave her something, she didn't give it back to me, and if she had told me she was being threatened, I would have definitely advised her to go to the police."

It was such a flimsy, bullshit lie, but I was looking so guilty in all of this. I had no idea what happened with Harvey, but I didn't kill Fiona, and I wasn't going down for a murder I actually *knew* I didn't commit.

"Tell me why you were at her crime scene."

"Because even though she didn't tell me she was being threatened, I could see she was worried about something. I kept asking her about it, but she wouldn't tell me. I kept thinking about my own accident. I remember being worried and afraid of something, and I didn't want the same thing to happen to Fiona. So, I followed after her. I figured she would take the coast highway home, but when I didn't see her, I thought I'd lost her. I was about to turn around when I came upon the roadside diner and saw the police cars and the crowds outside. I think I might have just missed the murderer."

Only part of that was true. I wanted to talk to Fiona, to make her see reason and to help me. I wanted us to go to the police together. I thought it was a stroke of luck when I saw her car outside that diner and figured she was either having an early lunch or using the bathroom before heading back to San Francisco. I waited for her, but I waited a long time, and no one came out that front door. Then, I heard a scream from inside and ten minutes later, EMTs and police vehicles began to show up. I should have left then, but I couldn't move without knowing if she was all right.

"All very convenient, Carrie."

Eve interjected. "I don't care how you feel about Ms. Wallace's diagnosis, Sergeant, but the fact still remains that she's undergoing psychiatric therapy for the loss of her memory. I will not have you badger and force her to try to recall or admit to anything she doesn't remember."

Harris looked at me the entire time my lawyer was speaking, and I could read the look in his eyes all too clearly. He thought I was faking it all.

"You want to know what I think," he said, putting a fist underneath his chin and looking thoughtful. "I think what we have here is a setup for blackmail."

That got a reaction out of me. "What?"

"Sergeant, please," Eve said, at the same time.

But Harris continued on, raising his voice above us. "I think you were setting Adams up for a big payday. Whatever you gave to Fiona that night was evidence to blackmail him. You visited Adams to let him know what you had on him, and he didn't take it too well. Maybe there was a fight. Maybe he even hit you, but you don't strike me as a fool, Ms. Wallace. You thought ahead and brought protection with you just in case things got ugly. And they did. He came after you, and you shot him."

"This is ridiculous," Eve said, rolling her eyes.

But Harris wasn't done. "But it turns out Fiona was no fool, either. She found out what happened to Harvey and probably came to the same conclusion I have. But she wants no part in it, she finds out your address, and brings you back whatever you gave to her. She tells you she's done, but you can't just let her go, knowing what she knows. She's a loose thread. So, you killed her, too."

I stood in an instant, shoving the steel chair away from me. "You're wrong. You're so fucking wrong! I would never do that. I didn't kill anyone!"

I could hear my lawyer's pleadings with me to sit back down, but my attention was all on Sergeant Harris. This man held my freedom in his hands, and I had to make him believe me.

"I didn't kill anyone," I said again.

"How would you know if you can't remember a damn thing?"

"Sergeant!" Eve raised her voice in admonishment and the room went silent. When she had his attention, she continued. "You've laid out quite a theory, but I'm going to need to see some proof, or we're leaving."

CHAPTER THIRTY-THREE

By the time Brian arrived at the precinct, the interview was over. Whatever had happened was obviously not enough for Carrie to be arrested because her parents flanked her on each side and her lawyer walked behind them as they all escorted Carrie down the hallway toward the precinct's exit. However, she may not have been arrested, but judging from her facial expression, Brian could see she'd been put through the ringer. She looked utterly and thoroughly defeated.

"Carrie," he said as they all passed by him.

"Not now, Brian," Andrew said. "She's worn out. We're taking her home with us."

"What about her sessions?"

"We'll make sure she keeps up on the exercises you've given her, and she'll resume her sessions with you next week."

As soon as he said that, Natalie looked to her husband with chastisement in her eyes. She obviously wasn't on board with that plan.

Brian stepped in front of them, ignored her parents'

annoyed glares and looked directly at Carrie and tried to get her attention again. "Are you all right?"

She'd been staring straight ahead, looking lost in thought, but at the sound of his voice, she focused her brown eyes on him.

"Carrie, are you all right?" he asked again.

She opened her mouth to speak, but Natalie took her arm, sidestepped him and continued their trek down the hall.

"She's fine. She just needs some rest."

Brian stopped and watched the three of them exit the precinct. As always, they were a unit, and he was odd man out. He started to pull out his phone and text Shawn an apology for not getting there on time but stopped when he heard his name. He turned to see Sergeant Harris coming out of what must have been the interview room.

"Dr. Kessler," Harris said, walking up to him. "You're a little late to the party."

Brian nodded but wasn't about to elaborate on the reasons why. He immediately thought of Rachel and how understanding she'd been. She'd deserved honesty, and he wanted to be forthright with her. Yes, Carrie was his patient, but she had plenty of support around her. He felt like an asshole having to leave Rachel alone after admitting to her he was beginning to feel things for Carrie he had no business feeling. Feelings that should have been remained dead and buried the day their divorce was finalized.

"Yeah, I was detained." He looked back down the hall, but Carrie and her parents had already disappeared. "Who was killed?"

"Fiona Richards. Ms. Wallace's paralegal."

Brian turned to the sergeant. "Was Carrie the last person to see her alive?"

"Not exactly," Harris reluctantly admitted. "But she knows something. However, her lawyer whisked her out of here so fast that I didn't have enough time to push her and get her to open up."

"Knowing something isn't proof Carrie killed her."

"Which is why I let her walk out of here."

"Does she even remember Fiona?" Brian asked.

Harris subtly rolled his eyes and let out a tired groan. "The amnesia defense. Tell me something, Dr. Kessler. How sure are you that she hasn't already recovered her memory of that night?"

"There are tests and studies designed for that. Also, I can recognize in my sessions with her that her amnesia continues to be genuine."

Sergeant Harris didn't seem to like that response, and a sudden and unfamiliar feeling of protectiveness came over Brian. This man suspected Carrie of committing two heinous crimes, and Brian felt the need to deny it all— not only as her therapist but as someone who once loved her.

"Sergeant, I understand Carrie's amnesia isn't helping your case, but calling her in every time someone is murdered is also not helpful to her therapy. She doesn't remember what happened the night Harvey Adams was killed, and all of us will just have to wait until she does."

"Yes, I'm sure his family would love to hear that," Harris replied dryly. "And Fiona Richards? Don't tell me she conveniently forgot what happened this afternoon."

"You had her in interview. What did she tell you?"

"Only that she didn't do it."

"Maybe it's time to try the other suspects on your list, if there are any."

"As a matter of fact, there is one other."

Brian turned and prepared to leave. Now that Carrie and her family had left, there was no point for him to be here. But the tone in Sergeant Harris's voice made him pause. He looked the man in the eyes and realized what he wasn't saying.

"Is there something you want to ask me, Sergeant?"

"Where were you between nine and midnight on March 17th?"

"At home."

"Was anyone with you?"

"My girlfriend, Rachel." Brian didn't elaborate that she was now his ex-girlfriend, but that didn't matter. All he needed was a confirmed alibi.

"So, you were in Gypsy Bay the night Harvey was killed, and your ex-wife, Carrie, who you say you haven't been in touch with in three years all of a sudden comes to visit you out of the blue on that particular night. Why?"

"You don't know she was coming to see me."

"What other possibility is there, Dr. Kessler?" Harris stepped back and shoved his hands into his dark gray slacks. "So, for argument's sake, let's say she was coming to see you. Can you think of any reason why she'd do that after three years of no contact?"

"None at all."

"Do you think she was coming to ask for your help in covering up a crime?"

Brian shook his head with growing exasperation. "No, Sergeant, I don't think that."

"Would you help her if she did?"

"Of course not."

"Even if it was to protect you?"

Brian paused and thought about what the man was saying. "What are you getting at? What would Carrie be protecting me from?"

Harvey shrugged. "I guess that's something only you would know, Doctor—for the time being."

CHAPTER THIRTY-FOUR

*I*f Carrie had any choice in the matter, she would've no doubt made her way back to her car, driven herself all the way back to Gypsy Bay and then found a way to get herself into more trouble.

Natalie wasn't having it. So, after a couple of rounds of Natalie arguing back and forth with her daughter, Andrew finally stepped in, sided with Natalie and pronounced that Carrie was coming home with them, and the matter was final. Carrie stared at the two of them with aggravation, but she finally got into the car, silently accepting defeat.

When they returned to their home, Natalie attempted to smooth things over with her daughter. "I can show you where your room is, honey."

"I'm sure I can find it," Carrie replied shortly and marched up the stairs. She then paused on the steps and turned around. "When are we going to talk about my ex-husband?"

Natalie shook her head. "We have other things to worry about. He's not important, Carrie."

She nodded solemnly and turned around, resuming her tread up the stairs. "That's what I thought. Good night."

A few minutes later, they heard a door open and close soundly somewhere upstairs. Andrew, who in that time, had shed his coat and fixed himself a drink, finally turned to Natalie.

"You've got to stop treating her like a child."

She tried her best to look affronted, although she knew in the back of her mind he was right. Still, that remark had put her in a defensive mode, and she now felt obligated to explain herself.

"I'm just trying to look out for her. Jesus, Andrew, she was caught fleeing the scene of a murder!"

She kept her voice low so as not to alert Carrie upstairs, but she could still hear the desperation and worry in her own voice.

"I know that, but she's still a grown woman, and the last thing we need is to push her away because she feels trapped. Eve is a good attorney. Let her worry about her defense."

"I would worry a lot less if she was nearby."

He put his empty glass down and sighed. She could feel his exasperation and growing impatience with her. Under normal circumstances, Natalie would have backed down, remembering her mother's advice to always give her husband his needed space. Well, not this time.

She continued to plead her case. "She's a murder suspect. We need to keep her as close to us as possible. It was already bad that she was suspected of murdering that man Harvey Adams, now Fiona Richards? She never should've gone to Gypsy Bay, but I let you talk me into it."

"This has all been discussed and decided. I'm not the biggest fan of Brian Kessler either after what happened between him and Carrie, but he's a brilliant therapist…next to Gerald."

Natalie saw the look of regret pass over Andrew's face and waved it away instantly. "Let's try to get through this discussion without bringing Gerald and all of what happened into this. The issue is Carrie, and it's time we bring her back home."

"What does her living in Gypsy Bay have to do with Fiona Richards's murder?" Andrew asked.

"Maybe nothing and maybe everything. The point is she's there with *him*, when she should be up here with us. We can support her. We can take care of her. You didn't listen to me before, but I'm begging you, Andrew. Listen to me now."

Andrew looked at her, and she knew she was getting through to him because she saw the same fear in his eyes that mirrored her own. Could their daughter really have done the things the police are accusing her of? Parental instincts were shouting *no*, but there was still that small inkling, that small whisper of doubt somewhere deep inside of her.

CHAPTER THIRTY-FIVE

*B*rian smiled as he watched his mom float around the kitchen, preparing breakfast. She was in her element. Cooking was a passion for her, and it always seemed to bring her great joy to have someone to cook for, namely him and his father. He remembered growing up, when even after working twelve grueling hours in the box factory, she'd come home in the evenings and make sure her family was fed a delicious and hearty meal—simply because she loved to do it. After his father died, Brian made it a point to visit her every other weekend, because he didn't like the thought of her being alone, as well as to give her someone to spoil with her cooking skills.

Once he left the precinct, he'd crossed the bay and decided to stay the night with his mom. With Carrie staying at her parents, their sessions were temporarily suspended, and he didn't have any other patients scheduled until next week. After last night, he figured Rachel wanted space and time away from him to clear her things out of the house. He'd texted her and tried once again to get her to talk to him and possibly rethink this decision to break up. Her response was:

I'll be back for the rest of my things. I'm sorry, Brian.

When those words didn't hurt him but rather gave him a tiny feeling of relief, he told himself to stop being selfish and just let her go. He texted her to call him if she ever needed anything and left it at that. He liked being with Rachel. She'd been just what he needed when the seclusion of a small town was getting to him. They'd met when he was looking for an ally with the SFPD—someone who would reopen his father's case and start investigating it as a murder, rather than death by natural causes. Somehow, Rachel had heard about it in the DA's office and called him. She seemed interested and told him the circumstances of his father's death always puzzled her. She agreed to go over the case with him again, and if they found the tiniest bit of evidence of foul play, she'd take it to her contacts in the homicide division. But even Rachel didn't have as much clout as she'd thought. Brian was disappointed but never gave up. And Rachel kept calling and coming by to check on him until one evening, he asked her out to dinner.

However, after months of dating, he had to admit to himself that he wasn't in love with her, and it wasn't fair to either of them for him to hold onto her because he wasn't ready to face these conflicting feelings with his ex-wife. Yes, he needed to stay away from Carrie, but it didn't mean stopping Rachel from moving on and finding her own happiness.

"You're frowning."

Brian broke away from his thoughts to find his mom staring at him as she stood over a pan of sausage links.

"Am I?" he asked, taking a sip of his coffee, and then he smiled and winked at her. "Not anymore."

She shook her head. "Don't try that charm on me this early in the morning. What's on your mind? Did you and the new sweetheart have a fight and that's why you had to sleep in my spare bedroom last night?"

Brian cringed. "You're partly right."

Her pale, round face began to slowly turn to a frown, and he decided to just get it all out. So, he told her about the events of last night, starting with Rachel's decision to break up, the reason why, and his growing unprofessionalism with Carrie. By the time he finished retelling the drama that was beginning to surround him, Marie had laid a heaping plate of steaming eggs, sausage, and toast in front of him and sat down in the chair on the opposite side of the small kitchen table. In that time, her frown had also morphed into concern. She was quiet for a long time, but Brian knew that was just her habit as she sorted out her thoughts before rendering her opinion.

"I'm sorry about you and Rachel," she said. "I never got a chance to meet her, but I could hear in your voice when you talked about her that you were very happy with her." She paused and lowered her eyes to fiddle with a fork. Then she looked up and said hesitantly, "But with Carrie…"

He was chewing a mouthful of eggs, and when she paused, he swallowed and it felt like a lump in his throat.

"With Carrie…what?"

She shrugged. "With Carrie, you were different. You lit up. You seemed to like yourself more whenever she was around."

He sat back in his chair, now agitated. "Then all of that shit with Dad happened—"

"Don't curse at me, Brian—"

"And she turned her back on me. I left and never looked back. End of story," he said.

"I'm just saying that if I can see you're a different man around Carrie, Rachel must have seen it, too."

"It's over with Carrie, Mom. We've been divorced for a

while, and I was trying to move on. I wanted to move on with Rachel."

But did he really want to move on?

That silent, unasked question sat heavily between them.

Marie sighed. "When Gerry told me about his partnership with Andrew, I was happy for him. Then, when he told me how it would involve you and Carrie, I drew the line. I didn't want the two of you pushed into a loveless marriage simply because of your fathers."

"So, what changed?" He asked. "From what I remember, you took it hard when I told you about my divorce. You liked Carrie."

"I did like her very much because I could see that despite Andrew and Gerry's manipulating and planning, they had a good idea because you two were absolutely gone over each other."

She paused and a smile warmed her face as Brian guessed she was seeing him and Carrie together during the better times of their marriage. He couldn't help but reminisce a little too. However, his anger and broken heart wouldn't let him stay there.

Marie continued. "When you told me about the accident, I knew you would accept their pleas for you to treat her because no matter what happened between the two of you, you still care for her. You're an incredible therapist—just like your father. Carrie is in good hands. You treating her is the best thing for her. But I'm beginning to worry that it may not be the best thing for you."

Brian shook his head, his plate of eggs now forgotten. "I thought I could keep it strictly professional, but helping her uncover her memories is bringing back my own memories, and I don't want to remember all of that."

She gave him a knowing look. "You're going to stop treating her, aren't you? You've already made the decision."

"I have to. Having her in my life has already ended my relationship with Rachel. I'm not going to risk my license, too."

"What about her legal troubles? Isn't she still a suspect in the murder of that lawyer?"

Brian shrugged. "She has money. Her family has money. They'll hire a slew of lawyers to beat it if it even goes to trial."

"And that's it? You're sure you can just turn your back on her like that? You've never been able to do that before."

He leveled a hard gaze at his mother, looking into the same dusky blue eyes she gave him and hoped to God he looked indifferent, even though he felt far from it.

"Things change."

* * *

He ended up spending the remainder of the day with his mom until it was time for her to go to her weekly poker night with some women she met at the YMCA. There was never money involved, but Brian had once witnessed how intense the game could get with those women, and he figured it may as well involve money. He wished her luck, kissed her goodbye, and stole a few solitary moments in front of the TV. The next thing he knew, he was being awakened by his ringing cell phone. He sat upright on the couch with a start, looked at the time on his cell, and saw he'd only been asleep for forty-five minutes. The sky had grown darker, and from a large picture window in the living area, he could see clouds beginning to form over the bay. It would soon begin to rain.

He looked at his cell again. It had stopped ringing, but before he could check through the missed calls, it started up again. He saw whom it was, and for a moment, he considered not answering. But her name kept flashing on the screen, weakening him with every ring. He finally pressed the talk button and slowly put the phone to his ear.

"Carrie?"

"Dr. Kessler? Yes, it's me, Carrie."

Brian closed his eyes the moment the sound of her sultry, low voice greeted him. That entire conversation he'd had with his mom about severing his relationship with her had been demolished in the blink of an eye the second he heard her voice on the other end of the line. He knew she wasn't deliberately trying to sound sexy. It was just her natural timbre. It was the reason he used to always make up an excuse to call her when they were married—even if it was just to ask if she needed him to pick up detergent on the way home.

"What is it?" he asked.

"I need you."

He felt himself grow hard. Damn her. He didn't trust himself to speak, so he let the silence reign between them while he sat there in agony and willed himself not to hang up on her.

"Dr. Kessler…Brian? Are you there?"

He pinched the bridge of his nose. "Yeah, I'm here. What do you need?"

"Are you still in the city?" she asked. "If you're back home in Gypsy Bay, I can just call—"

"What do you need, Carrie?"

"Come get me. Please."

CHAPTER THIRTY-SIX

The three of us sat at the elegant dining table, having dinner. Even though it was among fine china and crystal, the mood was hardly festive. My mom had long stopped trying to force the conversation, and like my dad, found the food on her plate a lot more interesting. As for me, I picked at my dinner, because I couldn't eat from the nervousness swirling in my stomach. They didn't know what I'd done, because telling them would just start an argument. But I knew there was no avoiding it.

When the doorbell sounded, everyone looked up in surprise but me.

"Who could that be?" Mom asked.

Dad rose from his chair and tossed down his napkin all too eagerly. I got the sense he was happy to escape the tension. "I'll get it," he said, heading for the door.

She glanced at his retreating back and then turned to look at me. "Were you expecting someone?"

I opened my mouth to speak, not sure how I was going to answer her, when the raised voices coming from the foyer answered my mother for me. She jumped up and left the dining room in a hurry, whereas I slowly stood and took my time following after her.

By the time I made my way into the grand two-story front room, I saw that my parents were standing on either side of Brian like two pillars. My mother wore an angry scowl, while my father kept demanding he leave.

"It's late, Brian. Whatever this is, it can wait. We'll talk about our plans for Carrie's treatment tomorrow."

Then Brian's blue eyes lasered in on me, and I knew he was silently telling me to open my mouth.

I stepped forward. "Dad, I told him to come."

My father turned to me. "What? Honey, why would you do that?"

"Because I'm going home. There's no reason for me to be here. I need to get back home, continue my treatment with Dr. Kessler and try to get my memory back."

I noticed Brian shift slightly as I spoke, but I figured he was feeling awkward about being in the middle of my family drama.

"No, Carrie. That's not a good idea." Mom came toward me and put a hand on my shoulder. "We were going to talk to you about this after dinner."

I narrowed my eyes at her. "Talk to me about what?"

"Your father and I have been talking to Eve, and we feel the best thing for you right now would be to stay low-key until this is all over," she said.

I gaped at her. I wanted to address the topic of why my attorney was in communication with her and my father without my presence, but that was a discussion for another day.

"I'm already staying low-key right now in Gypsy Bay."

"I mean that it would be better for you to sever all contact with everyone, except the attorney and us."

I scoffed with laughter. "You want me to go into hiding? Why?"

My father came forward to stand directly behind her. Together they appeared to be a united front—against me. "This isn't funny, Carrie. There's too much murder surrounding you. We believe you're in danger, and the best thing for you right now would be to stay out of sight. Hopefully, more evidence will surface that will prove your innocence, and Sergeant Harris will focus his attentions on someone else. You can get back to your life"—he paused to look back at Brian— "and your sessions."

As they spoke, I could feel the frown on my face deepen. I looked to Brian to see if he'd heard the same thing I did, and his confusion seemed to match mine. Silence filled the room because my parents were waiting for my reply, but I was at a loss for words.

"Carrie didn't kill anyone," Brian said, and all eyes turned to him.

"Of course, she didn't," Mom said, appalled. "We never said she did!"

"But you want her to go into hiding as if she actually has something to hide."

"That's not it at all," Dad said, his annoyance showing.

"And the last thing she needs to do is quit her therapy because the two of you are afraid she'll be arrested for murder. If the sergeant had any concrete evidence, he would've arrested her by now. I'm sure the high-priced attorney told you that much."

"Frankly, Dr. Kessler"—Dad's voice dripped with derision — "this doesn't concern you. If it's your fee you're worried about—"

He stopped abruptly when Brian took one menacing step forward. "Sir, with all due respect, don't ever insult me like that again. This isn't about money. It's about Carrie's mental health. Interrupting her treatment could be detrimental."

"We have plenty of fine doctors who can pick up where you left off. You're not the only specialist in town," Natalie said.

"So, we're back to that again?" Brian turned his gaze on her. "Your problem isn't Carrie being treated for amnesia. You just don't want me treating her."

"That's right!"

"Well, maybe it's time you put your ego aside for the time being, Mrs. Wallace, and think about your daughter's care."

My mother exploded, my father chimed in to defend her, and Brian battled them both. All of this time, I had kept quiet, watching as Brian argued with my parents. My head swung back and forth as though witnessing an aggressive tennis match. As their voices grew louder and more intense, it all reminded me of the morning I woke from the coma and they all stood around my bed arguing about my treatment. I was now even more convinced that this behavior was typical of my family and wondered if I'd ever been allowed to make a decision on my own. Whether it was true or not, it was stopping today.

I stepped closer to the shouting match and started speaking, but no one heard me. I then raised my voice to an octave that could be heard above all of them.

"Brian is right!"

Everyone turned to me in shocked silence, but I wasn't sure if it was my shout or what I'd just said that had them giving me this odd look.

I moved away from my parents and went to stand by Brian's side.

"Brian—I mean, Dr. Kessler is right. I'm not running away from this. I'm staying in Gypsy Bay, and I'm continuing my treatment." I stared at them, hoping they could see the pleading look in my eyes. "I want to remember everything, even the memories I'm afraid of. I didn't kill Fiona. I know that for a fact. Harvey's death is still a mystery, and I'm not going to wait around for Sergeant Harris to find proof that I'm guilty. I need to know what happened, and because of that, I need to stay in Gypsy Bay—near Brian."

I paused, realizing it was the third time I'd called him by his first name. My mother must have noticed it, too, because her eyes squinted with concealed anger at the two of us. But she left it alone.

"It's not just the investigation that has us worried, Carrie," Dad said. "Your mother and I know you would never harm another human being, but if you didn't kill Harvey, you may have seen who did, and that same person likely killed your assistant. You could be in danger."

"Just stay here another night and think about it," Mom pleaded. You'll be safe here."

Once again, she was trying to get me to leave Gypsy Bay and stay in the city with her, and I was absolutely sure that ninety-five percent of it had to do with the man standing beside me.

I went to grab my purse by the hall table. "I know you love me," I said, talking to them both. "But you need to trust that I know what I'm doing. I may have lost my memory, but I haven't lost my sense of self-preservation. I know how to take care of myself."

"Carrie—" Mom began.

"Let's go," I said to Brian and headed for the door.

As I stepped onto the front porch, I turned to see that Brian had not followed behind me. Instead, he had been halted by my parents, and they were speaking to him in hushed undertones. By the looks on their faces, they were very angry—and very scared.

CHAPTER THIRTY-SEVEN

"I'm sorry you had to get into the middle of all of that," Carrie said, waving her hand back in the general direction of Natalie and Andrew's immaculate Sea Cliff home. "I don't like how I left things with them, but I had no choice. They worry so much."

"They're your parents. They can't help but worry about you."

"They're also afraid for me," she said. "Afraid I may be a murderer and just forgot I was."

Brian turned down the radio and let the driven sheets of pouring rain fill the silence. He looked over at Carrie who was staring out the window, looking lost and forlorn. Every part of him wanted to reach over and touch her to tell her everything would be all right, but he resisted, knowing the slightest compassion he showed her would undermine everything he'd said to his mother earlier. He had to leave her alone, and once he dropped her off at her car, he was going back to Gypsy Bay and contacting his colleagues to refer her to another psychiatrist. At least that had been the plan in the beginning. He had agreed to come get her for one reason, and that was to tell her face to face that he would not be her therapist anymore. He'd crossed a professional line, and it had to end. Being around her wasn't good for him or his peace of mind. But what he'd just witnessed back there, her interaction with her parents, her standing beside him, defending him—it all had him torn, and once again, second-guessing himself.

"You seem to know the roads pretty well," she said, grabbing her purse from the back seat.

"I've been up here before," he said, simply.

"Oh yeah, when?"

He didn't answer her but instead pulled over to the shoulder of the road and switched the ignition off. Without the engine, the rain pour was almost deafening with its heavy drops.

"What's wrong?" she asked.

"Carrie, I came over here to tell you…" He paused and saw that her mouth was moving and her head was bobbing. "What are you doing?"

She continued to do it, and then Brian realized with a start what she was doing. He turned to the radio and slowly turned up the volume. *September* by Earth, Wind & Fire was playing on an oldies station, and she was singing along.

Carrie halted and spoke quietly. "I know this song."

Brian laughed, his somber mood momentarily forgotten. "Keep singing!"

And she did. She sang the entire song and danced in her seat until they were both singing and laughing uncontrollably.

"I love seventies music!" she screamed at the top of her lungs with tears shining in her eyes.

"Yeah, you do," he said, speaking more as a man from her past.

"Oh, my goodness," she said, flopping back in the passenger seat. "Do you know how wonderful it is to discover something you like that you didn't know you liked?"

Brian couldn't help it. He found himself smiling at the way her eyes lit up from laughter. He couldn't remember her ever laughing this much when they were married and wondered if maybe they'd laughed more together that things would have turned out differently. He suddenly wanted to kiss her and the impulse only annoyed him. Just that quickly, he remembered what he had to tell her.

He must have been showing some of that annoyance on his face, because she turned to him and her laughter died instantly.

"Brian? What is it?"

She doesn't know. But she should know, dammit! She should know everything they put each other through. She should share in the guilt, agony and misery of what was once their relationship. Why did she get to just forget everything as if it never happened?

He couldn't do this anymore. He'd been a fool to think he could remain professional, but he hadn't managed to fool Rachel. She told him he was flirting with trouble when he agreed to counsel his ex-wife. Carrie had been the love of his life once, and then she'd turned into his enemy. Those feelings couldn't be so easily brushed aside, and the more she was in his presence, the more memories that assaulted him. Some good, some bad, and he was taking them all out on her.

"Dr. Kessler? Brian? What's the matter?"

He lowered the volume back down on the radio and turned to her. "I'm referring you to another therapist."

"Why?"

There were too many reasons to list, but one of the main reasons was that, in all truth, he did have a birthmark on his inner left thigh.

"I don't feel that I'm benefitting you anymore."

She bowed her head and laughed with self-deprecation. "If this is about me showing up at your doorstep unannounced or that kiss, then let me apologize—"

"It isn't any of that."

"Then what is it? Tell me. I think you're helping me tremendously, and I don't want to start over with someone new."

"I have plenty of excellent colleagues who would readily agree to treat you. Most of them in San Francisco, You'll be closer to home and to your family."

She opened her mouth to speak, but no words came. She looked so lost, and despite what he'd told his mother earlier, the feeling of abandoning her made him sick. He gripped the steering wheel with both hands, only to keep from leaning over and enfolding her in his arms. It was something he'd been feeling the urge to do more and more these past weeks, and it had to stop.

But Carrie didn't fear touching him as he did with her. She touched his forearm. "Please, don't do this. I don't want anyone else. I want you. Just you."

He looked across at her in the darkened car as the rain beat down heavily around them. "What you did back there... I've never seen...You stood with me."

The sudden change in topic seemed to confuse her and then she shrugged. "What else was I supposed to do? You were right. Hiding isn't going to solve anything, and I know there's still more for me to remember."

"Yeah, I know. It's just...if only you'd..."

He was stammering all over the place and finally broke off the rest of what he was about to say. She still didn't know who he was, and telling her that if she'd stood a united front with him while they were married, the way she just did with her parents, he'd never even thought of divorcing her. Whatever shit they'd been going through, he would've tried to work it out—especially if he knew she was on his side. That was all he'd ever wanted from her: from the days of when they were newlyweds, to his father's scandal, to her parents distancing from him, to his father's death—he could have faced it all if she was there with him. That Carrie, his wife, didn't have his back then. But this Carrie, his ex-wife and a stranger, she was magnificent in the way she stood up to her parents.

He couldn't believe the words coming out of her mouth, and he knew Andrew and Natalie had been just as surprised. He nearly took her in his arms right there in front of them, telling her all the while: *"This is the woman I want. This is my Carrie. This is my wife!"*

She was frowning at him. "What is it? What's wrong?"

He didn't say anymore. He couldn't think anymore. He reached across the console, grabbed the back of her neck, and kissed her.

The moment his lips met hers, she opened her mouth immediately to him, drawing him in closer and drowning him. There was no hesitation and no flinching from her—just an immediate welcoming as though she'd been expecting, anticipating, and waiting for him.

She grabbed the back of his head, too, with both hands, forcing the kiss deeper. The two of them moaned from delight, but it wasn't enough. Brian needed her closer to him. He needed her body to meld with his.

To his delight, Carrie rose until her knees were on the passenger seat, which pushed her breasts firmly against his chest. Brian's hands moved to her back and down to her soft, round ass. He was recalling every inch of her, every curve he thought he'd committed to memory for those long, lonely nights, but nothing compared to the real woman in front of him.

"Get over here," he growled, breaking the kiss long enough to relieve the hard-on straining against the zipper of his jeans. He shoved his jeans down to his knees and felt his ego soar as Carrie admired him.

She tore off her shirt and bra, lifted up her skirt, and shoved down her panties. She then climbed her full and toned thighs over the console to straddle his lap and slowly sink her body down over his.

"Christ," he said, grasping her waist. The moment he felt her surrounding him like a warm glove, he sent her bouncing up and down on him, creating a fiery friction that quickly drove him beyond all reason. Waves of her black hair fell across his face and chest as she writhed and rode him in pleasure. Outside, heavy pouring rain beat against the car's roof and windshield while inside the moans, groans, and cries filled the space like an erotic song.

"Oh, Brian!" she cried out as she braced her small hands on his shoulders and rocked her hips back and forth, searching for her release. "Brian! Who are you?"

God, he wanted so much to tell her right now. He moved her hair away from her face and stared into her eyes, urging her to remember him, right now at this moment while he drove himself inside of her over and over. But the lost look he recognized from amnesia victims was still there, and he knew she was certain he was someone to her but couldn't quite piece it together. He kissed her again, silently telling her it was all right. She didn't need to know him, because he knew her, and he wanted her. He sat back and let her continue to ride him and watched with wonder as the intensity of pleasure showered her face. And just as he remembered, she looked so beautiful when she finally succumbed to it.

He wrapped his arms around her bare back and pulled her close to him, feeling her body shudder from the effects of their lovemaking. The tiny quivers coming from her sent him over the edge, and he was soon hurtling through wave after wave of his own incredible pleasure.

CHAPTER THIRTY-EIGHT

For a long while, Brian and I stayed in that position. Me straddling his lap, while he held me tight against his chest. We listened to each other's breathing go from heavy and heated to calm and cool. As the seconds ticked by, his arms around me began to relax, and my thighs began to ache from the cramped position and the realization of what we'd done began to slowly make its way between us. I sat up and shook my hair away from my face. I covered my exposed breasts with my hands and moved off of him and settled back into the passenger seat. I hastily slipped my bra and panties back on, followed by my top, and then straightened my skirt. I even finger-combed my hair in an effort to make myself look halfway decent—even though I felt far from it. I could hear Brian dressing himself beside me, but I couldn't make myself turn my head to look at him for fear there would be regret in his eyes like the last time we kissed.

But as time further lapsed, I couldn't take it anymore. I slid a sideways glance toward him and took in his strong jaw, firm mouth, and soft blue eyes, which had only moments before been watching me intently as I came. I grew excited from the memory and already wanted to feel him inside of me again.

He must have realized I was staring because he turned toward me, and I instantly looked away, feeling embarrassed.

"Are you all right?" he asked.

I nodded my head, now focused on the wet terrain outside.

"I'll take you back to your car."

* * *

We said very little to each other on the thirty-minute drive back to my car where I'd left it after being taken in for questioning. By the time Brian pulled beside my car, I was thoroughly done with the entire awkward scene. So, I said a quick thank you and goodnight and then hopped out as if I were on fire. When I was tucked inside my SUV, I pretended to be looking for something in my purse while in my peripheral vision, I watched as Brian slowly pulled away. I glanced up to the rearview mirror and trailed his headlights until I couldn't see them anymore. Finally, I felt like I could breathe again. I wondered sadly if this would be the last time I saw him. He had come to tell me he was no longer going to counsel me anymore, but that had been postponed for the moment because we couldn't keep our hands off each other. As much as I relished every single second of that man's hands all over me and of him deep inside of me, I knew that I'd made a mistake that would cost me my therapist.

I took another glance into the rearview mirror and saw he was long gone. In fact, there was no one on this stretch of road only yards from a murder scene. I opened the driver's side door and eased out of my car, paying no mind to the rainwater drenching my hair and clothes. I slowly knelt down and moved my hand underneath the car. I felt blindly along the asphalt until my hands landed on the object. I breathed a sigh of relief and got back into my car, shutting the door. I switched on the interior light and looked down at the flash drive clutched in my hands. I'd barely had time to drop it and kick it underneath my car while Sergeant Harris chased me. Thank God, he'd been distracted by an angry driver and hadn't found this.

I was now a suspect in two deaths, and unlike Harvey, whom I could barely remember, I actually remember interacting with Fiona. I remember the fear and apprehension in her eyes as she handed me the flash drive that I'd given to her for safekeeping. This had brought her nothing but trouble, and I was feeling so much guilt for her death. She'd done her best to find me in order to return it to me, and it had gotten her killed. Not for the first time, I wondered if it would've been better for everyone if I hadn't survived that crash. But that was my dramatic self talking, and just like the many other times, I ignored that little voice and went back to strategizing about what the hell I was going to do about all of this. But there was nothing to do until my brain decided to wake up. For the time being, I was going to go in search of answers—and I'd start with this flash drive.

CHAPTER THIRTY-NINE

Widow Lake 10:47 p.m.
She wrapped her jacket tightly around her as the breeze from the lake whisked in and blew across her face, sending wisps of her hair flying. Tucking the strands away, she thought about how much he used to play with her hair. He'd take errant strands between his fingers and remark how soft and delicate it felt to him.

"You're so special to me," he would say. "I just want to keep you safe."

The way he looked at her, with so much love… She kept that memory close to her and retrieved it whenever she felt like this. Whenever she felt his anger, pain, and disappointment. Whenever he was looking at her as though she were a mistake.

"What's the matter with you?" he asked, pacing up down the gravel pathway.

It hadn't been the first time he'd asked her that question since she broke the news to him. At first his anger had frightened her, but after a half an hour, she'd grown used to it, sat down on a park bench, and waited patiently for him to calm down, but that hadn't come yet.

"Your role was so crucial," he bellowed. "All you had to do was stay put and keep tabs on him. Now, you're sitting here telling me that you decided to just break up with him." He stopped and bore down on her. "Why?"

Rachel calmly looked up at him. "I told you why. I could see it in his eyes. He's still in love with her. I'm not going to stand by like a fool while he wars with himself to stay loyal to me when all the while he wants to be with her."

"So, where the fuck does that leave me?"

She shook her head and for the first time, saw something in him she'd refused to see before. The selfishness.

"You," she said, sneering derisively. "That's all this is about —*you*. Oh, how silly of me. You and Eliza."

She got up from the bench and started to walk toward her car, but he halted her arm with one hand and turned her around to face him.

"Rachel, wait."

She snatched her arm away and stepped back. "You're still in love with her, aren't you?"

Marcus stood under the dimly lit lamppost with his hands out to his sides. "I love you. I've told you that over and over. I only want justice for her. That's it."

She didn't believe him, but even though she was ready to walk away from him and his memories, she wouldn't have walked out of his life completely, because no matter how he felt about her, she still loved him. She always had, from the moment Eliza brought him home for Thanksgiving and introduced him to the family as her fiancé. Out of respect for her sister, she kept her feelings to herself, but the love she felt for Marcus had been immediate and completely out of her control. However, as much as she loved him, she could see he was completely smitten Eliza. A love that passionate and fierce didn't just go away when someone died.

After her sister's death, Marcus distanced himself from the family, and Rachel missed him terribly. She'd tried to move on with her life, focusing on her career at the DA's office and finding new friends. Then one afternoon, they'd run into each other, completely by chance, caught up on old times, and Marcus invited her to breakfast the next day. She realized, sitting across from him in a booth eating pancakes, that her love for him had never gone away; however, she could also see he was still affected by Eliza's death. From that day, Rachel took it upon herself to be Marcus's comforter. She didn't instantly reveal her love for him, because that would be seen as disrespectful. No, she only kept in contact with him, continued to invite him to family barbecues and holiday dinners, and whatever else she could to remind him that even though Eliza was gone, he was still a welcome member of their family. Soon, the time they spent together became even more frequent, and one day, after they'd just left a movie, he kissed her, and Rachel was floating on cloud nine ever since.

It was only after they'd made love that she began to see the darkness in him and the heartbreak he still carried. But she chose to ignore it and agreed to participate in this scheme because of her love for him. Marcus was going to go after Brian, and he needed her help, and she realized with both exhilaration and sadness that she'd do anything for him —even sleep with a man she wasn't in love with.

When she first put herself in Brian's path by feigning interest in his father's murder case, she was so nervous he would immediately find her out, even with her change in name, hair and eye color and four years of aging. But she never saw any hint of recognition in his eyes, so she continued on with the plan as though their meeting was purely by chance. At first, it was difficult letting a man she wasn't in love with touch her in places she'd only allowed Marcus to touch her, but then it became frighteningly easy. She'd found herself looking forward to Brian's tenderness, especially when the man she really loved withdrew into a dark place.

Now, months later, she began to realize that while she blamed Gerald Kessler for Eliza's suicide, she didn't blame Brian. She'd even come to like him. Then she started to sense he was pulling away from her, and her woman's intuition told her it was because of Carrie. One morning, instead of going to work, she snuck back into the house during his session with Carrie. She had been so curious about the woman Brian had once been married to, and although the woman had been beautiful with her smooth caramel skin, long raven-colored hair, dark brown eyes and low, hypnotic voice, Rachel didn't feel a hint of jealousy. For weeks, she'd been looking for an excuse to end the relationship with Brian. She was tired of the scheming and plotting. She just wanted to run away with Marcus and leave all of this behind.

"He wants you, Rachel," Marcus said. "You could've used that."

"He doesn't want me at all," she said, fishing in her coat pocket for her cell phone.

She pulled it out and swiped through her gallery of pictures before she came to a particular photo. She pointed to the image of Carrie and Brian sitting in his office during that session. Brian had mistakenly left the door ajar, and neither one of them heard or saw her come near the office.

"I took this when she came for one of her sessions with Brian. They didn't see me, but I could see them."

She didn't finish her thought, because what she wanted to tell him was that she'd seen Brian look at Carrie in a way he'd never looked at her. But she knew what it meant because it was the same way Marcus used to look at Eliza. There was love there.

Rachel envied it, but she wasn't in love with Brian. She had come to respect him, and with the way he looked at Carrie, talked to her, and just being the man he was, she seriously doubted he would ever ask any woman to sleep with another man in order to satisfy his revenge.

Marcus didn't say anything more with his face now hardened stone, and Rachel took that as her cue to leave. There was nothing more to say. She tucked her phone away and leaned forward to brush a kiss on his lips.

"I'll help you do whatever you need," she said, "but find another way because this part of the plan is over."

She started to walk away, and he grabbed her wrist again, but this time there was more force in it, and it was painful.

"Ouch, Marcus, stop! You're hurting me."

"Give me your phone," he said.

Even under the night sky, she could see his eyes had turned cold. "Why?"

His grip on her wrist tightened even more.

"Stop, let go of me!"

"Give me your phone," he said again.

She used her free hand to hurriedly pull her phone out. He snatched it out of her grasp and instantly released her, but it was more like a shove. She watched as he unlocked her screen and scrolled through the picture gallery until he came back to the image she'd just shown him. Rachel rubbed her wrist and looked at him with anger and hurt.

"What are you looking for?"

He shoved the phone in her face. "This is Carrie Wallace?"

"Yes."

"You're sure?"

"Yes. Why?"

He didn't say anything immediately and continued to

look at the picture of Carrie as if he were in shock. Then without warning, he began to laugh.

"Jesus Christ. All this time and she was right under my damn nose."

Rachel frowned. "What are you talking about?"

"She's the bitch that was seeing Harvey. She was there that night. She saw me."

"That's her?"

He didn't say anything more but forwarded the picture to his own phone and gave her phone back to her.

"It's time for the final part of the plan. Can I count on you, or have your feelings for Kessler clouded your judgment?"

"You know you don't have to ask me that but, Marcus, tell me what's going on."

"Not now. I need to think. I'll call you later."

Without another word, he walked up the path leading away from Widow Lake and left Rachel with the realization that she despised him as much as she loved him.

CHAPTER FORTY

The digital files Fiona had returned to me had officially become a blur. Not only did I not have a clue as to what I was looking at, but I had no memory of gathering all of this together—and I wasn't even going to begin to guess why I created a digital file about Harvey Adams to begin with. I needed help, and with Fiona as my only link gone, I called my firm to get the contact information for Samuel Collins, the investigator who Fiona said I'd hired to surveil Harvey. Sam had told me that I confided in him that I was seeing Harvey on a casual basis, so, in a nutshell, I was sleeping with a man whom I was also investigating, and may or may not have killed.

"I was sorry to hear about Fiona," Sam said. "I wanted to help her, but my policy is to never reveal my client's documents. I feel like now, maybe I should've at least given her something."

I closed my eyes at the sound of regret in the man's voice. I couldn't take any more of it, because I was already overwhelmed with my own feelings of it. It came over me in waves whenever I thought of Fiona and her senseless death.

Sam had no need to blame himself. I had brought Fiona into this mess by showing up at her door that night. She'd been trying to help me and was killed for it. Harris was right in suspecting me. Even if I didn't kill the woman myself, I sure as hell was the cause of it.

"Please don't blame yourself," I said. "You were doing your job. But I need your help now. Maybe something in these records could point me in the direction of her killer. Tell me what I had you doing."

"It's just like you guessed, Ms. Wallace. I was surveilling Mr. Adams for you and looking into his bank records. Aside from the inconsistent but large cash deposits from Magnolia Trust, there was nothing else out of the ordinary."

"Did you ever find out the owner of the trust?" I asked.

"No, that was the only hold up. They're called blind trusts for a reason. You have lawyers and corporations that take ownership of the trust and run it on their client's behalf. It protects the privacy of the owner."

"And let me guess: I never told you why I wanted you to do all of this investigating to begin with."

"No, ma'am. You said the less I know the better. You said you only had conjecture and were still preparing your case."

I sighed and scrolled through the documents one last time. I supposed Sam had given me all he could, and there was nothing more to do but sit back and wait for my mind to connect the rest of the dots. I came to the end of the file.

"If you need anything else from me, Ms. Wallace, you can reach me at this number day or night."

"All right, Sam, I appreciate you answering my questions." I paused and noticed an address at the bottom of the last page. "Oh, one more thing. There's an address here in San Francisco. 481 Callahan Street. Apartment 2B. Do you know it?"

There was a long silence on the line, and then Sam

chuckled to himself. "Oh, forgive me, ma'am. I keep forgetting about your amnesia. That's the apartment in Potrero Hill. It's your place."

"What? No, that's not mine. My townhome is in Presidio Heights. I know that much, at least."

He chuckled again. "I thought it was a little rundown for a senior litigator. Still, it may not be where you live, but you must go there once in a while. You told me to forward all the hard copy documents there."

I frowned at the address, but nothing came to mind. Thinking quickly, I minimized the file, pulled up the internet, and typed the address into the search bar. When it came up with an image of a building, I stood up fast, knocking the desk chair over behind me.

Sam was right. I did know that place.

* * *

The rainy season had come, and something told me this was my favorite time of year. I had the sudden urge to go for a drive, but it wasn't just because of the rain—I was in search of answers. I found myself outside Brian's house and could see him through the window. I shouldn't have stopped, but the sight of him sitting in an armchair with a pen and notepad in his hand and his glasses slipping forward tugged at something in my heart. He was the image of comfort, security, and homecoming. I wanted to come home to him, and I didn't even know why.

Leave him alone.

I shook my head at the flash of memory. That was my voice. I had told myself that recently. But when?

He's happy now. Just let him be happy.

I'd been here before.

Go home. He's with her. But why is he with her?

A quick, successive rap came on the window, and I jumped. Brian was frowning through the window, his hair growing damp from the rain. He motioned for me to roll down the window, and I did. As the glass pane disappeared, his blue eyes grew clear.

"I saw you sitting out here," he said. "What's wrong?"

"Nothing. I didn't mean for you to come outside. You're getting wet."

He shook his head as if it was no matter to him. "Do you want to come in?"

"No."

My quick response surprised him. It surprised me too, but suddenly, the little voice inside my head rang all too true. This was his home, he was happy here, and I would only destroy all of that for him. But how?

I looked away from him, stared outside at the wind and rain rustling through the tall pines, and inhaled a deep breath.

"What did I do, Brian?"

"What are you talking about?"

I faced him. "What kind of woman was I?"

"How would I know?"

I turned to him in a flash, my patience now gone.

"Don't! Don't do that! I know you. I feel it in my gut. You were someone very important to me, and I don't care how fucked up my memory is right now, my intuition is working just fine. I know you!"

His tone, on the other hand, remained cool and leveled. "Come inside. If this is about what happened after leaving your parents, we can talk about it."

"I was here that night."

He stilled.

"The night of my accident. A memory came back to me. Well, not actually a memory, but a voice. I must have been sitting outside this house, and I was convincing myself to leave."

"Carrie, I don't know what you're talking about."

"Damn you!" I pounded my fist against the steering wheel. "Don't you see that I'm afraid? I'm afraid I was someone bad for you, and I don't want to remember her. I don't want her to come back."

"It's all right."

"No, it's not, because I have a feeling that woman is the reason why you pretend to not know me." I dug in my purse and pulled out the printed directions to the apartment building in San Francisco. "Do you know where this is?"

He took the paper from me, his strong, broad hands clutching it as the raindrops pelted his jacket. As his eyes roamed the paper, I could see those strong, broad hands begin to shake ever so slightly.

"Where did you get this?"

"Apparently, I own it. Do you know that address?"

When he looked at me again, his face had once again assumed a mask.

"I just want to know if you know that address—"

"I don't know it."

I watched him, hoping to see any kind of reaction, but all that rested between us was the lie he'd just told, and I knew with absolute certainty, we'd long ago grown used to lying to each other. I looked away and turned on the ignition.

"I have to go."

"Wait, Carrie. Look, just come inside and talk to me."

"No. No more therapy, no more journaling, no more memory exercises. I've said enough."

I pulled away from the curb and saw him staring after me in the rearview mirror. But I didn't go back. He would only try to explain it all away, and I was so damned tired of the truth being hidden from me. I'd have to chase after it myself.

CHAPTER FORTY-ONE

"Ms. Wallace? Ms. Wallace, it is you! How are you? I haven't seen you in a long time."

I stopped midway through the store and look oddly at the older black man behind the counter, who was serving the customers in the convenience store. He was beaming at me, and I felt terrible for not knowing his name. So, I pasted on a smile that was not quite as bright as his and faked as if I knew him.

"Hi. I, uh, was just trying to get upstairs."

He frowned at me, and I knew instantly I'd forgotten some other critical piece of information.

"Oh. Well, the residents never use the store entrance. There's a private entrance in the back that leads upstairs."

"Thank you. It's good to see you," I said and left the store as quickly as possible before he quizzed me on something else I knew nothing about.

I rounded the back of the store, and sure enough there was a private entrance that needed a key. I pulled out my key ring and flipped through the set until I found one I had not used yet. It opened the main door, and I climbed the stairs until I arrived on the second floor. There were only two floors and there was only one apartment to an entire floor. The key slid easily into the lock of 2B and turned. I stood there, breathing in and out slowly, not sure what was waiting for me on the other side. I turned the knob and the door swung open. I immediately stepped into a living area, a small kitchen was straight ahead, and farther in the back were two bedrooms that shared a bathroom. It was a small unit, much smaller than my own apartment on the other side of the city. Three bottles of water and two cups of yogurt were all that was in the refrigerator. The cabinets and pantry were empty. The closets had no clothes in them. The bed, in what was probably the master bedroom because of its slightly larger size, was made with older linen. The only semblance of living was in the smaller second bedroom that housed a large desk with a computer and paper files strewn across it.

I crossed to the desk and turned on the computer. As it booted up, I went through the files and paperwork to see exactly what I had been working on. From what I could tell, it was all legal documents, but before I could really delve into it and see what it all meant, something peeked out of the corner of one of the files. I slowly pulled at it until I could see it in full color. It was a 5 x 7 photograph, and my hands shook as I lifted it and stared at the two smiling people. My heart began to race feverishly, and tears welled in my eyes as I stared down at the proof I had been looking for all of this time. But seeing me wrapped in the arms of the man I knew as Dr. Kessler and laughing up at him as he stared at the camera with a wide grin made me wonder what happened between us. What had gone so wrong that he wanted to pretend he didn't know me?

"What are you doing here?"

I whirled around to find Brian standing in the doorway of

the bedroom. He was looking at me with shock painting his handsome face. A face from my past.

I stood, clutching the picture down by my side and began to stammer.

"I—I didn't know I had this apartment. I think I come here to work on my cases."

He hesitantly came forward, and he looked as if he was unsure of what to do with himself.

He looked past me at the desk covered with files and slowly shook his head. "I don't understand this," he said more to himself. "Why did you…" He paused, then looked at me. "This is my apartment, Carrie. This is where I grew up. Why do you have this apartment?"

I threw my hands up in the air, beyond consumed with frustration. "You're asking me? I don't know! I don't know anything, and I can't depend on you to tell me the truth."

"Fuck," he said, running his fingers through his still damp hair. Then to my surprise, he turned to leave.

"Wait!" I grabbed the sleeve of his overcoat. "Don't go!"

"I can't do this. I can't be here. None of this makes sense."

He spoke over his shoulder at me, as his long strides carried him toward the front door, causing me to slightly run to catch up to him. I managed to grab at his coat sleeve again, halting him.

"It makes even less sense to me. I just want to know, Brian. I just want to remember things!"

He turned around and it suddenly felt like he was towering over me with anger. "But *I* don't want to remember these things!"

That stunned me, but I couldn't back down now.

"Please," I said on a whisper. "I don't know what happened between us, and maybe it's best I don't remember, but there's a reason I bought this place and why I still have it. Help me put it all together."

We stood there together in what I now knew was his childhood home, and even though he said nothing, I could tell his thoughts were warring with themselves. Finally, his shoulders slumped with defeat and he slowly returned to what had been his bedroom growing up. He crossed to the desk where the computer had finished booting up, brought up the internet, and typed something into the search bar. He clicked on the first link, and the next image I saw was that of a beautiful woman with green eyes and blonde and brown streaks of hair. She was dressed in a lavender floor-length gown and giving a dazzling smile as she posed for the camera at what looked to be a Hollywood red carpet event. I gasped when I read the caption above her photo:

Eliza Watley Falls to Her Death.

CHAPTER FORTY-TWO

Four years ago...

"What's this?" Eliza asked, sitting down on the bed across from Rachel holding the small wrapped gift box in her hands.

Rachel rolled her eyes. "Do you really think I'm going to tell you? Open it."

Eliza laughed and tore open the wrapping paper like they used to as kids. They had gotten a kick out of making a mess of wrapping paper on Christmas day only to be forced by their mom to clean it all up before she allowed them to play with their toys. Rachel laughed at her sister because this didn't have as much of an effect since it was a small box.

Eliza gasped with joy as she pulled the sterling silver pin from the satin and held it up.

"Ray bird, it's beautiful!"

"I know it doesn't come close to the diamonds and the dress you're going to wear tonight, but I wanted you to wear something from me."

"Oh, shut up," she said, laughing. "I'm going to pin it to the front of my gown so everyone can see it. To hell with those diamonds. When *US Weekly* asks about the dress, I'm going to say: 'Oh yeah, it's cool. Did you see this pin my sister gave me? Isn't it gorgeous? I just love this flower.'"

Rachel laughed again because she knew Eliza was true to her word. No matter how famous she got or how much Hollywood loved her, she didn't want to be anywhere else but there with her family, and Rachel loved and admired her for that. She admired her because if the shoe were on the other foot, Rachel wasn't sure if she, herself, would be just as humble.

* * *

"Are you sure you don't want to take this case?"

Rachel shook her head and tried to concentrate on the conversation she was having. She had been lost in the memory of the last time she saw her sister. She didn't know why the thought came to her all of a sudden, but she was glad of it. Eliza had looked so radiant that day.

"My load is full," Rachel said, waving her hands in dismissal of the folder. "Take it. I know you could use a win since the mistrial last week."

Quentin, the young and eager ADA, nodded and she could see the excitement filling his eyes as he contemplated his good fortune. It was the reason she chose him to carry out the rest of the plan—well, to carry out the rest of Marcus's plan. She wasn't obsessed with it as much as he was. She simply wanted to take her inheritance, elope somewhere on a beach, and live the rest of her life in simplicity with Marcus. They could leave all of this death and revenge behind, but he wasn't having it. According to him, he would not be able to live in peace until the ones linked to Eliza's suicide were brought down. She thought about Brian and how he was in Marcus's direct line of sight. If only he hadn't written that book about his father and included the chapter on suicide. There was no stopping Marcus after that. He was on the fast track for revenge. Even though Brian had nothing directly to do with Eliza's death, Marcus was hell-bent on righting the wrongs he believed were made against her.

Not for the first time, Rachel wondered why she was doing this. Despite Eliza's wealth and stardom, Rachel knew her sister suffered from depression. Her fans knew it too, since she was always so open about it. But was she really honoring Eliza's memory by doing this? She was angry with Gerald Kessler, because he was her therapist and well…she still needed someone to blame for her sister no longer being with her. But Brian didn't deserve her blame, and she knew that deep in her heart. Was this what happened when a woman was blinded by love?

"Rachel?"

She focused her attention on Quentin, who was giving her a quizzical look.

"What?"

"I said it's a shame Harvey couldn't be here to see this one through. It would've been good for his career."

She smiled indulgently. "You're a good attorney. I'm sure you'll do him proud."

He nodded and stood enthusiastically with his ego now boosted by her praise. "I'd better get going. With this new evidence, I should be able to get him served today."

As he practically skipped out of her office, her eyes trailed him with a mixture of satisfaction and regret. There was no turning back now. The wheels of justice were in motion—no matter how underhanded.

As soon as Quentin was gone, Rachel got up and shut her office door to prevent anyone from eavesdropping. Then she sat back down at her desk and made the phone call that would be the final nail in the coffin.

"San Francisco Police Department. Downtown Precinct."

"I'd like to get a message to Sergeant Derek Harris."

"Hold please."

After a few moments, a man's deep and firm, no-nonsense voice picked up the line. "This is Harris."

She hadn't expected him to be there, but all the better. It was the last part of the plan. "I'm Carrie Wallace's neighbor here in Gypsy Bay, and I'd like to report some suspicious activity at her home. It involves a gun."

CHAPTER FORTY-THREE

"Eliza Watley was my father's patient. She was what they call a *celebrity darling*. The media and fans loved her. Most of her fame was made from starring as the lead role in romantic comedies. But despite her fame and beauty, she suffered from depression. She spoke candidly about it and that she was seeking therapy. What endeared her even more to the public was that she often donated to foundations and organizations that supported further studies and treatment on depression. My father treated her for years and said he was proud of her progress. In fact, when it became known she was his client, his got the attention of many influential people in his field, including your father."

"My father?" she asked, frowning.

"Yes. Your father and my father were partners in a medical practice."

She shook her head, obviously trying to sort out all of this new information. This wasn't how he wanted to do this. He wanted her to remember on her own, in drips and drabs. Not all at once to overwhelm her.

"Carrie, maybe we should—"

"Go on," she said.

He sighed heavily. "When Eliza committed suicide by jumping off the Golden Gate Bridge, her family and the world blamed my father for not doing more to prevent it. He became an outcast, the Watley family sued, and he lost his license."

He watched as she scrolled through the news story while at the same time listening to his retelling. He had to pause many times and take a deep breath because just like her, he was remembering things he had long ago forgotten.

"As the months passed, my father began to experience his own kind of depression. He was unable to do what he loved to do and found himself at a loss of what to do with his days."

Carrie now turned to him, her eyes wide with fear. "He didn't..."

"No," Brian said outright. He could feel fury slowly rising inside of him as he retold this story. "He didn't kill himself. He was murdered. At least, that's my belief. The cops believe he died of natural causes, and I've been trying to prove otherwise for years."

Her face saddened, and with her eyes downcast, she turned back toward the screen and continued to stare at the photograph taken on the evening Eliza jumped from the Golden Gate Bridge. He'd seen the same image more times than he knew, appearing in several different major and not so major publications, but this was the first time he paused to actually study the photo. She was wearing a silver pin clasped to the front of her gown, and he wondered to himself why it looked so familiar to him.

But the moment for curiosity was lost as Carrie continued to scroll down the page until she came to another link that related to the story. She clicked on it, and Brian saw his father's photograph. Carrie leaned forward, and he knew she was reading the caption that reported his name. She then turned to Brian with an accusatory stare.

"That's him. That's the man I saw in my visions. Gerald Kessler. All of this time, you knew who I was describing. You knew I was remembering him, and you said nothing to me?"

His temper was beginning to peak, and he had to walk away from her to the opposite wall of the room. He remembered having his dinners in this room. His mom would make him a plate of food and let him go play with his toys while he ate his supper. But every now and then, he would put down his toy trucks and get up to peek out from his room and watch his mother sitting at the small kitchen with the dimly lit lamp overhead. She was flipping through bills, trying to decide who would get paid that month. Maybe it was at that moment in time when he'd subconsciously decided he would never be in that same position. He would never allow his children to see him contemplating which bills to pay. It was probably then he decided he would always have money, no matter what it cost him.

"This man was your father. You said he was partners with my father? Is that how we know each other?"

He didn't answer her. Christ, why was this all coming back now?

"Brian. It's time to tell me everything." She rose from the desk and came to stand behind him. Although her frame was much smaller than his, he could feel her strength behind him.

"Who am I to you? Quit being so selfish, and just tell me, Goddamn it!"

He turned around with eyes fierce and boring into hers. "Selfish? That's rich!"

"What else would you call it? You agreed to counsel me, help me get my memories back, but you've been delaying everything, because you didn't want me to find out who you are to me. I could've been miles ahead of where I am if you'd just told me from the beginning. Instead, you let me wander through the fucking dark and question why the hell I feel a strong attraction to you. When all of this time, there was a perfectly good reason for my feelings."

He moved in closer to her and suddenly wanted to kiss her. It was that same feeling he always got when he came near her. Yes, they were a comfort to each other, familiar to each other, but they were also two dormant volcanos of sexual tension. There was something raw and passionate between them, and every time he got within several feet of her, he felt it and was damn sure she felt it too and was dying to erupt just as much as he was.

"And what is that reason?" he asked. "Tell me why you have these strong feelings for me?"

"I don't know."

"You do know," he said. "Tell me."

"Because I was…" She shook her head in confusion.

"Say it. Deep down, you've always known. You've told yourself over and over. Now say it out loud to me."

And then he waited, just to see if she would work it out herself. She walked back over to the desk and picked up the photo of the two of them. He'd forgotten about that picture. His mother had taken it the day after they were married, and they had been on their way to the airport to board a flight to Greece for their honeymoon. He remembered being completely satisfied because he had a beautiful woman on his arm, a thriving practice, and his parents were no longer struggling. But behind his smile, there was an inkling of something in the back of his mind, and it was fear. Fear that everything that was going good for him was all just temporary.

He watched her as she kept studying the photo and this time, he knew she saw the matching rings on both of their fingers. She dropped the photo back onto the desk and looked at him, stunned.

"I was your wife." She slowly sat back down at the desk chair. Then she looked up at him again. "I figured there was something between us, but marriage? How long?"

He hesitated and then finally told her the truth. "Five years."

"Are we still—"

"No. The divorce was finalized three years ago."

"You, Shawn, my mother and father...you all kept this from me."

"We all agreed that it was best for now while I treated you. I didn't want our past to cloud any progress you would make." He came toward her, rubbed a hand down his face, and looked defeated. "I knew eventually you would begin to remember everything about us. I just wanted it to come naturally."

"You didn't want to treat me," she said. "I could tell from that first session how uncomfortable you felt around me."

He nodded.

"Because you hate me."

"No! Not at all. It's because I was trying to forget that part of my life. I hated the man I became, but I never hated you. I didn't know you anymore."

"Join the club. So, what happened with us?"

Brian shrugged. "Too many things. We weren't right from the beginning, and with your family's influence and my father's troubles, it only widened the gap between us."

"What did your father have to do with anything?"

Brian paused, put his hands in the front pockets of his jeans and looked around the near empty room. "Like I said, after Eliza killed herself, her family sued my father in civil court for damages. The Watleys hired your firm for the civil case."

She closed her eyes briefly and looked down as if ashamed.

"You weren't on the case, of course. That would've been a conflict of interest. But you had colleagues on the case who would feed you information, and as you can guess, it caused even more problems between us."

He flashed back on an argument he and Carrie had:

"I'm sorry for what's happening to your dad, Brian, but the Watleys lost their daughter. What do you expect them to do?"

"I expect them to mourn for her, and not honor her passing by suing my father for every last penny they can get!"

"You're right. I have been lying to you. At first, I wanted to keep all of this from you and let you regain your memory without our relationship affecting your treatment. But it began to turn into lie after lie, and I'm sorry for that. As soon as you remembered my father, I should have told you everything. It was only a matter of time before you'd begin to piece it all together, but I still didn't want to rush things, and I didn't want you to know who I was to you."

"None of that explains all of this," Carrie said, waving a hand at all the legal papers and files on the desk. "What was I doing here? What does all this paperwork mean?"

"It looks like you were working on something that had to do with my father and me," Brian said.

Carrie looked around the apartment. "The store owner downstairs may have a spare box," she said. "I want to get these things packed up and take them back with me. Maybe something will help to jog my memory."

Within thirty minutes, they had everything boxed up on the desk, including the laptop, and loaded into Carrie's car. As they worked together in silence, Brian realized the connection and intimacy they shared after leaving her parents' home a few nights before was no longer there. He blamed himself for that. It seemed as though after every kiss and every touch, he pulled further away from her, and she must have been tired of his hot and cold moods.

"I'm heading back now," Carrie said. "Are you?"

"Yeah, follow me back."

She nodded and just as she turned to head toward the driver side of her car, Brian gently took hold of her forearm and halted her.

"You remember my father, you remember this apartment, now you see pictures of us together." He paused. "Do you remember me, Carrie?"

Guilt and regret filled her eyes, so he knew the answer before she uttered a word.

"No," she said. "I'm sorry, but I still don't remember you."

CHAPTER FORTY-FOUR

Throughout the entire ride back to Gypsy Bay, Brian kept checking the rearview mirror to ensure Carrie was behind him. She'd had a breakthrough today, no thanks to him. It had been his job to guide her into recovering her memory, and up until today, he had been more hindrance than help.

When he finally pulled up to his house, he groaned at the sight of another car parked just outside and a man getting out. He didn't have time to interview or take on any potentially new clients. He wanted to help Carrie as she was probably experiencing a swarm of memories right now. He parked his car, got out, and headed the man off before he got to his front door, preparing to tell him to please make an appointment for a later time.

"Dr. Brian Kessler?"

"Yes, that's me, but I'm very busy at the moment—"

Brian's words halted as the man revealed a legal-sized envelope that Brian hadn't seen earlier.

"You've been served." He handed the envelope to Brian and walked away, back to his car.

Brian stood there, paralyzed with momentary shock until Carrie came to stand beside him.

"What's that? Who was that man?"

Instead of answering her, he ripped the envelope open and pulled out a small stack of official-looking documents—court documents. After reading the front page, he began to see red.

"I'm being indicted. For my father's murder."

"What? Let me see that." Carrie took the papers from him and read them over. When she looked up at him, there was a mix of confusion, anger, and worry in her brown eyes. "I don't understand."

"I do. Look at the original signature on the back."

Brian waited but knew the exact moment she read the name because her entire body went still. She looked up at him again, but this time, he couldn't see any emotion in her eyes.

"Why would Harvey do this?"

"You tell me. You tell me what proof your boyfriend had that I killed my own father?"

"I don't know."

"Were you working with him on this?"

"Of course, not—I mean—I don't know." She handed the papers back to him and began to pace. "Harvey was a prosecutor. I'm a defense attorney. There's no way I would've been helping him bring murder charges against you. If anything, I would be…"

She trailed off, but he'd heard enough. He headed toward the house. "I need to call my lawyer."

He unlocked the door and opened it only to find she was still right behind him. He blocked her entrance into the house.

"I need you to go home."

"Brian, wait. Don't you understand? This is what I was preparing for."

"What are you talking about?"

"Somehow, I must've found out that Harvey was planning to indict you. All those case files and documents at the apartment—maybe I was preparing to defend you. That's why I think I was driving here that night. I was coming to tell you everything."

"But you didn't tell me," he said. "You turned around and headed back to the city. Why?"

Now, defeat fell across her face. "I don't know why."

But he was feeling even more defeated. "Go home, Carrie."

"Brian please—"

"Go home!"

She stood in his doorway, her eyes wide. He couldn't remember ever shouting at her like that, not even when they were married.

But instead of turning around to leave, she stepped closer to him and he could see from her narrowed eyes that she'd lost all patience with him.

"Do you want to hear something stupid? When I first realized I'd been married, I wanted so badly for it to be you. I knew you and I had a connection, and I wanted it to be something as strong as marriage. Then I see how you act toward me now, and if being your wife is what made you like this, I don't want to be her anymore. I don't want her to come back."

Before he could respond or even apologize, she turned away and headed back down the pathway toward her car. He closed the door, and stood there, breathing in and out until he could feel his pulse slowing back to its calm state. That was when he heard a throat clearing behind him.

He turned and saw Rachel standing by the stairway, holding a duffel bag.

"I just came to grab the rest of my things and give you back your key," she said. "But it sounds like I came at a bad time."

CHAPTER FORTY-FIVE

There was no talking to Brian. There was no reasoning with him. I couldn't convince him of anything other than my complicity in his downfall. I was seeing Harvey, and we were both lawyers and colleagues, so it stands to reason I knew he planned to serve Brian an indictment. But an indictment for murdering his father?

After everything Brian had told me, I couldn't believe I would stand by and allow this to happen to him. Had our marriage been that contentious? I smacked my hand hard against the steering wheel, not for the first time, cursing my foggy memory. I was remembering things but not fast enough to get through this fucking nightmare that is now affecting a man I once loved. A man I still love?

Yeah, that was foolish. Brian couldn't stand to be around me. One moment we were making love that was so hot it left me wanting more, and the next, he was pretending he didn't know me. Hell, he wouldn't have even told me we were married if I hadn't seen that picture. He wanted me out of his life, and it had only been out of his sense of professional duty that he agreed to be my psychiatrist. I don't remember what it felt like to have him love me. Maybe, I'll never remember, and maybe that's for the best. But he had been there for me since my accident, so I owed it to him to get him out of this mess. After that, I would leave his life and finally give him the chance to move on.

Before I knew it, I was rounding the street that led to my house. Whether Brian wanted to hear me out or not, I believed I was preparing his defense, but I was in no way capable of being his lawyer now. I worked for one of the top firms in San Francisco, and I was going to get him the best and meanest power-hungry criminal attorney they had to offer. In my mind, I could see the firm's business card on a desk in the corner of the living area. Someone there would help, and I'd hand over all the case files and documents I'd gathered—including the information from the USB key Fiona had given me. That key proved Harvey's negligence. He was taking bribes from someone who wanted Brian ruined, and that information alone had to be enough to get the case thrown out.

My eyes widened as the truth slapped me in the face. That's why I was having Harvey investigated. I was going to discredit him in court. But then I wondered why would I discredit my boyfriend to save my ex-husband?

I was pulling up to my house, coasting on the adrenaline I was riding on, excited for the plans I was making to turn everything around. Then I pulled into my driveway and slammed on the brakes.

The force of my car coming to a halt effectively knocked me back to reality. A reality where I was still a murder suspect of two people. Sergeant Harris stood in the middle of my driveway, wearing a stern expression and holding a piece of paper. I grabbed my purse and quickly got out of the car, keeping my eyes on him the entire time. I made my way to him, but he didn't wait until I was within arm's length before he was shoving the document in my face.

"Carrie Wallace, this is a warrant to search your home and premises."

I snatched the warrant out of his hand and quickly scanned it. "Search my home for what?"

"We'll know when we find it," he said and gestured for me to precede him up the porch steps. "Please, open the front door. I don't want my men to have to force their way in."

I scowled at him, then marched up the steps to the porch, pulled out my house keys, and unlocked the door. As soon as the door swung open, police officers filed in and invaded my living room, kitchen, and the upstairs bedrooms. Others stayed outside to search the small lot surrounding the house, all looking for something I obviously wasn't entitled to know. Several neighbors began to come out from their homes and stand on their porches to watch the show, and I cringed with embarrassment. Then I became furious. I really didn't have time for this. I stalked back inside the house and over to Sergeant Harris who was conducting his own personal search of my belongings.

"Don't bullshit me. You know what you're looking for, and you can tell me what it is."

He was feeling along the crevice of the couch with a latex-gloved hand. "We received a tip that an item relating to Harvey Adams's murder was found on or near these premises." He paused in his work and then stood to his full height to look at me. "You're more than welcome to contact your attorney, Ms. Wallace, but she'll tell you that we are well within our rights."

I was sure my eyes were telling him I wanted to scratch his eyes out, but he looked as if he was hoping I would do something just to give him an excuse to put handcuffs on me, so I mentally counted to ten, stepped back, and waited to see if the anvil would fall on me. And in just under fifteen minutes, it did.

An officer called for Sergeant Harris from outside, and I hurried close behind him to see what had been found. All the excitement was coming from behind the garden shed. I froze before nearly colliding into the back of Harris when I saw the officer holding an automatic gun by the handle in one of his gloved hands.

Sergeant Harris stepped forward with an evidence bag already opened, and the weapon was dropped in and sealed. He then turned and walked slowly back to me, holding the evidence bag up for me to see it clearly.

"Do you recognize this?"

I stared at the gun, knowing my fate was being sealed just as easily as he'd sealed that bag. "No," I said. "I've never seen it before in my life."

Then I looked up at him and gone was the judgment he normally kept reserved in his eyes for me. Now, he was looking at me with pity, as if he really hadn't wanted to find something so incriminating.

"We're going to take this back to the lab to get it tested against the bullets found in Harvey Adams. Because it's the same make and model as the murder weapon, I'm going to have you taken back to the precinct while we wait for the results. Officer Lowell will escort you back there. Officer Lowell?"

I wasn't really listening to his words anymore, but I knew what the gist was. Something told me that weapon would be a match, and that I was going to be formally charged for murder. Funny thing is, I wasn't worried about myself. I was more concerned about Brian. How was I going to help him if I was locked up?

But those thoughts instantly vanished when I noticed the younger-looking officer with the close buzz cut and medium height coming toward me with his handcuffs out. I instinctively backed away and began to tremble. My mind was racing, but my thoughts were so jumbled I couldn't sort any of them out. He was going to put me in the back of his police car, but out of all my racing and jumbled thoughts, the only one I could make out, the only one I could latch onto, the only one that repeatedly screamed at me was:

Don't get into the car with him. Don't let him take you away.

CHAPTER FORTY-SIX

Rachel had been hoping to avoid Brian because she knew exactly when that indictment would be served. If it hadn't been for a last-minute meeting her supervisor had called, she would've made it back to Gypsy Bay an hour earlier, had the rest of her things packed, and been gone before Brian returned home.

She was in the master bedroom upstairs, but she could hear him downstairs in his office, making phone calls to find a lawyer for his case. She tried not to allow herself to feel sympathy for him, but there was no use. He really didn't deserve to be in Marcus's crosshairs, but Marcus couldn't be convinced otherwise. Brian's book was an effort to exonerate his father's name, But Marcus took it as a personal attack. Even her parents hadn't taken as much offense to it because Brian in no way insulted Eliza's depression. In all honesty, he'd shed light on it and created an understanding of the diagnosis that even Rachel admired and appreciated. With that thought she knew it was time to leave before she went against Marcus's wishes and did something drastic like call her boss and confess to what she'd done. She re-doubled her packing efforts and got up to go to the hall closet to grab her last suitcase. That was when the doorbell rang. Brian's home had a two-story living area so from the balcony of the second floor, she could see as he made his way to the door and opened it. And it was from there she saw a woman practically fly into the home as if death were right on her heels. It was the same woman Brian had told earlier to go home. It was Carrie Wallace. And before Rachel had the idea to return to the bedroom and shut the door, Carrie paused in whatever she was frantically telling Brian and looked directly up at her. When their eyes clashed, Rachel felt instantly that Carrie knew her.

* * *

"Who's this?" I paused in eating my lo mein and reached for the picture Harvey laid in front of me. It was a colored photocopy of a woman's employee badge.

"Rachel Manning," Harvey replied. "She's a colleague at the DA's office. She brought me the case in the first place."

I studied her face, shrugged, and pushed the picture away. "You still haven't told me anything about this case. Is it a secret?"

"No, it just has the potential to be high-profile, and I don't want the details getting leaked before I have a chance to serve the indictment."

I put a forkful of noodles in my mouth and chewed, all the while narrowing my eyes at him. I then swallowed and spoke. "I'm going to try not to be offended by that."

"Relax," he said. "That's the reason I invited you over here."

"Not for my charming company?"

He leaned over the kitchen counter and open Chinese food containers to kiss me. "Okay, it's part of the reason I brought you here."

We smiled at each other at the thought of our lovemaking that ended only a half an hour earlier, after which we were both starving and made our way into my kitchen for some leftover takeout.

"I wanted to tell you what's going on as a matter of professional courtesy and well, because I care about you."

I frowned. "This sounds serious."

"It is." He continued to eye me warily as he fiddled with the plastic top of the juice bottle on the counter.

"Carrie, the indictment will be against Brian. There's proof that he murdered his father, Gerald Kessler."

* * *

"Carrie? Carrie, are you all right?"

I took my eyes off the woman standing on the landing above us and looked at Brian. Did he know? Did he know that this was the same woman in the picture Harvey showed me? She had brought proof to Harvey that Brian killed his father. The two of them were working on an indictment to serve Brian before Harvey was killed.

"I—I'm sorry. I forgot what I was saying."

"You were talking about some cop. You said you hit someone." Brian took hold of my elbow and tried to peer deep into my eyes. "What's going on?"

I looked up at Rachel again and snatched my elbow away, my crisis momentarily forgotten. "She was here that night."

Brian followed my gaze up to the striking brunette on the second floor. She hadn't moved an inch, but I could tell she knew as much about me as I knew about her.

"I came to see you the night Harvey died, but I stopped and turned around, because..." I trailed off, turned to look at the window that faced the street. There was an armchair that looked inviting enough to sit and relax in on cold, windy nights. Which was exactly how I came upon the two of them.

"You were sitting in that armchair. She was sitting on your lap, and the two of you were laughing about something. I didn't understand it at first, because I saw her in the picture that Harvey—"

"Brian, what's going on?" The woman I now knew as Rachel Manning finally spoke. "Is she all right?"

"Give me a minute," he said, still not taking his eyes off me. "You remember coming to see me that night?"

"Yes."

"Why did you turn around and head back to the city? What changed your mind?"

Leave him alone. He's happy now. Just let him be happy. Go home.

He's with her. But why is he with her? That's the woman from the photograph.

What does it matter? I need to go to the police. Brian can't help me. He wouldn't even want to help me, not after the way I abandoned him.

"Brian, I'm calling the police," Rachel said.

"No, wait!" he said, now looking up at her and raising his voice. "Don't call anyone. Let me handle this."

The police. I looked behind me, sure I would find a trail of police cars coming down Brian's quiet street to arrest me. I had to get out of there. I was wasting time trying to explain things to him when I couldn't even explain everything to myself.

I began to back away. "It's okay. I'm going."

Brian leapt for my arm, but I backed even farther out of his reach and turned to head for my car. "I have to go."

"Carrie, wait! Where are you going?"

I got in my car and drove away. I couldn't have answered him if I wanted to, because I had no idea where the hell I was going. I just knew I had to get away.

CHAPTER FORTY-SEVEN

Brian stared, frowning after Carrie as she drove away down the street. It took him only a matter of seconds before he acted. He turned, grabbed his jacket and car keys, and turned to look up at Rachel, who was now coming down the stairs.

"Will you be all right here alone?"

"I'll lock up when I leave, but where are you going?"

"I shouldn't have let her leave like that. She was in the middle of a breakthrough."

"She'll be fine."

"In her state, she might get into an accident or worse."

"Brian, please. Will you just let her go?"

"She was scared, Rachel!" He could see his raised voice shocked her, but he didn't have time to cater to her feelings or mince words. He did, however, take a couple of breaths and lowered his voice. "In all my years of knowing her, I've never seen Carrie scared. I'm going after her."

He paused at the door and turned back around to look at her. "I'm sorry for yelling."

She smiled weakly. "It's all right."

"Listen, there's something I saw earlier…"

She waited him out and when he couldn't seem to find his words, she prodded him. "What is it?"

"Your tattoo of the flower. You never told me what kind it is."

She frowned. "It's a Magnolia. Why?"

He stared at her, not exactly sure if any of these details really meant anything. He shook his head, dislodging his suspicions and turned to leave once again.

"We'll talk about it later. I have to go."

But just before he opened the front door, a blinding pain shot from the back of his skull, and the world immediately descended into black nothingness.

* * *

A short time later…

Rachel got nervous when she saw the police cruiser pulling up at the entrance of the park. Had Brian regained consciousness already and called the police on her? But how would he have known where to find her?

The cruiser pulled right up beside her so fast, she had to jump back, but her panic instantly subsided when the passenger door swung open, and she saw who was inside.

"Get in," Marcus commanded.

She did as he asked and barely closed the door before he was peeling away from the entrance to Widow Lake. She looked back at the spot that had been their meeting place for the past eight months and wondered if this would be the last time they would be there together. She then turned to Marcus, who had a furious look on his face, and she just now noticed the ugly gash on the side of his head.

"Oh my God, what happened?"

She tried to reach for him, but he angrily jerked away.

"That bitch knocked me over the head with a vase. It's a fine time for her memory to return now."

He quickly filled her in about accompanying Harris to serve the search warrant for Carrie's house.

"Where's the sergeant now?" Rachel asked.

"Organizing a search for Carrie. He's got an APB out for her car already. If the cops find her before we do, we're screwed. I gave Harris the slip by telling him I needed to get to the hospital to get this checked out," he said, gesturing to the bandana pressed against his head to stop the bleeding.

Rachel sighed. It was now her turn to give bad news. "I had to knock Brian out. He was going after her. And there's something else." She waited until he turned to look at her. "Carrie remembers me, too."

Fury flashed in his eyes, and he pounded the steering wheel over and over again.

"Fuck! How the hell does she know you? You weren't even in the apartment that night."

"Harvey must have told her about me—I don't know. But I saw it in her eyes the way she stared at me…"

"Yeah, I know. She looked at me that way, too. Where do you think she'd go?"

"If she's starting to remember, she'll want more answers, so let's try Harvey's place."

"Hold this against my head," he said, and Rachel pressed the bandana firmly against his wound. She watched him steer with one hand while the other pulled a Glock and fully loaded clip from his holster. She guessed instantly it wasn't his police issued firearm. This gun's sole purpose was to rid him of his enemies.

CHAPTER FORTY-EIGHT

It was the insistent pounding that pulled him out of the darkness. Brian slowly opened his eyes, looked around, and realized he was on the floor directly in front of his front door. The pounding sounded again, and it was enough to pull him further out of the groggy state. He sat up and then instantly regretted it when his head roared with pain. He groaned, clutching the back of his head, and felt something wet and slick. He pulled his fingers back to see they were covered with blood.

"Brian!" The door pounded again and even shook a little from the force of whoever was trying to get inside.

"All right," he called. "Hang on!"

"Are you okay in there? Open the door!"

He recognized the demanding tone as belonging to Sergeant Harris. Instead of answering, he cautiously rose to his feet, not sure what else on his body had been injured. Then he reached for the front door lock and unlatched it.

Harris didn't even wait for him. He surely heard the click of the lock and immediately opened the door. He had his gun out as he looked to Brian with wariness.

"I'm fine," Brian said, still holding his head.

"What happened to you?" Harris asked, holstering his weapon and coming inside.

"I got hit over the head."

"Who hit you?"

Before Brian could answer, he noticed movement behind Harris. Andrew and Natalie Wallace were now standing hesitantly at the threshold of his front door, but instead of the disappointed looks he typically received from them, this time he saw fear and apprehension in their eyes.

"What happened?" Brian asked, although he could almost certainly guess it had everything to do with Carrie.

Carrie.

He was going after her. That's what he'd been doing. He had his jacket and car keys in his hand and was heading out the door to go after her when…

Rachel?

"What the fuck?" he whispered to himself.

Harris stepped around Brian to examine the back of his head. "Why do I get the feeling that whatever you're about to tell me is related to what happened at Carrie's house a half an hour ago?"

Brian winced when he touched a sore spot. "It probably does, but right now, I need to go after her. She left here, and she looked scared. I think her memory is coming back, and I need to help her through it."

"We have an APB out for her car. She bashed one of my officers over the head with a vase." Harris frowned. "Don't tell me she did the same to you with that fire poker."

"No, and I don't have time to explain. I need to go find her."

"We're going with you," Andrew said, coming forward. "If Carrie is in any danger—"

"She's not in danger," Harris cut in. "She's going to be arrested." He then turned to Brian. "You can ride with me. You're in no condition to be driving. I should send you to the hospital like I did Officer Lowell, but I have a feeling you'll just leave and go find her on your own."

Brian frowned. "Did you say Lowell? As in Marcus Lowell?"

"Yeah. Why, you know him?"

Before Brian could answer, Harris's cell phone on his hip began to chime, and he answered it on the first ring. "Harris."

As he spoke to his caller, Brian tried to get his mind to think about why that name was so familiar to him. Confusion slowly morphed into realization, and he quickly excused himself from Andrew and Natalie and hurried down to his basement, where he kept boxes of his father's old cases. It only took him two boxes to rummage through before he came to the third box, and what he'd been looking for was resting on the top. It was a legal pad filled of notes from his father's final sessions with Eliza Watley. He flipped through the yellow pages until he found the entry he was looking for. His father noted that Eliza had gotten into a fight with her boyfriend Marcus who was a police officer with the SFPD. He wanted them to elope, which Eliza was ecstatic about, but he insisted that once they were married, she would get rid of her name *Watley* and become Mrs. Eliza Lowell.

"Dr. Kessler, are you down there?" Harris called from upstairs.

"Yeah, watch your step," Brian called back, not taking his eyes off the notes.

He had not used these notes when he wrote the book about his father, because many of these details were protected by doctor-patient confidentiality. And back then, his only goal had been to exonerate his father in not recognizing Eliza Watley's propensity for suicide. He'd wanted to give him a voice. To this day, after reading through the notes, he was still not convinced that anyone could have predicted she would've ended her own life. He put aside the yellow legal pads as another idea came to him. He then rummaged through another banker's box until he found the object he was looking for and began to hurriedly thumb through the pages.

"I just got a call from the local ER in Gypsy Bay. Officer Lowell never showed up," Harris said, looking around the basement. "I'm worried he may have blacked out from his head wound on his way to the hospital."

Brian didn't believe that all. Something else was going on —something more sinister. He'd begun to suspect it when he saw the picture of Eliza Watley in the news article and the sterling silver pin she was wearing on her evening gown. Apparently, he'd spooked Rachel when he asked about her tattoo, and the fact that she hit him in the back of the head was further proof that he was getting closer to a secret he was never meant to find out. But there was one more piece of the puzzle he needed in order to be certain. It had to be the nickname, *Ray bird*. Rachel said her sister got it from a movie, but that wasn't it. He'd heard it somewhere else. She'd also told him her sister's name was Lily, but that could've been a lie.

"Kessler, what are you looking for? We need to get going. In case you forgot, Carrie Wallace has money, and she could be on her way out of the country by now."

"My daughter wouldn't do that, Sergeant. She's scared," Natalie Wallace said indignantly.

"Mrs. Wallace, if you could just wait upstairs, I'll be right with you," Sergeant Harris said. "In fact, you should be contacting Carrie's lawyer right about now, because when I find her—"

"Let's go," Brian said suddenly as he headed toward the basement steps. "Natalie's right. Carrie won't run. She wants answers. She's confused and she wants to remember more."

"Wait a minute," Sergeant Harris said, grabbing Brian's forearm as he stalked by him. "You want to tell me what you found in those boxes?"

"Not what. Who," Brian said. "Eliza Watley had a younger sister. She was a freshman in college at the time of her death, but Eliza and her parents did their best to keep the younger sister out of the public eye to maintain her privacy. Otherwise, I would've recognized her when she first introduced herself to me."

"Who?" Harris asked.

"I remember," Andrew said, coming to stand behind his wife. "She didn't even testify at the trial against your father, but they took her deposition. Rita or Renee…"

"Rachel," Natalie finished. "Rachel Watley."

Sergeant Harris whipped back around to Brian. "Tell me it's a coincidence that the woman you're dating is also named Rachel."

Brian held up a bright yellow journal and flipped to an open page. "They're the same person. She must've changed her last name after Eliza's death."

Harris frowned. "What does this have to do with Harvey Adams and Carrie Wallace?"

"I'll tell you on the way."

Andrew stepped from behind Natalie and looked at Brian with fearful and imploring eyes. "You know her, Brian. Where would she go?"

"Harvey's place. Back to the scene of the murder," Brian said. "Like I said, Carrie wants answers, but she also remembers both Marcus and Rachel, and they're going to want to get rid of her."

Brian stepped past them and raced back up the basement

stairs with his mind consumed by that chilling thought. He could feel time slipping away from him, and when it ran out, Carrie would be dead.

CHAPTER FORTY-NINE

That cop. He had been there that night. He tried to shoot me but Harvey had gotten shot instead. That bullet had been meant for me. But that woman was involved somehow, too. Harvey had been working with her to bring an indictment against Brian.

What did it all mean?

I wanted so much to just drive to the bank, empty my accounts, and keep going. But all that would do was have Sergeant Harris and the SFPD on my ass for the rest of my life. I looked down to the console at my phone, which lit up again from an incoming call. It was my father this time. The last ten calls and texts had been from my mother. They must have heard about me bashing the guy's head with the vase. They also probably needed me to meet with Eve to discuss my impending murder charge. But I wasn't going anywhere or meeting with anybody until I had proof of my innocence. But then again, how or where was I going to get proof? How could I even begin to defend myself when I couldn't get my mind to remember every detail?

Harvey's apartment.

The thought came instantly. I had just been driving aimlessly, putting as much distance between Gypsy Bay and me as possible. But now I had an idea. I took the exit on the highway that would take me over the bridge and to downtown San Francisco. I'd begun to remember things when Brian took me there that day, but it had all been too much to take at the time, so I'd shut it down. But I was desperate now and had no other choice but to try to endure it all again.

Harvey's place was where the murder happened, and if I wasn't his killer, I was definitely a witness.

* * *

I played a hunch that the second unknown key on my key ring would open Harvey Adams's apartment, and I was right.

When the lock clicked, I swung the door open and hesitated there on the threshold. My last time there was a short visit, but I couldn't afford to run away now. While I stood there, at that very moment, Sergeant Harris was mobilizing his team of officers and conducting a hunt for me with only one objective in mind and that was to arrest me. My mind was beginning to remember—that was what I wanted. Only I was still so afraid of what I'd forgotten.

Stepping inside the furnished apartment, I immediately noticed the kitchen, dining, and living area all shared the same open space. The master bedroom, guest bedroom, and bathroom were to the right and down a hallway. The subtle floral scent of air freshener mixed with an even more faint smell of bleach wafted around my nose. I guessed the police had gathered all of the evidence they'd needed from the place and turned it back over to the property manager. For the first time, I wondered who Harvey's next of kin was and if he had any family who would come to pack his things up. No one from his family had reached out to me, so if he did have loved ones, he and I obviously hadn't made that step to meet each other's family. My parents claimed they didn't know about him until after his death.

As I made my way through Harvey's apartment, I had no idea what I was looking for. I just knew the answers I wanted were somewhere in this place. It was a last-ditch effort, a way for me to start the inevitable. Eventually, I would have to pull out my cell phone and make the call to Sergeant Harris to let him know where he could find me. Outside, the afternoon sky was beginning to darken, and shadows from the setting sun were beginning to dance across the wood floor. Still, I continued on through the open space toward the kitchen. Then I was stopped when I bumped into the metal wastebasket, and it toppled over to the floor with a loud clang. I started to reach down and set it upright, but once my fingers touched the metal, they began to tremble. Just like that, a memory soared to the forefront of my mind with stark clarity.

"Carrie, calm down," Harvey said, when I tried to leave the apartment in such a rush that I bumped into the trash can by the kitchen and sent it toppling over its side.

"Don't tell me to calm down! I'm out of here." I grabbed my purse and keys and looked around for my coat. "You're taking bribes. You're accepting money to get a man put in jail. And not just any man—this is Brian. I don't even know you anymore."

"The evidence is clear and damning. I'm prepared to take this to trial."

"Yes, and I'll bet that money you're getting is to ensure a conviction."

I stopped in my search for my coat and got a good, long look at him. "What's the matter with you? How could you even consider something like this? You're about to dig up the past and destroy his life all to suit your mysterious sponsor."

Harvey's brows knitted together. "Are you more upset about my taking a bribe or the fact that this involves your ex-husband?"

I wanted to say both. Harvey was a colleague. We'd gotten to know each other during trial when our cases pitted us against each other. He was a good attorney and Prosecutor, and I hated to see him go down this road, all for money. It reminded me of my failed marriage. Money brought Brian and me together, and it was money that broke us up.

Brian.

I knew this all had to be a set up. He would never kill his father—not after fighting so long and hard to protect his name and reputation after Eliza Watley committed suicide. He stood by Gerald's side against the medical community, my parents, and even me. That was what I always regretted. The fact that there had been a line drawn between us was devastating. I had loved Brian so much, but in the end, the loyalty to my family had been stronger. So yes, it did piss me off to know the man I was casually dating was going after a man I'd once loved. A man I still loved—whenever I had the courage to admit it to myself.

"Whether I take the bribes or not, this is still a strong case. If I win, it will be great for my career."

I narrowed my eyes at him. "If by some miracle you even make it to the courtroom, you won't win this case. I will be representing Brian."

Harvey's voice turned evil and malicious. "That man can't stand you. You've told me so yourself. He wouldn't accept help from you. And what makes you think I'm going to let you stand in my way?"

I was floored. "You're really going through with this?"

He exploded, slamming a fist down onto the high-top counter that separated us. "You weren't even supposed to find out!"

"Well I did find out, so now what?"

The moment I asked that question, Harvey got a strange look on his face. I couldn't tell what it meant, but something inside me told me this wasn't right. This whole scene was wrong.

He'd invited me over here to explain himself, but he was only justifying what he was doing. He wasn't looking for me to change his mind. His mind was already made up, and no matter what I said, he was going to continue to do what he wanted to do. So why invite me over there? Then it hit me. He was stalling. He was waiting for something to happen. Fear began to grip me, and without saying another word to him, I turned with my purse and keys in hand and headed for the door. Fuck my jacket. I had to get out of there now. I didn't know why, but I had the feeling I was in danger. And when I turned toward the door, that danger was staring right at me.

* * *

"That's her car," Marcus said the moment he pulled up to the condo building.

Rachel had never been to Harvey's place, but she knew where he lived and had given his address to Marcus when Harvey called her in a panic that night, telling her that his colleague had found out everything, and that he needed her taken care of. It occurred to Rachel that he'd never said Carrie's name, and that had been unfortunate. If he had, their little problem could've been taken care of a long time ago. Instead, Carrie had gotten away from Marcus that night, and they'd been chasing their tails ever since, never realizing the eyewitness they'd been after had been under their noses all along.

"Stay here," Marcus ordered as he grabbed the door handle and jerked the car door open.

Rachel grabbed the sleeve of his jacket to halt him. "What are you going to do?"

He frowned with irritation and impatience. "What the

hell do you think I'm going to do? She knows our faces. She saw me that night. You think I'm just going to let her continue walking around, waiting for her to name me as a killer?"

Yes, it had been obvious what he was going to do, but she only asked to slow him down because she was having second thoughts about this. Maybe there was another way. But a little voice inside her head told her they'd already gone too far down this particular road to turn back now. No, she herself hadn't killed anyone. Marcus had done away with that meddling paralegal bitch and Harvey had been an accident. Still, Rachel had attached herself to him, and she was not willing to let him go or leave him alone to take the fall for everything. She had to keep going.

"Be careful," she said, just as he had stepped one foot out the door.

He turned around and the look he gave her was enough to warm her heart.

"We're leaving here after this," he said. "I promise you that." He leaned back and gave her a long, sensuous kiss before hurrying out of the car and shutting the door behind him.

She watched him go and prayed he would be quick. She had this feeling they were outracing time. Someone would eventually find Brian unconscious and Sergeant Harris would realize Marcus didn't go to the hospital. She'd kept both of their passports in her purse from the day he'd told her about this plan of his. She knew that once everything was complete to his satisfaction, they would have to take the rest of her inheritance and leave the country. But so much had gone wrong that she wasn't sure anymore if it would be that easy.

She looked with worry toward the doors of the apartment building that Marcus just entered. She had a terrible feeling, and if something happened to him, she'd never be able to go on without him. She'd promised to see him through this, and that's what she was going to do.

She opened the glove compartment where she knew he kept a spare gun and clip. She pulled them both out and slammed the clip into place. She was just about to close the glove compartment when something shiny stopped her.

It was tucked deep in the back of the glove compartment, hidden among some papers like a dirty secret. When she moved the papers aside and saw what it was, she snatched her hand back as if what she was seeing wasn't real.

Dear God, please don't let it be real.

Her hand shook with fear as she reached for it again. She clutched it and pulled it out of its hiding place. Tears of disbelief and anguish welled in her eyes as she stared at the object in the palm of her hand that was so small and innocent yet caused her so much despair. Rage slowly began to build up from somewhere deep inside her until it could no longer be contained, and finally, it erupted from her with a scream that went on forever.

* * *

A man had entered the apartment silently without me noticing. Horrified, I looked from him to Harvey, but I saw that Harvey didn't share my same look of fear. He had left the door unlocked and allowed whomever this man was to come in.

"What's going on here? Who are you?" I asked, backing away from the stranger.

He didn't answer me but had a predatory look on his face as he stood completely still in all black and blocked the doorway.

"Harvey?" I said, turning to the man who had not only been a lover but someone I thought was a colleague, a friend, and at the very least, someone I thought I could trust.

His eyes filled with regret. "I'm sorry, Carrie, but I hoped you would at least see reason. Brian is guilty, and I'm going to prove it. If a little extra money came my way in the meantime, what did it matter so long as I was putting a murderer behind bars?"

"Brian is not a murderer, and don't give me that fake nobility! You just want the money. You don't care whether he's guilty or not, you fucking greedy bastard."

His jaw tightened and the regret he'd shown me earlier was now replaced with barely concealed anger. I knew he wanted to say something more, but he was too much of a coward to utter it. Instead, he looked to his silent guest and gave him a nod that had been so slight and subtle I would've missed it had I not been looking for it. That was the signal. He was done talking to me. Now he just wanted me gone.

I turned to the man and widened my eyes at the sight of a gun now in his hands. Thinking fast, I grabbed a jade green Chinese ornament from a nearby end table and threw it at the man. He dodged it, but that move was all I needed to dash around Harvey, out of the kitchen and into the darkened hallway for a place to hide. A bullet hit the frame leading to the corridor, and I screamed but kept going.

"What are you doing?" I heard Harvey yell. "Don't do her here. Knock her out, then take her somewhere else."

His words sent chills down my spine as I ran to the master bedroom. I needed to get to one of the windows, let myself out, and take the fire escape down. It only took seconds to get there, but it felt like I was already out of time because I could hear the scuffling of racing feet right behind me. Once inside his bedroom, I turned to shut the door, but one of the men put their weight against it, and we were both fighting for control. I shoved at the door as hard as I could. It would only be a matter of time before the other one joined to help, and I would be no match to the weight of two men. The door only had inches to go until it was closed. I shoved again with all my might and screamed from frustration and fear, knowing if they pushed that door open, I was a dead woman.

"Get over here and help me," I heard one of them say. It was Harvey.

I saw his four fingers peeking out on my side of the door, so I bent down and bit those motherfuckers as hard as I could. Harvey hollered and instinct had him instantly jerking his hand back. I used my final reserve of strength to shove the door the rest of the way, slammed it closed, and locked it. I knew that would only buy me a short amount of time because the silent guy out there only had to blast the lock open with his gun.

I ran toward the windows where the fire escape was, tried to lift one of them, but it didn't budge. I tried another one. It didn't move. I frantically checked the rest of the windows and by now could feel my hands shaking from adrenaline and trepidation. I was in fight or flight mode, and I wanted so much to flee. Tears flowed down my cheeks as I desperately tried to get one of the windows opened.

The lock was shot open, and I knew then I was going to die. I thought of Fiona and thanked God I had the foresight to give her the flash drive about Harvey before coming here. The truth about him would come out and maybe that would save Brian from the embarrassment and shame of being arrested for the murder of a man he adored.

I tried one last window, shoved, and to my relief, it slid up and the cool downtown air whisked across my face. I started to climb out but felt a hand grab for my leg and try to pull me back inside. I screamed out into the night, hoping to God someone would hear me and call 911.

"Get in here," Harvey said, grabbing me around the waist and pulling me back into his room.

He had my back pressed tightly against his chest and I tried kicking and clawing at him, fighting him like an alley cat. Out of the corner of my eye, I saw the young man with the close buzz cut raise his gun with its silencer and point it at me.

"I said don't do her here," Harvey said above my screams.

The man flipped the gun to its handle and headed toward us. He was going to knock me unconscious and then take me somewhere to kill me. I renewed my efforts to get away from Harvey. As the man got closer, I used Harvey's weight to swing my body upward and kick the man in the face. He stumbled back, and I took my nails, reached back and scratched Harvey down his face.

"Aaargh!" he screamed, letting me go. I dashed around him back to the open window, but Harvey reached out with one hand and tried to stop me. We fought each other, and he looked maniacal with the bloody scratches staining his face and rage in his eyes.

"You bitch!" Harvey put his hands around my neck, attempting to strangle me.

I grasped his forearms and tried to get him off me while noticing the other man come up behind Harvey, also full of rage and raising his gun to point it at my head one last time. He wasn't waiting anymore to take me to some unknown destination to kill me. He was ending this now. But Harvey couldn't see the man aiming his gun at me behind him. His focus was on strangling me. With his hands around my neck, he made the fatal mistake of cocking his head to the side, right into the bullet's path.

Blood exploded in my face and the two of us went down instantly. I lay there in shock as Harvey's unmoving body covered mine. I didn't know where the gunman was, but I could hear knocking coming from the front door. My screams must've finally alerted someone. Next, I heard a muffled string of curses and then the gunman moved into my sight. He was climbing out the window to the fire escape and racing down the metal stairs.

I couldn't think. I couldn't feel. I was in survival mode, and my instincts were telling me that no one would know this gunman had been here. I was the last to see Harvey alive. I had his blood on me. I needed help. I needed some place to think. I needed Brian.

I was shivering by the time the memory had ended.

Harvey had tried to kill me. He and that cop had tried to kill me because I knew too much.

I had to get out of there. I had to find Sergeant Harris. Hell, I'd even let him lock me up as long as he listened to everything I had to say. With so many thoughts colliding with each other in my mind, I hurried toward the front door, but it was already swinging open, stopping me in my tracks. It was him. The cop I'd hit over the head with the vase, but this wasn't a cop who would protect me. He was a killer. He was the killer from that night, standing in the same spot and blocking my escape.

"I would say this is déjà vu, but you really have been through this already, haven't you?" he asked, his voice hard and his face emotionless. Danger seeped from him as he stood in his uniform, clutching a gun in his right hand with the silencer on.

I began to slowly move backward, inch by inch.

"I had a hell of a time finding you," he said. "I knew I should have killed you that night, but I thought I'd be able to get to you eventually. I never figured you'd lose your fucking memory and get tucked away somewhere."

I kept moving away from him, not exactly sure of my escape route. I just needed to put as much distance between him and me, between that gun and me, as possible.

"Where are you going?" he asked, taunting me.

I didn't think anymore. I turned and ran, and just like that night, I sprinted toward Harvey's bedroom. But this time, my assailant guessed at my move. He shot the gun and a bullet hit the door frame, just inches from my head. I screamed as loud as my lungs could bear and changed directions toward a spare bedroom. A storm of bullets got there ahead of me, slamming into the door with rapid and lethal pops that had my adrenaline and fear skyrocketing. I made a dead run to the last door, ducking low and screaming all the way. I opened the door and threw myself inside before closing it behind me. It was then I realized why he hadn't shot at me when I went for this door. I'd ran straight into a goddamned closet.

"Shit!" I screamed as tears flooded my eyes.

It was a walk-in closet that served as a storage area, but there were no windows or any place for me to escape.

"There's nowhere to go from inside there, bitch!" he shouted.

Two bullets shot through the door, and I ducked to the ground, screaming louder, praying a neighbor heard me, called the police, and that by some miracle they got here in time. The bullets struck within inches of me. I got as close to the corner as I possibly could, trying to make myself small, but I knew it was no use. Surely, one or all of the next several bullets would strike me, and I would be dead. I thought about my parents and my brother. Instead of running, I wish I'd taken the time to tell each of them how much I loved them. And there was Brian. I didn't know if what I felt for him could be called love, but it was something. It was a strong enough feeling that I wished to God he was there right now and that I could tell him about it.

"You're making this harder on yourself," he said, shouting through the door at me. "Just come on out here. Let's get this over with."

I didn't know how close he was to the door. If he was close enough, I could run out, ram the door against him and catch him by surprise. Maybe it would give me just enough time to get away.

Another shot right above my head, and I ducked and screamed. "Please stop!"

"Come out of there, now!"

"Please just let me go! I won't say anything, I swear!"

Several more shots and one of them got my left shoulder.

I cried out as pain and terror gripped me by the throat. I didn't want to die like this—trapped and frightened like an animal. I took several breaths, grasped my wounded arm, and looked around the closet in a panic. On the upper shelf was a toolbox. Warm blood seeped through my fingers as I used my free hand to reach up and snatch the toolbox off the shelf. It came tumbling down and metal crashed to the floor. I dove for the first weapon I saw, a hammer and took hold of the doorknob. I prepared myself to burst from the closet, swinging wildly. If I was going to die, I would make sure I wounded him before I went.

Suddenly, it was deathly quiet from the other side. I waited a few moments and still didn't hear anything. Just as I was about to push open the door, two more rapid shots came, and I thought I'd been hit. But I didn't feel any pain. I moved away from the door and checked my body. But I still had the one wound on my arm and no new pain. The bullets hadn't struck me. He hadn't even aimed at the closet door. Then I heard a groan and a string of curses coming from him. Then another shot rang out, and I pressed myself against the wall.

"Jesus Christ, Rachel," I heard him yell. "You shot me! What the fuck is wrong with you?"

CHAPTER FIFTY

Rachel looked at the man she fell in love with years ago, now collapsed to the floor and bleeding from wounds in his left leg and stomach. It was all surreal. Never had she thought she would ever pick up a loaded gun and use it on Marcus. He was supposed to be the man she spent the rest of her life with. He was supposed to be her companion when they finally left all of this sadness and revenge surrounding Eliza behind. They were supposed to be each other's salvation.

"Why would you shoot me?" he asked while clutching his gut.

In answer, she opened her palm and dropped the magnolia pin she'd found in his glove compartment to the floor.

When he saw what it was, he looked up at her, and his eyes were so full of sorrow that she knew the truth without him having to say a word.

"Rachel—" He tried to explain, but she cut him off.

"I gave it to her to wear that night. She had it pinned to her dress. She would never have taken it off. I thought it was lost in the bay when she jumped, but you ripped it off, didn't you?" she screamed. "You ripped it off when you pushed her!"

"I didn't mean to," he said, one hand raised in a pleading gesture. "I pushed her, yes, and she tried to hold onto me to stop her fall. I grabbed the pin, and it came off when she fell over."

Silent tears streamed down Rachel's face. "Why? Why would you do that?"

"She was going to leave me!" he shouted, his face now covered in sweat. "She was going to leave me all because that quack Kessler told her to. So yeah, I met her after the awards show. We crossed the bridge to a lookout point. It was late. Not many cars passed by, and I let her stand there and lie to me about how much she loved me, only to tell me she wouldn't see me anymore."

Rachel shook her head in disbelief. "All this time, all these years, we thought she'd killed herself. You let my parents and me think she would actually take her own life."

"I'm sorry, baby. I just reacted. I tried to take it back. I tried to stop it from happening, but she was just gone."

She burst into sobs and raised the gun to his head.

"Wait a minute," he said, speaking slowly. "Wait a minute. I told you it was an accident. I was angry. I wasn't thinking, but you need to understand that if it hadn't been for her fucking therapist, she'd still be here. He's the enemy, not me. That's why I got rid of him!"

She hesitated, the truth now becoming so clear. "You killed Gerald Kessler because he advised Eliza to leave you. That's why you had me get close to Brian."

"Baby, please listen—"

"It was never about the book. You were just using me. You sent me in to distract him because he was getting too close to finding his father's killer, finding you."

The gun shook in her hands as she tried desperately to get ahold of herself. She was in a battle between loving and hating him, and there was no clear victor.

"Listen to me, Rachel. I need to get to a hospital. Let's finish her off," he said, angling his head toward the closet door. "Then we can leave here, just like you've always wanted. We can go anywhere you want."

"I'm sorry, Marcus but I can't do that," she said, her face wet with tears. "I love you, but I also loved her. And you took her away from me, you selfish son of a bitch."

Just like that, the love in his eyes was gone as though it had never been there. It had transformed to something evil; it was the darkness inside of him that she'd been trying to ignore, only this time it was aimed at her. In a flash, he reached for the gun he'd dropped and aimed it at her. But his wounds hindered him, and Rachel was much faster. She screamed as she shot him in the chest over and over until she was out of bullets and he was lying at her feet, completely still and staring through her at nothing.

* * *

"You can come out. I won't hurt you."

After the shouting and the gunshots had stopped, I heard a soft and familiar voice call to me, but if it was whom I thought it was, I wasn't so sure if an enemy was waiting for me on the other side of this closet.

"Carrie, it's okay. I promise I'm not going to shoot."

I'd dropped to the floor when the shooting began, trying to protect my body. I now slowly rose to my feet, twisted the doorknob, and opened it while still clutching the hammer. The door opened onto the hallway, and I immediately saw Officer Lowell lying lifeless on the ground with multiple gunshot wounds to his chest. Just a few yards away, stood Rachel Manning with a gun in her hand.

"Are you all right?" she asked.

I continued to look from the dead man to the woman who'd just killed him. I'd heard the conversation from inside the closet, was able to put the story together, and now couldn't help but feel sympathy for her and the pain she must be feeling right now.

"We should call the police," I said.

"No need," she said just as the sound of sirens wailing outside pierced the air. "I called them before I came up here."

Moments later, a swarm of officers entered Harvey's apartment. Rachel, who had been looking at Marcus's dead body the entire time, woodenly dropped the gun and held up her hands in surrender.

Once the officers cleared the place of any danger, Sergeant Harris rushed in, followed closely by my parents and Brian. As soon as my parents saw me, they assaulted me with hugs and tears of relief. I held them both close while looking over their shoulders at Brian. He was standing off to the side, watching with sorrow and regret in his eyes as Sergeant Harris put Rachel in handcuffs. She, on the other hand, still had her eyes on Marcus as the EMTs looked over him and pronounced him dead.

Once Rachel was taken away, Brian walked over to us and an awkward silence amongst him, my parents, and me filled the room.

"Are you all right?" he asked.

I nodded. "Yes. I came here, hoping to remember some more, and I did. I didn't kill Harvey."

"It's okay, honey. Don't think about it anymore," Dad chided.

"Your arm is bleeding," Mom said, gasping. "Sergeant, we need the EMTs over here, now!"

"It's okay, Mom. I think the bullet grazed it." I was speaking to her, but my eyes were still on Brian, and he was still watching me.

I turned to my parents. "Could you give us a minute, please?"

"You need to get that looked at," Mom protested. "And Sergeant Harris will need to get your statement—"

"It's fine, Natalie," Dad said, stepping in and taking her gently by the arm. "We can give them a minute."

She gave us both a curious stare before allowing my father to lead her away. I watched them walk down the hallway, and when they were finally out of earshot, I looked up at Brian to find him still watching me.

"I'm sorry," he said, "for the way I spoke to you at my house. I was blindsided by those

papers, and couldn't hear anything else. Then when you came back, I saw that something had scared you. I never should've let you walk out of there alone."

He paused and looked at Marcus's dead body now shrouded. "Was he the one who killed Harvey?"

"Yes, and I witnessed it. But there's something else you should know. He told Rachel he killed Eliza. She didn't commit suicide."

Brian's eyes hardened. "Are you sure?"

"He pushed her over the cliff nearby the bridge. Your father didn't make a mistake." I paused and then said softly, "Marcus killed him too, Brian."

He nodded slowly, as though he were trying to take in all of this news at once. Then, as if on instinct, he drew me into his arms and held me tightly. I could feel his chin resting on the top of my head. It was only then I could feel myself finally breathing easily. I sank into his warmth and comfort and inhaled his natural scent, which smelled so wonderful it almost pained me. It couldn't be this way forever.

Sergeant Harris stepped up to us. "Sorry to interrupt, but I have to take Ms. Wallace to the station." Noticing the glare on Brian's face, he rushed to say, "I only need to get her statement as to what happened here, and I overheard that she remembers more details from Harvey's murder. You're welcome to join us, Dr. Kessler."

"No," I said quickly, moving away from Brian's arms. "It's fine. I can do this on my own. Let's go."

"Carrie—" Brian tried to reach for me again, and I held up a hand to stop him. "You were right. I need a new therapist. I haven't got it all back, but I think we can both agree that I can't see you anymore."

He frowned. "You mean professionally, right?"

"Right," I said, knowing that it was a lie.

CHAPTER FIFTY-ONE

*S*ix weeks later…

Brian stood when the doors to the visiting room opened and Rachel walked out. She came toward him with a hesitant smile on her face, and Brian returned it with an even brighter one of his own.

He gestured for her to have a seat, and then they both picked up the phone at the same time in order to hear each other.

"You look good," he said, meaning it. Her face was devoid of makeup, but the clean and freshness of it enhanced her youthful beauty.

Rachel smiled shyly and then tears began to well in her eyes. "I never thought you'd come to see me. Not after I tried to ruin your life."

He ignored that for the moment and then reached into his bag. "I have something for you. I'm going to see that it gets to you once I leave here."

"What is it?"

He pulled out the bright yellow journal he'd found in the boxes of his father's notes. The little book had a bedazzled

Eliza on the front.

"I found this in my father's things. It belonged to your sister, and I think she gave it to him for safekeeping. She writes about you a lot in here with so much love. I'm sure she'd want you to have it."

Tears welled and overflowed in Rachel's eyes. She held the phone with one hand and put her other hand to the glass pane. Brian put the journal up to the pane and gave her a moment to look at it.

"Thank you."

He nodded and put it away. When he looked at her again, he spoke with regret. "Why didn't you come to me first?"

She laughed bitterly. "And say what? That our relationship was a complete fake? That I was helping the man I thought I was in love with to bring you down, only I found out too late that I was trying to ruin the wrong man?"

She paused and shook her head in self-deprecation. "He was a murderer, Brian. I knew that in my heart. But I told myself Harvey was an accident. Then with Fiona, I figured all he needed to do was scare her to get her to back off. But she didn't, and I pretended to be okay with her death. With all that happened, it never crossed my mind that if he could kill two strangers so easily, why not the woman he idolized? I didn't want to believe that about him."

Brian wished he could reach through the glass and hold her hand. He knew what it felt like to fall in love with someone and then to have that love shattered when you see something about them that should've been seen a long time ago. Carrie had been his love, and no, their circumstances hadn't been as extreme as this, but the decline of their marriage began when the two of them began to see things in each other and in themselves they did not like. The problems only worsened when they refused to acknowledge it or even work to fix it. Now what they had was gone, and he was certain there wasn't second chance at love coming for him.

"I don't know if you've heard, but I have a new lawyer, thanks to Carrie. It seems one of her colleagues owed her a big favor and she got him to take on my case, so there's hope I won't be in here for the rest of my life, even though it's what I deserve."

"You saved her life, Rachel."

She shrugged. "Yeah, well, her statement helped a lot, too, so if you ever see her again, I'd like you to thank her for me. Even after everything I did—"

He held up a hand to stop her. "When I was married to Carrie, she used to always tell me that the past didn't concern her. She wanted to think about the future and do what she could do in the present to make it better." Brian paused and for the moment, lost himself in memories of her. "Even with the amnesia, I guess that belief hasn't left her. I think she wants to do the same for you."

Rachel smiled, knowingly. "So, when are you going to do the same?"

"What do you mean?"

"You told me once she's not the same woman she was when you two were married. When are you going to stop punishing her and yourself for the past and focus on who she is now and who she might be in the future?"

"And who is she now?" he asked, flippantly. "A woman with amnesia, who as soon as she gets her memories back will revert back to the woman who I didn't want to live with?"

"Or," Rachel said, drawing out the word. "She reverts back to the woman you couldn't stand to live without."

* * *

"So, all charges against you have been dropped, the trial is underway, and best of all, Sergeant Harris and his department have issued you a formal apology. How do you feel?"

I smiled at Dr. Jenkins, my new psychiatrist. I'd been seeing her for several weeks now after leaving Gypsy Bay and moving back to my home in San Francisco. It was still slow-going, but I remembered Sheriff Gray Spencer's advice and was trying to be patient with myself.

I shrugged. "The sergeant is a nice guy, but I feel bad for who will be in his crosshairs on his next murder case. After my testimony for Rachel Manning's defense, I haven't returned to the courthouse, but from what I'm reading in the media, she's getting a fair trial."

"Any residual feelings of guilt at the memorial service?" Dr. Jenkins asked.

Fiona Richards's families held a memorial service, and I had attended with my parents. I'd received a mixture of looks ranging from sympathetic to concealed hostility. Some of Fiona's family members probably blamed me for her death, and I had a hard time not blaming myself either.

"Let's just say I'm human."

She nodded her head, accepting that answer. "When do you go back to work?"

My smile widened this time at the thought of returning to law. "Next week, but I'll just be assisting other litigators for the moment. No need to rush into things too soon."

"That's good to hear," she said. "Well, I'm pleased at everything I'm hearing." A pause and then she continued. "So, it's all over?"

"It's all over," I said, then held up a finger. "Well, not quite. I still haven't got it all back. That's why I'm here with you, Doctor."

Dr. Jenkins smiled indulgently, crossed her legs, and

leaned forward in the armchair to study me. "Yes, you're right, but I wasn't talking about your memories."

"What then?"

Her eyes narrowed in the square-shaped frames she wore. "I read online that the DA is dropping the indictment charges against Brian Kessler." She paused. "Should we talk about him?"

I stared at her for a long time and then slowly shook my head. "No."

CHAPTER FIFTY-TWO

Brian saw that the front door was open, allowing the autumn air to float into the house through the screen door. He stepped up onto the porch with his hands tucked deep into the pockets of his hooded sweatshirt. He raised one fist and hesitated before knocking on the door frame. He then turned away and looked down the quiet, tree-lined street of Cherrybell Drive.

"Hello, Brian."

He turned at the sound of the familiar voice and smiled. "Good morning."

"You know Carrie isn't here, right? She's in San Francisco. She left last—"

"I know," he said, raising his hand to stop Natalie. "I actually came to see you."

There was surprise in her eyes. "Me? Why on earth would you want to see me?"

"Because you're her mother. You understand her better than anyone. I should've come to see you when she and I were first married, but I didn't. I'm doing it now."

She looked him over once, with the same cool gaze that Carrie was known for, and he knew she was warring with whether to continue the hostility they've shared for years or to finally let it all go and try something different.

He silently exhaled in relief when she pushed the screen door open to allow him to enter.

"I'm going to need help taking some of these boxes to the car. We can talk while you help me with them."

"Sure," he said, "I'm dressed for moving."

She eyed his hooded sweatshirt and jeans and raised a brow. "No patients today?"

"No, I'm unofficially on vacation for a couple of weeks."

She picked up a pile of folded towels and dropped them in an opened box.

"Given everything that's happened, that sounds like a good idea."

She closed the lid but didn't tape it shut. Brian watched as she paused in her movements. Her head was bowed, and her shoulders began to shake. She was crying silently, and he immediately stepped forward and put one hand on her shoulder. She looked up at him. Tears and the stress of all the events that happened up to now were streaming down her face in rivulets. She then started to breathe deeply as if releasing every burden and worry she'd been carrying for her family—especially her daughter.

Then a laugh escaped her lips. "You're the last person I would ever expect to give me comfort. Not because you're not a compassionate man, but because I was such a bad mother-in-law to you. Both Andrew and I were horrible to you and your father."

"You were protecting Carrie."

"No, don't do that." She sniffed. "Don't make excuses for me. The moment your father fell on hard times, we both cast judgment on him and you—me especially, because I'm the one who pressured Andrew into buying Gerald out and cutting ties with him completely. I didn't want your name associated with my family, because even at my age, I was stupidly obsessed with what my friends and colleagues thought."

She paused to look up at the ceiling. "I blame my own father for that. He was a pastor of a large congregation, and my brothers and sisters and I were constantly warned not to do anything that would embarrass the family. 'Appearances are everything,' he would say. Those words stuck with me to the point I married a man with the same beliefs as him and together we pushed those beliefs onto our children."

She resumed folding more towels as the memories seemed to come at an onslaught now. "Shawn was the rebellious one and didn't buy into all the social status stuff. But, Carrie...Carrie was our angel. She was the one who would do whatever the family needed. We could always count on her to make us proud and never do anything that would soil the Wallace name—not until she met you."

"You're saying I was a bad influence?"

"Not in the way you think. Andrew and Gerald brought you two together for their own gain. I hate to say this, because it sounds so archaic, but it was supposed to be a marriage of convenience."

Brian nodded. To his dismay, he agreed with her. That is what it was supposed to be, and it would've been. He could've happily continued being married in name only to the independent woman with the sexy frame, beautiful spirit and intelligence that made him proud while enjoying the perks of being associated with her family. But, some time between the moment he first set eyes on her to the day his father died, Brian had fallen in love with his wife. And he couldn't pretend to not be hurt by that same woman turning her back on him and choosing to side with her family while they ostracized his family.

"Of all the men she dated and introduced to us, you were the only one who made her want to rebel. I saw her warring with herself daily to be loyal to us or throw it all to the wind for you."

"After the divorce, she stayed with us for a few days while you moved out of the house, and I would hear her crying at night in her room. But I never went in to comfort her. I was too afraid that the moment she looked at me, I would know I'd gone too far and cost my daughter her happiness."

Natalie took in a long breath and exhaled. "I never doubted your ability as her therapist. My problem was that the moment I saw the two of you together again after so many years, the guilt came back. I'd been trying to deny it for so long, but I can't anymore. I saw how you were with her, and I saw that you never stopped believing her—even when I did."

"Stop blaming yourself," Brian said. "There was a lot of evidence and she'd lost her memory."

"But I never should've lost faith in her."

He didn't like it, but he realized she needed this moment to admonish and then ultimately, forgive herself. So, he stopped speaking and allowed her the time she needed.

Soon, Natalie began to breathe easier. "You didn't come here to listen to me babble on. I know you care about my well-being, but more than anything, you're concerned about Carrie."

"I hear her sessions are going well."

"She's slowly remembering things, but she hasn't gotten it all back." Natalie paused and gave him a knowing look. "And that still isn't what you want to know."

Brian frowned, only to mask the look of surprise that she'd guessed at his intentions.

"Just before you came by, she called. She said she was packing up that apartment you grew up in to sell." Natalie stepped forward and laid a gentle hand on his shoulder. The soft touch was unfamiliar to him, but he knew he could grow used to it. "Maybe if you hurry, you can help her remember why she bought it in the first place."

CHAPTER FIFTY-THREE

Childhood memories assaulted Brian as he walked up to the apartment building where he grew up. He'd always hated this place that sat atop a convenience store in a lower-class neighborhood. It only made him think of his parents struggling. He'd even vowed to himself he would never return to this place when his family had finally afforded to move to a middle-class neighborhood. That vow had been broken during the first year of his marriage to Carrie when she insisted he show her where he grew up. He'd felt shame when he showed her the place, which at the time was vacant and for sale. But Carrie walked around the place and smiled.

"It's intimate and peaceful here," she said. *"It's a good place to come and shut out the world. And the fact that you were a boy here makes it even more special."*

At the time, he thought she was nuts, but he'd underestimated just how drawn she'd been to the place. Never in a million years could he have imagined she would've bought this place as her own peaceful haven—all because it had once belonged to him.

Now, as he made his way up the flight of stairs to the old apartment, he found himself thinking of the good times he'd had here as a boy. In treating Carrie, he realized he'd also treated and healed himself. He now came to appreciate all of his memories—good and bad. They may not have had much financially, but his parents had love for each other and love for him. He wished he understood that when he was married to Carrie. They were more than comfortable financially, the very thing he'd wished for as a child, but given a second chance, he'd refuse it all in exchange for the two of them telling and showing each other how much they loved one another.

The front door was slightly open, and he figured he'd catch her packing up just like her mother had been doing. But he didn't hear any movement inside, so he knocked once, called her name, then stepped inside. He passed the tiny kitchen and living area with no sign of her. He then made his way to the back of the apartment where the two bedrooms were. The first room belonged to his parents and when he didn't see her in there, he guessed he must've missed her heading down the stairs to load things into her car. Then he came to the threshold of his old bedroom and saw her sitting at the desk with photographs scattered about in front of her.

For a moment he stood there watching her, with her brows knitted in concentration. From his vantage point, he could see the pictures were of the two of them taken during vacations, office events, and parties her family had thrown at their house. She paused on one picture of the two of them bundled up in snow gear, huddled together and drinking hot chocolate at a café. She ran her fingers over the photo, and he wondered if she remembered that during that time, she was six weeks pregnant. But two weeks later, after they had returned home and news of Eliza Watley's death swept the nation, she'd had a miscarriage.

"Where did you find those?"

Carrie jumped and the picture fell from her hands. "Jesus! You scared me. How long have you been standing there?"

He entered the room and came forward until he was standing over her and the pictures of their past and asked her again. "Where did you find those?"

"On a shelf in the closet. I must've put them there a long time ago." She began to gather them all up and put them back in the box. Then she covered them with the lid and stood from the desk. She left his old bedroom and he followed her out to the living area.

"I was only looking at them to see if they would help me remember…help me remember you."

He didn't want to tell her how much it pained him that she still couldn't remember the things about them that he did. He was still a stranger to her. As a doctor, he understood it and logically knew her memories would return in time. However, as a man, it was unacceptable. They'd been in love, he couldn't keep away from her, she'd been everything to him, and then they'd broken each other's hearts. She had to remember him and remember him soon, because he couldn't saddle all of these memories on his own.

"Natalie tells me you're selling the place," he said.

She nodded. "I wanted to donate the proceeds to Eliza Watley's memorial fund."

"That's very kind of you."

"Speaking of the Watley's, I saw them on TV the other day. It was decent of them to publicly apologize to your family and your father, especially."

He looked around the small room, only in an attempt to keep his eyes off her. "Yeah, well, Mom appreciated it."

"And you?"

He shrugged. "Part of me says it's a little too late, but I

know it's in everyone's best interest if we let the past rest, so I called and thanked them."

"That was decent of you, too."

He didn't say anything more. Suddenly, he didn't even know why he was there. She looked to be doing well, and if he thought that a few weeks of therapy, two murder investigations and intense danger warranted talks of a future with her, that was stupid. They still had their own lives, and with everything that had happened, she didn't need him coming around and complicating things with his renewed love for her. It was still a surprise to him, but maybe he never stopped loving Carrie. Maybe after his father died and their marriage ended, he buried the feeling so deep inside of him, that he convinced himself there was no love for her anymore. But it had always been there, waiting patiently for her to come back into his life and rise to the surface with an intensity he couldn't even begin to deny.

"Brian?"

He finally looked at her, searching for the same feeling in her eyes, praying he wasn't in this alone.

"I know why you're here, but I think it's best we don't see each other anymore."

The breath was instantly stolen from him.

"Carrie, wait a minute—"

"I remember this place, but I still don't remember you, and I don't want to remember. These pictures of us show how happy we used to be. We once loved each other, then we hated each other, and I don't want to know why."

"I'm so sorry I kept this from you."

"Forget it! I don't want an apology. I don't want to go back down this road with you," she said. "I don't know how we came to despise one another, but I'm not going to risk going through it all again. Your memories are clearer than mine, so why should you want to?"

"Because, we're not the same people."

"How do you know? Yes, you might have changed, but how do you know I'm not the same woman? I don't even know myself."

"But I know you! I knew you back then, and I know you now, and you're not that selfish woman, and I'm not that immature man. Give us a chance."

She shook her head adamantly. "I'm sorry."

The look in her eyes told him she would not be swayed. He waited a moment longer, silently praying she'd change her mind, but when she kept silent, he finally accepted defeat.

"You say you're not sure of anything, but you're so sure that we won't work a second time around."

She didn't respond, and he didn't expect her to. He walked to the door, opened it and was ready to walk away from her for good, just like before.

But this time, he stopped. He stood at the entrance with the door held open, and then seconds later, he stepped back, slammed it shut and turned to face her. He was about to lay into her and ask her how the fuck she could stand there and give up on them again. They were being given a second chance, and she was slapping it away, as if it didn't matter. He was going to tell her that she may not remember him, but he remembered her, and that they could start from this day and begin to make new memories together that the both of them would remember. He would do all of this if she would just have him and not push him away. Not like he did to her. He was ready to say all of this because he knew when he turned around, she was going to yell and scream at him to get out and leave her alone. He was ready to argue with her and fight back. But when he faced her once again, she wasn't angry at all. She was relieved.

"Brian," she said on a shallow breath.

He reached her in two strides, took her face between his hands, and kissed her soft lips. They let out a pleasurable moan in unison at the first touch and then began immediately attacking each other, trying to touch every part of each other. Without breaking contact, Brian shrugged off his jacket and then lifted her blouse above her head. He felt the lacy fabric of her bra and reached behind her to unclasp the hooks. The bra fell to the ground at their feet, and he went to his knees to take each of her breasts into his mouth. Carrie cried out in delight and held the back of his head to draw herself as close as possible to his tongue as it rapidly flickered over each erect nipple. While he paid homage to her breasts, she attacked the buttons on his shirt and removed it. It followed the rest of the clothes to the ground as she caressed and stroked his bare chest.

"Take me to the bedroom," she demanded just as he lifted her into his arms and wrapped her legs around his waist.

She clung to him as he carried her into the master bedroom and lay her down on the bed. The moment her back touched the mattress, she tugged away her jeans and panties. Brian watched her, mesmerized as he discarded his own jeans and underwear. It had been a long time since he'd seen her fully naked and lying before him, and he wanted to savor the moment and not be as rushed as they had been in his car.

He put one knee on the bed, spread her legs, and put his face to her womanhood. Carrie's back arched at the first contact his lips and tongue made to her. He slowly and deliberately reacquainted himself with her taste while she undulated and squirmed. He kept at it, moving his face to match her hips as she urged him to go deeper and get his fill. When he felt her body begin to quake and shiver, he rose up, grabbed her full thighs, pulled her to him and entered her swiftly. Carrie released a cry, clutching him to her as an orgasm came on strong and swift and rocked her body. As Brian stroked her over and over again, he buried himself into the crook of her neck, inhaling the sweet scent of her perfume and tasting her with his mouth. She cradled the back of his head, running her fingers through his hair while he whispered the most erotic sounds into her ears. He felt pleasure building inside of him as with each word, he could feel her body growing hot and her center growing wet.

"Give me another one, Carrie," he ordered her as the intensity of his strokes increased.

He sat up, braced his hands on the side of her hips and drove himself into her until he was close to the edge himself. But he wouldn't go over until his woman came in his arms one more time. He stroked from above and she answered from beneath. Sounds of pleasure filled the air as the sensual dance brought them closer together, until finally, Carrie's moans were all that were heard but music to Brian's ears. He watched the beautiful sight of ecstasy overtake her, like liquid pouring over her body.

"I love you," he said, and then he, too, went soaring.

* * *

"You're thinking too hard," he said, moving a strand of hair away from my face and bending low to kiss my bare shoulder.

We were embraced face to face in a full-sized bed in a bedroom that once belonged to his parents. I still didn't know what it was that possessed me to buy this place and keep it for myself. The memories from here belonged to Brian. What did it all have to do with me? I'd probably never know, but it had to be something wonderful about it all.

"What is it?" he asked.

"I want so badly to remember you," I said. "I'm so sorry it hasn't happened."

"Stop. I of all people know how much time and patience this is all going to take. It will come back."

"I know, but let me just say this. I may have forgotten you, but these feelings I have for you..." I hesitated, gathered my thoughts and then continued. "From the moment I saw you standing over my hospital bed, I knew there was something. I could feel it. I don't know if it's love or just the fact that I don't want to be without you, but I want you to know that whatever it is, it never went away."

I focused on his eyes and felt myself drowning in the cerulean blue. It was the first time since waking from my coma that I felt safe and completely sure of everything.

"I never forgot that feeling," I said.

The blue in his eyes grew darker, and he looked at me with such love I could feel it surrounding and enveloping me.

"Neither did I," he said and then leaned forward and kissed me long and deep. It was as if he wanted to implant in my head this moment, and that whatever happened, he wanted it made known I would never forget him again.

EPILOGUE

*O*ne month later...
   I woke up remembering Brian.

The memory came back as clear as all of my other memories, and this one was just as cherished.

I slipped out of bed and padded my way through the house, skirting around luggage and boxes of my things. Items still left over of my recent move in. We hadn't yet decided if we'd stay in Gypsy Bay. He knew the town was just a little too slow for me, so every evening, we perused the real estate sites together, looking for a place we could both call home together.

But for the time being, I'd sold my townhome in the city and moved in with him, because of no other reason, except that I didn't want to spend another day without him. As it was, we'd wasted so much time apart, and I was in the mode of making up for it.

I found him in the kitchen, standing by the counter with a mug of coffee in one hand and watching the sports highlights on a small television that rested on the counter.

I smiled when I saw him, hardly able to contain myself.

"Brian," I said.

"Hmm," he replied, his attention still on the announcer's recap of last night's Warriors game. When he felt my presence just standing there, he finally turned the volume down and gave me his attention.

I was still smiling, and now I began to chuckle.

He started smiling himself, but I was sure he had no idea why. "What's so funny?"

I chuckled again and looked at him with so much admiration and love. "I just remembered my ex-husband wants to literally fly to the moon."

At first, he looked utterly confused, and then I saw the realization flood his eyes, and he looked down and shook his head. He stayed that way for a moment before finally looking up at me, and I saw the sheen of unshed tears glistening in his eyes and the most handsome smile broadened his face.

"You really remember that?"

I nodded. "And the margaritas."

"Damn right," he said, pulling me into his arms and bursting with laughter.

* * *

Thank you for reading EXPLOSIVE! If you enjoyed Brian and Carrie's exciting love story, you'll love the next book in the EX FILES series, EXPOSED.

When married couple Eric and Havilland Sawyer find themselves on opposite sides of a high-profile investigation, what could possibly go wrong?

Everything.

ONE-CLICK EXPOSED NOW >

"A plot twist you do not see coming."

"This book will take you on a ride and just when you think you've figured everything out, she surprises you and takes you in a different direction."

SIGN UP FOR LISA'S NEWSLETTER:

www.lisaryancampbell.com/newsletter

And if you love Christmas with romance and suspense, make sure you check out EX O EX O, my EX FILES Christmas novella.

It's three days until Christmas and Agent Roman Walsh has one assignment: Get Senator McIntyre's ex-wife into protective custody. It's supposed to be a simple job to drive her from California to Washington, and he'll be home in time to see his kids on Christmas morning. It's his kids he's thinking about when he secretly accepts money from a mysterious stranger who asks him to take a slight detour in his trip. But what he soon finds out is the money he took comes with strings and will ultimately put his life and the life of the woman he once loved in danger.

Dana McIntyre is in possession of a list that belongs to the Senator, detailing the names of those he accepted bribes from during his term in office. She plans to hand it over to the District Attorney in exchange for protection from some very dangerous people who also want the list and will stop at nothing to get it. When she finds out her escort to Washington is the man who walked away from her years ago, a pain she thought was long gone resurfaces, and she wonders what she has gotten herself into.

With each mile Roman and Dana travel together, they relive memories and buried feelings of a young love that ended too soon. However, they will have to learn to trust each other again if they're going to survive the enemies on their trail and make it to Christmas morning. But that won't be so easy, because one of them has been lying from the very beginning.

. . .

ONE-CLICK EX O EX O and warm up this holiday season with this steamy, suspenseful novella.

ALSO BY LISA RYAN CAMPBELL

The Ex Files

Exiled

Exchange

Explosive

Exposed

Ex Files Box Set

Execution

Extortion

The Ex Files Novellas

Explicit

Ex Factor

Ex O Ex O

Ex Appeal

Historical Romance

Deceit and Seduction

ABOUT THE AUTHOR

Award-winning Author, Lisa Ryan Campbell began writing as a small child using her mother's pink typewriting paper. Years later, she decided it was important to get a "real job" and attended Arizona State University to major in English with the goal of continuing on for both a Master's and Doctorate degrees in English and teach at the college level.

In 2002, Lisa graduated with a Bachelor's degree in English Literature and an Ancient Egyptian romance novel she wrote in her spare time. She decided then she would not be continuing on to graduate school, but instead joined Romance Writers of America and focused on her true love.

Lisa is an avid traveler and has seen many of the world's treasures in Egypt, Peru, Spain, France, Morocco, England, Mexico and the Caribbean. She spends her time mostly at her home in Colorado writing, reading and watching 1940's noir movies. She also loves to laugh, so you may frequently catch her watching reruns of Archer, Veep and The Office.

Sign up for Lisa's newsletter and find out more about her books at www.Lisaryancampbell.com and connect with her on social media.

Made in the USA
Columbia, SC
14 October 2024